T

BRIAN FLYNN was born in 1885 in Leyton, Essex. He won a scholarship to the City Of London School, and from there went into the civil service. In World War I he served as Special Constable on the Home Front, also teaching "Accountancy, Languages, Maths and Elocution to men, women, boys and girls" in the evenings, and acting in his spare time.

It was a seaside family holiday that inspired Brian Flynn to turn his hand to writing in the mid-twenties. Finding most mystery novels of the time "mediocre in the extreme", he decided to compose his own. Edith, the author's wife, encouraged its completion, and after a protracted period finding a publisher, it was eventually released in 1927 by John Hamilton in the UK and Macrae Smith in the U.S. as *The Billiard-Room Mystery*.

The author died in 1958. In all, he wrote and published 57 mysteries, the vast majority featuring the super-sleuth Antony Bathurst.

BRIAN FLYNN

THE SPIKED LION

With an introduction by
Steve Barge

DEAN STREET PRESS

Published by Dean Street Press 2020

Copyright © 1933 Brian Flynn

Introduction © 2020 Steve Barge

All Rights Reserved

The right of Brian Flynn to be identified as the Author of the Work has been asserted by his estate in accordance with the Copyright, Designs and Patents Act 1988.

First published in 1933 by John Long

Cover by DSP

ISBN 978 1 913527 43 3

www.deanstreetpress.co.uk

INTRODUCTION

"I believe that the primary function of the mystery story is to entertain; to stimulate the imagination and even, at times, to supply humour. But it pleases the connoisseur most when it presents – and reveals – genuine mystery. To reach its full height, it has to offer an intellectual problem for the reader to consider, measure and solve."

BRIAN Flynn began his writing career with *The Billiard Room Mystery* in 1927, primarily at the prompting of his wife Edith who had grown tired of hearing him say he could write a better mystery novel than the ones he had been reading. Four more books followed under his original publisher, John Hamilton, before he moved to John Long, who would go on to publish the remaining forty-eight of his Anthony Bathurst mysteries, along with his three Sebastian Stole titles, released under the pseudonym Charles Wogan. Some of the early books were released in the US, and there were also a small number of translations of his mysteries into Swedish and German. In the article from which the above quote is taken, Brian also claims that there were French and Danish translations but to date, I have not found a single piece of evidence for their existence. Tracking down all of his books written in the original English has been challenging enough!

Reprints of Brian's books were rare. Four titles were released as paperbacks as part of John Long's Four Square Thriller range in the late 1930s, four more re-appeared during the war from Cherry Tree Books and Mellifont Press, albeit abridged by at least a third, and two others that I am aware of, *Such Bright Disguises* (1941) and *Reverse The Charges* (1943), received a paperback release as part of John Long's Pocket Edition range in the early 1950s – these were also possibly abridged, but only by about 10%. These were the exceptions, rather than the rule, however, and it was not until 2019, when Dean Street Press released his first ten titles, that his work was generally available again.

The question still persists as to why his work disappeared from the awareness of all but the most ardent collectors. As you may expect, when a title was only released once, back in the early 1930s, finding copies of the original text is not a straightforward matter – not even Brian's estate has a copy of every title. We are particularly grateful to one particular collector for providing *The Edge Of Terror*, Brian's first serial killer tale, in order for this next set of ten books to be republished without an obvious gap!

By the time Brian Flynn's eleventh novel, *The Padded Door* (1932), was published, he was producing a steady output of Anthony Bathurst mysteries, averaging about two books a year. While this may seem to be a rapid output, it is actually fairly average for a crime writer of the time. Some writers vastly exceeded this – in the same period of time that it took Brian to have ten books published, John Street, under his pseudonyms John Rhode and Miles Burton published twenty-eight!

In this period, in 1934 to be precise, an additional book was published, *Tragedy At Trinket*. It is a schoolboy mystery, set at Trinket, "one of the two finest schools in England – in the world!" combining the tale of Trinket's attempts to redeem itself in the field of schoolboy cricket alongside the apparently accidental death by drowning of one of the masters. It was published by Thomas Nelson and Sons, rather than John Long, and was the only title published under his own name not to feature Bathurst. It is unlikely, however, that this was an attempt to break away from his sleuth, given that the hero of this tale is Maurice Otho Folliott, a schoolboy who just happens to be Bathurst's nephew and is desperate to emulate his uncle! It is an odd book, with a significant proportion of the tale dedicated to the tribulations of the cricket team, but Brian does an admirable job of weaving an actual death into a genre that was generally concerned with misunderstandings and schoolboy pranks.

Not being in the top tier of writers, at least in terms of public awareness, reviews of Brian's work seem to have been rare, but when they did occur, there were mostly positive. A reviewer in the Sunday Times enthused over *The Edge Of Terror* (1932), describing it as "an enjoyable thriller in Mr. Flynn's best manner" and Torquemada in the *Observer* says that *Fear and Trembling* (1936) "gripped my interest on a sleepless night and held it to the end". Even Dorothy L. Sayers, a fairly unforgiving reviewer at times, had positive things to say in the *Sunday Times* about *The Case For The Purple Calf* (1934) ("contains some ingenuities") and *The Horn* (1934) ("good old-fashioned melodrama . . . not without movement") although she did take exception to Brian's writing style. Milward Kennedy was similarly disdainful, although Kennedy, a crime writer himself, criticising a style of writing might well be considered the pot calling the kettle black. He was impressed, however, with the originality of *Tread Softly* (1937).

It is quite possible that Brian's harshest critic, though, was himself. In *The Crime Book Magazine* he wrote about the current output of detective fiction: "I delight in the dazzling erudition that has come to grace and decorate the craft of the 'roman policier'. He then goes on to say: "At the same time, however, I feel my own comparative unworthiness for the fire and burden of the competition." Such a feeling may well be the reason why he never made significant inroads into the social side of crime-writing, such as the Detection Club or the Crime Writers' Association. Thankfully, he uses this sense of unworthiness as inspiration, concluding: "The stars, though, have always been the most desired of all goals, so I allow exultation and determination to take the place of that but temporary dismay."

Reviews, both external and internal, thankfully had no noticeable effect on Brian's writing. What is noticeable about his work is how he shifts from style to style from each book. While all the books from this period remain classic whodunits, the style shifts from courtroom drama to gothic darkness, from plotting serial killers to events that spiral out of control, with Anthony Bathurst the constant thread tying everything together.

We find some books narrated by a Watson-esque character, although a different character each time. Occasionally Bathurst himself will provide a chapter or two to explain things either that the narrator wasn't present for or just didn't understand. Bathurst doesn't always have a Watson character to tell his stories, however, so other books are in the third person – as some of Bathurst's adventures are not tied to a single location, this is often the case in these tales.

One element that does become more common throughout books eleven to twenty is the presence of Chief Detective Inspector Andrew MacMorran. While MacMorran gets a name check from as early as *The Mystery Of The Peacock's Eye* (1928), his actual appearances in the early books are few and far between, with others such as Inspector Baddeley (*The Billiard Room Mystery* (1927), *The Creeping Jenny Mystery* (1929)) providing the necessary police presence. As the series progresses, the author settled more and more on a regular showing from the police. It still isn't always the case – in some books, Bathurst is investigating undercover and hence by himself, and in a few others, various police Inspectors appear, notably the return of the aforementioned Baddeley in *The Fortescue Candle* (1936). As the series progresses from *The Padded Door* (1932), Inspector MacMorran becomes more and more of a fixture at Scotland Yard for Bathurst.

One particular trait of the Bathurst series is the continuity therein. While the series can be read out of order, there is a sense of what has gone before. While not to the extent of, say, E.R. Punshon's Bobby Owen books, or Christopher Bush's Ludovic Travers mysteries, there is a clear sense of what has gone before. Side characters from books reappear, either by name or in physical appearances – Bathurst is often engaged on a case by people he has helped previously. Bathurst's friendship with MacMorran develops over the books from a respectful partnership to the point where MacMorran can express his exasperation with Bathurst's annoying habits rather vocally. Other characters appear and develop too, for example Helen Repton, but she is, alas, a story for another day.

The other sign of continuity is Bathurst's habit of name-dropping previous cases, names that were given to them by Bathurst's "chronicler". *Fear and Trembling* mentions no less than five separate cases, with one, *The Sussex Cuckoo* (1935), getting two mentions. These may seem like little more than adverts for those titles, old-time product placement if you will – "you've handled this affair about as brainily as I handled 'The Fortescue Candle'", for example – but they do actually make sense in regard to what has gone before, given how long it took Bathurst to see the light in each particular case. Contrast this to the reference to Christie's *Murder On The Orient Express* in *Cards On The Table*, which not only gives away the ending but contradicts Poirot's actions at the dénouement.

> "For my own detective, Anthony Lotherington Bathurst, I have endeavoured to place him in the true Holmes tradition. It is not for me to say whether my efforts have failed or whether I have been successful."

Brian Flynn seemed determined to keep Bathurst's background devoid of detail – I set out in the last set of introductions the minimal facts that we are provided with: primarily that he went to public school and Oxford University, can play virtually every sport under the sun and had a bad first relationship and has seemingly sworn off women since. Of course, the detective's history is something not often bothered with by crime fiction writers, but this usually occurs with older sleuths who have lived life, so to speak. *Cold Evil* (1938), the twenty-first Bathurst mystery, finally pins down Bathurst's age, and we find that in *The Billiard Room Mystery*, his first outing, he was a fresh-faced Bright Young Thing of twenty-two. So how he can survive with his own rooms, at least two servants, and no noticeable source of income remains a mystery. One can also ask at what point in his life he travelled the world, as he has, at least, been to Bangkok at some point. It is, perhaps, best not to analyse Bathurst's past too carefully . . .

> "Judging from the correspondence my books have excited it seems I have managed to achieve some measure of success for my faithful readers comprise a circle in

which high dignitaries of the Church rub shoulders with their brothers and sisters of the common touch."

For someone who wrote to entertain, such correspondence would have delighted Brian, and I wish he were around to see how many people enjoyed the first set of reprints of his work. His family are delighted with the reactions that people have passed on, and I hope that this set of books will delight just as much.

The Spiked Lion (1933)

"Missing men; missing women; missing children. People of whom we never hear again. Unsolved tragedies, that, if we allowed ourselves to dwell on their dreadfulness, would pluck at our hearts until they bled. There is nothing so terrible, I think, as imagining what may have happened to these poor people . . . and in so many instances never knowing . . . anything."

THE US publication history of Brian Flynn's work is something of a mystery. Six of the first eight books were reprinted by Macrae Smith between 1929 and 1932, with *The Five Red Fingers* (1929) and *Invisible Death* (1929) being the exceptions. After a two year break, they resumed with *The Spiked Lion* and *The Case Of The Purple Calf* (retitled *The Ladder Of Death*). Following this, in 1937 and 1938, M.S. Mill & Co took over, producing *Fear and Trembling* (as *The Somerset Murder Case*), *Tread Softly* and the earlier, hitherto omitted, title, *The Five Red Fingers*. Following that, Brian's work never again appeared in print in the US. It is, in my mind, *The Spiked Lion*'s history that is the most intriguing. It was first published in the UK in 1933, but in the same year made a strange appearance in the US.

Ellery Queen Mystery Magazine, founded by the men behind the pseudonym, Fredric Dannay and Manfred Lee, has been published since 1941, each issue featuring a collection of crime fiction short stories. Eight years before this, however, their first attempt at a magazine was not such a success, running for only four issues. Rather than publishing short stories, they presented complete novels. The books in question were *Drury Lane's Last Case* by Ellery Queen themselves, *The Riddle of Volume Four* by Phoebe Atwood Taylor, *The Mystery Of The Black Gate* by B.G. Quin (another author lost to time) and, in the third issue, *The Spiked Lion* by Brian Flynn. We don't know why or how Brian caught the attention of Dannay & Lee, other than them clearly having impeccable taste, but we can perhaps assume that it was the magazine version that prompted Macrae Smith to give Brian another try with *The Spiked Lion*.

That's not the end of the story, however, as there is still the puzzle of an abridgement. The reprint in the *Mystery League* magazine appears to be complete, something quite impressive for a periodical, but a comparison of the UK and the US book publications shows that approximately ten per cent of Macrae Smith's US version of *The Spiked Lion* is missing. The cuts are varied in form – some replace British dialect of the time, such as the word "forrader", some truncate technical sections and some just remove chunks of text. An example of this would be the quoted paragraph above – the US edition stops at the word "tragedies" in the third sentence, completely robbing the text of its poignancy. One has to wonder why there was such a change. If a magazine could hold the full text, why not a hardback book? Page count may have been an issue but the font used in the US edition is not especially small, and could have been reduced. *The Spiked Lion*, moreover, was, in its UK edition, approximately the same length as Flynn's other novels, and it seems that the other US editions of his novels did not suffer a similar fate. The real reason will, alas, have to remain unknown.

On reading the book, one can see why both Ellery Queen and Macrae Smith would have chosen it for publication. There is certainly something eye-catching about the plot of *The Spiked Lion*. A codebreaker is found dead in Bushey Park with wounds all about his body as if he has been attacked by a savage beast. In his pocket is a hand-written note referring to an "animal that is not normal, it is spiked". However, when the post-mortem is carried out, it seems that the victim died not from his wounds but from cyanide poisoning . . . On top of that bizarre crime, there is also a locked room murder – another cyanide poisoning – for Bathurst to solve.

In case the reader is concerned about being sold short, do be assured that here, we present for the first time in over eighty years, the full text of the original version of *The Spiked Lion*. Enjoy!

Steve Barge

Chapter I
THE DEAD MAN ON THE GRASS

The Commissioner of Police turned in his chair and picked up the telephone receiver. He frowned in accompaniment; it was a frown that was unpleasant and vindictive, by no means a frown of the sympathetically parental sort. When Sir Austin Mostyn Kemble trafficked in frowns of this nature, those at the "Yard" to whom he said "come" for their coming, and "go" for their going, were excessively careful to mind their step and watch points. Chief-Inspector MacMorran had seen this frown's elder brother at close quarters about a quarter of an hour previously, and it still remained for him an acute reminiscence.

"Send Mr. Bathurst up at once," said the Commissioner with peremptory emphasis. "I'm ready for him immediately."

Anthony Bathurst came to him, smiled, and put his hat on the corner of the desk that fronted Sir Austin.

"A poor thing, sir," he said whimsically, "but mine own. The English weather must be held largely responsible. In addition to the fact that I abominate umbrellas. Morning, Sir Austin. What's the latest spot of bother? Head, tummy, gout, or just the 'Yard'? Can't a vet. do anything?"

Sir Austin turned gloomy attention from the hat to the hat's owner. He was not in the mood for dalliance. "The trouble over which I desire to consult you, my dear Bathurst," he remarked testily, "concerns me officially. That is to say, as Commissioner of Police. Had it been to do with my—er—physical self, I should have hesitated about dragging you into it, much as I respect your ability. Anyhow, sit down. Take that chair over there."

Mr. Bathurst was dutifully obedient. "I find it difficult to suppress my vivid qualities—the feast of reason and the flow of soul—but I am ready, Sir Austin, to become the perfect listener. There are thousands, I am sure, who would cheerfully give their false teeth for the opportunity that is mine. May I help myself to a cigarette?"

"Of course, of course. Now listen. I want you to assess the facts that I am going to give you as carefully as you possibly can. When I've finished giving them to you, I shall call upon you to give me an immediate expression of opinion. Understand? An *immediate* expression of opinion. The years of experience that, happily, are mine, have taught me to rely more or less on *first* impressions."

"They are often the best, I admit," murmured Mr. Bathurst; "but it would be unwise to exalt them in a statement that went beyond that. Well?"

The testiness in Sir Austin's tone gradually gave way to gravity. "First of all," he declared, "I will deal with the extraordinary case of John Pender Blundell."

Mr. Bathurst caressed his chin. The significance of the movement was not lost upon Sir Austin.

"Heard of him?"

"M'm. The name's familiar, certainly. Just trying to pick up the threads. They will come to me in a second or so. Still, never mind me—go on. Amongst other accomplishments, I can think and listen at the same time. When I get the connection for which I'm groping, I'll signal."

Anthony grinned. Sir Austin always had on him an effect which approximated an inordinate cheerfulness; there was no other man quite like the Commissioner in this respect, with the possible exception of Inspector Baddeley of the Sussex Constabulary.

"What I am about to say should assist you materially. If you want to stop me to ask me anything, don't hesitate. I know your knack of kernel-finding."

The Commissioner leaned a little farther forward in his chair. "John Pender Blundell was a man in the late forties. Between forty-eight and forty-nine, I believe. Comparatively well-to-do, as things go nowadays, and unmarried."

"Spare me these glaring redundancies," whispered Anthony; "they're definitely disturbing."

Sir Austin ignored the interruption and proceeded somewhat hastily: "He was independent. Lived a few miles the Brighton side of Hayward's Heath at a place called Hurstfold. There has always been money in the Blundell family, and it came to him fairly early in life. His mother died when he was at school, and his father was killed in the Hong Kong earthquake some years after the war. John Blundell, our man, may be classed as one of the best English type. Thoroughly sound and reliable in everything he undertook. Wrykyn and Luther. Not perhaps as hallmarked as Eton and 'The House', but in the ordinary way good enough for anything. But you understand that as well as I do." Sir Austin paused.

"One minute, Sir Austin. Let me get him as accurately as I can. Any war service?"

"I was coming to that. I will explain. He's always been a whale on ciphers and cryptograms and all that sort of thing—right from his early days at Wrykyn. He's the author of two standard books on the subject. Regarded in the circles that count as the English equivalent of Le Courvoisier. Can't give him higher tribute in his own department than that, can I? Well, because of this particular penchant of his, a special job of 'Intelligence' was found him during the five war years, and he acquitted himself according to all accounts with signal distinction."

"These details are all by way of news to me, Sir Austin, but I've linked up all right with regard to what I thought I knew of Blundell when you just mentioned the name. There was an S.O.S. message concerning him broadcast about ten days to a fortnight ago. Disappeared from his house one morning, didn't he, and hasn't been seen since? Am I right?"

Sir Austin's reply was delayed. When it came it was startling. "Almost—not quite. He was found in the early hours of this morning." The Commissioner drummed on his desk with his finger-tips. Anthony Bathurst, stung into acuter interest, looked at him with sharp enquiry.

"Where?"

"In Bushey Park."

Again Bathurst came in, rapid, insistent. "Wandering, do you mean? Loss of memory?"

Sir Austin shook his head in grave denial. "Worse than that, my dear Bathurst. Perhaps I misled you. *The body* of Blundell was found in Bushey Park. Dead as a door-nail. Moreover, had been dead some days, the doctor says."

Anthony stared. There was no levity now in any part of him; there was, on the other hand, work in front of him. Another man's death to be avenged. He was once again harnessed to the chariot of Justice. "How?" The question was almost curt.

"Well, that's rather peculiar. Poison. Sugden says cyanide of potassium—a form of prussic acid. Been sprayed up the poor fellow's nostrils. But there are other extraordinary features of the affair."

"Such as . . . ?"

Sir Austin drew a paper, towards him. "Fractured skull, three ribs and one leg broken. Tibia splintered, Sugden says. Body one mass of bruises, and a peculiar jagged slash down the right cheek."

Mr. Bathurst's stare developed. "Seems all wrong to me— somewhere, sir. Like so many of these cases do when you first start attacking them. Where exactly in Bushey Park was the body found? On a path? Near a seat? Beneath trees? On the grass? Tell me, please."

"On a stretch of grass beneath one of the biggest trees. I've a plan here. Look at it for yourself."

Bathurst took the paper that Sir Austin passed over to him. "Whose image and superscription is this?"

"An old friend of yours perpetrated that—MacMorran. He went along to the spot directly we got the news through. Chatterton went with him. You see, we'd combed the country for Blundell for a fortnight. Never picked up the slightest trace of him anywhere. He seemed to have vanished into thin air. Till this morning."

Anthony, after a moment's examination, pushed the plan back to the Commissioner. "Thanks, Sir Austin. That's no end of a help to me. MacMorran's an artist. The lines are hard and clear. When I see him I shall have to compliment him upon his versatility. Well?"

5 | THE SPIKED LION

Sir Austin Kemble was hesitant. Bathurst watched him silently. Several seconds elapsed. It seemed that Sir Austin was turning something over in his mind. Eventually the Commissioner broke the silence.

"What do you mean exactly by 'well'?"

Anthony grinned at him sympathetically. "Tell me the rest. Just that. Nothing more. You know. 'The primrose by the river's brim, a yellow primrose was to him.' Why the coyness?"

The Commissioner chose his words. "You must understand that we identified Blundell this morning entirely from what I will call 'physical' evidence. There was nothing *on* him, for instance, that screamed his identity. His features—his height . . . you understand what I mean? The suit that he wore was bought from a London tailor—not, for example, from anybody in the neighbourhood of Brighton or Hayward's Heath. There were no papers, letters or documents of any kind found in any of his pockets. But we had three photographs of him that had been supplied to us by his nephew two or three days after Blundell had first been reported missing, and thus we were enabled to establish the necessary identification. But . . . and here I come to the interesting—almost vital—point. In the lower left-hand pocket of the dead man's vest MacMorran discovered a small, crumpled piece of paper. A fragment of creased and folded notepaper—the ordinary stuff that can be purchased from a stationer in a small way of business. On it there were a few words written in pencil—very much rubbed by the passage of time, as you may well imagine, and, as a result, almost illegible. You shall endeavour to read them and make of them what you can. To me they seem fantastic, to say the least. Still, here's the piece of paper in question. Let's hear your views on it."

Anthony Bathurst extended his hand for the tiny fragment of notepaper. The writing, as Sir Austin had stated, was faint, bordering closely on a condition of erasure. Bathurst smoothed the paper out very carefully and took it to the light. After a time of examination, he turned to Sir Austin and made an announcement.

"I'll read it as I see it:

"To-night I heard that crackling voice use those same strange words that I have heard twice before in this house. But the animal is not normal, it is spiked, and remember, too . . . Wing . . ."

Bathurst looked up from his reading. "That's as near as I can get to it, sir. Some of the words are almost indecipherable, but I've supplied them by the context. The last word, I suggest, is probably, when completed, 'winged'. There are some more letters, I think, after the 'g', but it's impossible to tell what they are. 'Spiked' and 'winged' animals, eh? Wyverns and griffins and such-like almost indicate the Book of Revelation, eh? Do you agree, sir?"

The Commissioner caressed his cheek nervously. "My interpretation of the writing is almost identical with yours, Bathurst. Also, I am forced to remember this: John Blundell, whom I was seeking to protect, has been murdered. Why? How? By whom? By a spiked and winged animal? There's that slashed cheek, you know." Sir Austin stopped as he spoke and shrugged his shoulders. "You can't expect me to believe that, my dear Bathurst; unicorns and those things belong to the age of superstition; we are not living in a time or territory of—er—mythology."

"No, Sir Austin. And there's something else of which we ought to remind ourselves. John Blundell, poor devil, is not living at all."

"Exactly, Bathurst. Hence my sending for you. It seems to me a problem after your own heart."

Chapter II
INSPECTOR MACMORRAN CONTRIBUTES SOMETHING

Mr. Bathurst took his seat again, hard by the Commissioner's desk, and smoothed out the worn piece of paper for the second time. Sir Austin scented further developments.

"What is it?" demanded the Commissioner.

Bathurst turned the paper over. "Are you satisfied that this is Blundell's handwriting?"

Sir Austin pulled open a drawer. "I expected that you would ask me that. Yes—I am. Once again I will ask you to form your own opinion from what I am able to place in front of you. Blundell left his house on the morning of the fourth of May, fifteen days ago. As you know now, he never returned. After his disappearance had been broadcast and advertised everywhere, various data were brought to us and placed in our hands. All in the natural course of events. Amongst those data were these specimens of his handwriting. If you examine them you will be satisfied, I think, that these faintly pencilled words were written by Blundell himself. There is just enough of them to make the comparison possible."

Bathurst took the papers, and, scrutinizing them carefully, made the comparison. A quick nod was an indication of his agreement with the Commissioner's contention.

"I think you're right, sir. Who put the case in your hands? In the first instance, I mean."

"The dead man's nephew—the missing man's nephew, as he was then. By name, Hugh Guest. He and his sister lived with Blundell. I had a lengthy interview with him. Young Guest's still up at Oxford. Intends, so he told me, to come down next December, at the end of the Michaelmas Term. At the moment, owing to the special circumstances, the Varsity authorities have allowed him an extended leave."

Mr. Bathurst thrust his hands into his pockets and stared at the telephone. Sir Austin embraced discretion. He allowed the stare full latitude. A question from Bathurst was his reward.

"Is MacMorran handy, sir? If so, I'd like a word with him. If not, I'll ask you to—"

"Unless something's turned up he should be accessible. He was in here with me just before you arrived. We'll see. I'll send for him."

The Commissioner was as good as his word. MacMorran appeared, a little perturbed, perhaps, at this second summons from the "old man" coming so soon after its predecessor. His eyes falling on Anthony Bathurst, however, the perturbation was dissipated. He and Bathurst had hunted before in double harness. "There were amateurs," he was wont to say, "and amateurs."

"Cheer-o, MacMorran," Anthony greeted him.

The Inspector extended his big hand. "How do you do, sir? Pleased to see you again."

Sir Austin took the reins. "Er—sit down, MacMorran. We want to ask you a question or two. Concerning this Blundell murder. There are one or two things that are not quite clear. Go ahead, Bathurst."

"I understand that you found nothing in Blundell's pockets, MacMorran, with the exception of this crumpled piece of notepaper? No money, letters, keys, papers or anything?"

"That's so, Mr. Bathurst."

"Who examined them first of all? You or Constable Chatterton?"

"I did."

"Good. Now tell me. Would you say, from what you saw during that examination, that the dead man's pockets had been deliberately emptied and that this creased piece of paper had been left behind because it had been accidentally overlooked?"

The Inspector's eyes glinted. "That's exactly what I should say, Mr. Bathurst. I'll go further. I'll say, too, that there's precious little doubt about it. That creased piece was left behind because it escaped somebody's notice. Whoever murdered Blundell intended that nothing should be found on him. I'll tell you why. The quality of that notepaper is but poor. It's the cheapest stuff. It rubs easily. In a little while, for instance, it would crumble through ordinary friction and almost rub itself out of existence. It had worked itself into a kind of roughish spill, and was almost tight in a corner of the pocket where I found it. Like a little pill, it was, sir. That would be a better description. Does that help you, sir?"

"I think it does, MacMorran. Immensely. Thank you. Now tell me something else. What did you make of the dead man's bodily injuries? I'm a little puzzled. Why poison a man and knock him about as well? I'd like your views on that, Inspector."

"Well, Mr. Bathurst, Dr. Sugden's final autopsy hasn't come through yet. Unless, of course, Sir Austin has had it without my knowledge."

His statement bordered on the interrogative. The Commissioner nodded briskly. "I only know what the doctor has reported to me. That Blundell was murdered by poison. Cyanide of potassium. Administered through the nostrils."

"Now, MacMorran," supplemented Bathurst, "your own ideas. What are they? Never mind for the moment what you have just heard."

"Blundell was set upon by a gang, I should have said. Enticed into a house somewhere and robbed of something that the gang badly wanted. Either money or something else that we don't know about. They were afraid to dispose of the body until the hue and cry had died down a bit. Not very satisfying, perhaps, but that's as near as I can get to it."

"What about that piece of paper you found in the pocket? How are you going to explain that? Was this gang of yours attached to a menagerie?"

MacMorran grinned. "I wasn't doubting you'd arrange that I'd run into something of that kind. All the same—" He broke off with a shrug of the shoulders.

"Well?"

"Well, things aren't always what they seem, and because of that you can't jump to conclusions. When things are dark it's difficult to explain points which afterwards almost melt away, as one might say. How do you look at things yourself, Mr. Bathurst?"

Anthony shook his head. "Not looking yet, MacMorran, by a long shot. Just glancing furtively here and there—and hardly daring to do that in case I espy an inviting-looking turning that will only lead me astray. Hampered by that powerful force known to you and me as civilization. My dear Inspector, look at things for yourself. Don't forget that Blundell left his home near Hayward's Heath on the fourth of this month. Left his home, I should say, were I asked, for a *definite destination*. That he went out on no chance errand or journey. What was that destination?

It will bear looking into, MacMorran. Candidly, I am not satisfied with anything that has so far been brought to my notice."

He rose and walked towards Sir Austin's bookcase. Pausing, he looked into its glass front. For a brief period his two auditors watched him. Suddenly he turned and addressed them again. "Consider the dead man's bias, gentlemen. Appreciate his reputation in the country where the cryptogram is king. Supposing, for example, he were wanted secretly for any matter of—"

Again he paused. "A stray and fugitive reminiscence has just reached me, Sir Austin. From it I have extracted just the germ of an idea. What has happened once may happen again. These missing people of whom we hear. Missing men; missing women; missing children. People of whom we never hear again. Unsolved tragedies, that, if we allowed ourselves to dwell on their dreadfulness, would pluck at our hearts until they bled. There is nothing so terrible, I think, as *imagining* what may have happened to these poor people... and in so many instances never *knowing*... anything. Has there been anybody else reported missing, moderately recently, who could in any way be connected, for example, with the subject of ciphers and cryptograms?"

It seemed that he put the question with some degree of anxiety. The Inspector, at least, thought so. The Commissioner looked at MacMorran. MacMorran looked at the Commissioner. Sir Austin gave up this exchange of glances to use his telephone. Bathurst listened to his instructions with approval.

The three men waited in silence. The list of names that was brought into the room two minutes later was carefully scrutinized by Sir Austin. MacMorran and Bathurst rose and ranged themselves one on either side of him. The Commissioner shook his head slowly as he surveyed the detailed information. Suddenly an exclamation from Anthony Bathurst startled him.

"Sir Austin, look here! God—we're nearer to the truth than we thought!"

Sir Austin's eyes followed Bathurst's pointing finger. It indicated a name on this sad scroll of missing men. "Hubert Athelstan Wingfield, of Apperley House, Hurrilow, Wiltshire. Missing from his home since the 23rd of April. Age, 49.

Height, 5 feet 10½ inches. Hair, iron-grey. Features . . ." The Commissioner read on, but most of the details meant nothing to him—they were blurred and nebulous. He saw them, but that was all. He looked up for Bathurst's contribution. What was it that he read here that . . .

Before Bathurst made further comment, MacMorran vaulted the ropes and entered the ring. "Before you say anything about that case, sir," he said with quiet insistence, "you might be interested to see this."

He produced the mid-day edition of the *Bugle*. The headlines fascinated the eyes of the men who looked upon them and read: "Month-old Mystery Solved at Last. Missing Wiltshire Gentleman Found Dead near Sidmouth. Body Discovered in the Valley of Ferns. Is it Foul Play?"

"That last question," said Anthony Bathurst quietly to his two companions, "seems to me to be easily answered." He commenced to pace the room. "Too easily answered."

Chapter III
THE DEAD MAN IN THE FERNS

"I don't think that I quite . . ." muttered the Commissioner as he looked hard at the newspaper.

"The dead man's name, sir," returned Bathurst with immediate and forcible emphasis. "The word on that piece of paper that we originally took to be 'winged', I am going to suggest to you now, was 'Wingfield'. What the Inspector has told us since only serves to strengthen that opinion. The name aroused my blazing interest directly I spotted it. That 'wing' part of it made an irresistible appeal. Now that we know that this second missing man is dead in similar circumstances to Blundell, mere suspicion becomes moral certainty. Don't you agree?"

He turned to Inspector MacMorran, eager and questioning. "Who, and what, is the Wiltshire gentleman named Wingfield who has been found dead near Sidmouth? Does that paper of yours tell us anything more about him?" He rubbed his hands. "I could bear to hear a great deal more. What was his aim in life?"

MacMorran accepted the inevitable. He knew that when Bathurst was in this mood he would never rest until he had all the information at his finger-ends. He spread the newspaper on the Commissioner's desk. The three men bent over it, Sir Austin—seated—in the middle of the group. He read the paragraph at which they looked, aloud:

"The dead man, Hubert Athelstan Wingfield, whose mysterious death is reported above, was forty-nine years of ago and comparatively well known in literary circles. As recently as January this year he took the chair at the annual dinner of the famous Scripta Society. Educated at Clifton College and Selwyn College, Cambridge, Mr. Wingfield was a recognized authority upon the subject of legendary inscriptions and was frequently called into consultation thereon. Some few words on the subject may interest our readers. After the Renaissance, the works of the Roman poets were extensively used for legends and inscriptions, on medals, coins, jettons and seals. In this connection, it is interesting to point out that a Latin legend was very often a portion, commonly the end, of a hexameter. It may be remembered, in this reference, that Camden said, 'A motto is most commended when it is a Hemistitch or "parcel" of a verse.'

"Mr. Wingfield, in his best-known book, *Ghost Legends in Medallism, Numismatics, and Sphragistics*, throws a great deal of light on the disturbing practice of distorting unscrupulously Latin classical quotations for use on certain medals and jettons—particularly those belonging to Louis Treize. For an interesting example of this we quote the historic case of Martial's pentameter, 'Sospite/quo grat/um//credimus/esse Jov/em//' which has more than once been juggled with, and eventually tortured into, the form of 'grat/um quo/sospite/coelum/' in order to obtain the desired end of an obvious hexameter.

"Students, by reason of this mischievous habit, were constantly tempted to endeavour to remember what they never knew and so were sent hunting for the elusive will-o'-the-wisp.

There is little doubt that many empty hours have been spent by earnest seekers after 'the never was'.

"Mr. Wingfield was also the translator of Feuardent's *Jetons et Méreaux*, and the author of a brochure on Heraldry entitled, 'The Crown of England and its Former Possessions—Normandy, Guienne, and Aquitaine.'

"Mr. Wingfield, who married comparatively late in life, leaves a widow and sister, but no children."

"I'm a Scotsman," declared MacMorran dryly, "and I share the enthusiasm of my race for education. It's money well spent when it is expended on book-learning. All the same, would you mind telling me what a jetton is? I can't remember ever having heard the word."

Sir Austin rubbed his cheek and then, with a quick glance, sought refuge with Mr. Bathurst. Anthony waded gallantly to the rescue.

"A jetton," he explained, "is a small metal plate, or counter. The word is of French origin, of course, as you will have seen. The French also use it, you remember, in the phrase 'jetons d'abeilles', a 'swarm of bees'. That's all that I can tell you about it."

"H'm," remarked the Inspector. "I'm much obliged to Mr. Bathurst for the information, but I don't know that I'm much forrarder."

"Come to that, MacMorran," supplemented Sir Austin somewhat aggressively, "I don't know that you're the only one in that position. Mr. Bathurst seems to be sure that the deaths of these two men, Blundell and Wingfield, are connected, but I readily confess that I, for one, am not altogether satisfied. Cryptograms and legends seem to me to lie far apart from each other. I should require much more evidence than we have at the moment before I definitely laid it down that—"

"When we hear how Wingfield died, sir," intervened Anthony quietly, "perhaps it will help us all to understand. If you will pardon me a tiresome repetition, it is absurd to commence theorizing in the absence of authentic data. Send a message through to Devonshire, Sir Austin, and see what they can tell you from that end. They ought to have the facts by now. They may, or may not, prove illuminating."

When it was sent through to them, the news from the Sidmouth police was startling but, from Mr. Bathurst's point of view, eminently satisfactory. Hubert Athelstan Wingfield had died from an administration of cyanide of potassium. In the opinion of the doctor who had conducted the post-mortem, the poison had been sprayed, by some means, up the dead man's nostrils.

Anthony Bathurst, nerves taut and intelligence quivering, listened quietly while Sir Austin conveyed the information to him. When the Commissioner appeared to have finished, Bathurst taxed him with a question.

"Any mention of anything unusual about Wingfield's body? Face slashed? Any bones broken?"

"Yes," returned Sir Austin gravely, "the left arm is broken below the elbow and the body, generally, shows signs of severe bruising. I—er—accept your conclusions, Bathurst, in the light of all that we know now. I—er—tender you my apologies for having doubted you. You were able to see farther than I."

Anthony Bathurst rose from his chair. "An extraordinary case, sir . . . right from the start of it. But one, nevertheless, with a tremendous appeal. It has that hint of the bizarre that always intrigues the investigator. An animal . . . legendary inscriptions . . . two dead men . . . bruised and poisoned . . . one with his cheek slashed." He shook his head doubtfully. "I am in the dark, Sir Austin, equally with you," he said hopelessly. "It is clear that I shall have to seek the intimacies of both Blundell and Wingfield, and perhaps, too, see the places where they died."

As he spoke, the 'phone on Sir Austin's desk rang peremptorily and insistently. The Commissioner answered it.

"Hallo! Who? MacMorran? Yes, yes. What? . . . Who? Guest? . . . young Guest, do you mean? . . . the young fellow who came here? . . . Good God! . . . yes, yes, of course . . . get down there at once. Tell this Doctor Summerhayes that I sent you. Then report to me immediately you are able."

Sir Austin replaced the receiver and turned to the man at his side. "They come, not in spies, but in battalions. Young Guest . . . young Hugh Guest, John Blundell's nephew, was found dead last night in his bedroom at Sir Richard Ingle's place in the Isle of Wight. So far, cause of death has not been ascertained. Or, if it has, MacMorran hasn't heard yet. An ordinary young man this time, Bathurst. Mark that fact. Knowing nothing, I should say, of either cryptograms or legends. Just a commonplace young Englishman. Now what have you to say?"

"Only one thing, sir, that may seem in the slightest degree sensible."

"What's that?"

"That he's the nephew of our first murdered man, Sir Austin. He touches the fatal circle in the radius of relationship." Anthony Bathurst began to pace the room.

Chapter IV
THE DEAD MAN AT SIR RICHARD INGLE'S

Hearing his name called somewhat authoritatively, Hugh Guest halted in his tracks.

"Yes," he asked over his shoulder. "What is it?" Turning, he saw who it was had called to him. "Do you want me, Covington?" he enquired again.

"Shouldn't have bellowed out to you, you blighter, if I hadn't. Come in here for a minute, if you don't mind."

Guest slipped silently from the gravelled path outside the morning-room at Sir Richard Ingle's into the room itself. "Well, what's worrying you, Covington? Got something extra for the three-thirty?"

For a moment or so Barry Covington was silent. It was evident that he had ignored the raillery. Suddenly he burnt his boats. "Look here, old chap," he opened nervously, "don't think I've got cold feet, or anything like that, if I tell you something. Promise me. And forgive me, too, if I seem to be butting in on an affair that doesn't really concern me. I know how hellishly worried you are, and all that, and I know something that I think you ought to know. Is that O.K.?"

The lines of Guest's mouth tightened. Lines that hadn't been noticed before now showed plainly at its corners. What the merry hell was Covington dithering about? What on earth could he possibly know that . . . ? All the same, though, he supposed he'd better let him have his say—couldn't lose over it, anyway. Any thread thrown towards one was worth picking up.

"I don't quite cotton on, Covington, but I'm ready to listen to you. Is that what you want me to say?"

Covington, a little uncertain of his reception, gave him a sidelong glance. "First of all, Guest, is there any more news of your uncle?"

Hugh Guest was surprised at the question. "Up to the moment, Covington, none. Why? Why, particularly?"

"Just a minute, old son. Don't travel too fast for me. Let me get the hang of things. You've been to Scotland Yard, of course?"

"Naturally. Two or three times. I've interviewed the Chief Commissioner himself—Sir Austin Kemble. Got fed up to the eyebrows with the Sussex bobbies and decided to go to the fountain head. I thought you knew I'd been up there. What's biting you?"

"Have a spot of patience and I'll tell you. What have the 'Yard' done? That they've *told* you?"

Guest frowned. "Made the usual routine enquiries. People are always disappearing, you know, for one reason and another. It's only when you run up against it personally that you realize it. There's a special man on it—one of the 'Big Six'—MacMorran, his name is, I believe. Struck me as being pretty capable. So far he's toiled for days and days and caught nothing. My uncle seems to have disappeared without leaving the slightest trace. Pretty sickening, what?"

Covington looked round anxiously—privacy at Sir Richard's country house was not usually of long life. "Tell me, Guest, do you suspect foul play?"

Guest bit his lip. He was troubled. "I do. Most certainly. What else can I suspect? I think—I am almost sure—that my uncle has been murdered."

Barry Covington eyed him shrewdly. It seemed that he was assessing the strength of Guest's convictions. When he spoke his words were startling.

"Guest," he said, "if Scotland Yard know nothing, *you do*. I'm *sure* of it. Tell me—that's right, isn't it?"

Guest shrugged his shoulders with a superficial nonchalance that he was far from feeling. "Perhaps. But you tell me something. Let's get back to the position from which we were supposed to start. There's a reason behind your saying all this. What do *you* know?"

Covington returned question for question. "Guest, think carefully over what I'm going to say to you. Do you think that you yourself may be in danger? That the murderers of your uncle may be out to get you?"

Guest turned sharply, "Out with it, Covington. What do you know?"

Covington came to the point. Guest's manner impressed him. "Directly after breakfast this morning I went out for a stroll. Nowhere in particular. Just footled round on my own. It's a habit of mine. I may say that my original idea when I came down was eighteen holes with Ella. We fixed it up the night before. But she wasn't keen, she said, when the morning came, so it fell through. Well, I went over the downland in the direction of Lashey. Past the old bridge and then on beyond the church. Do you know that big bush as you go up the first slope that leads to Lashey Down—on the Vesey side?"

Guest nodded impatiently. "Yes—quite well. Go on."

Covington needed no second invitation. "Halfway up that slope I came over abominably lazy. It was warmish walking, and I was growing a mammoth thirst. I decided on a pipe and a rest—in the shade of the big bush that I mentioned. I had the pipe, and the 'rest' became a 'snooze'. As far as I can tell I suppose I must have dozed for about three-quarters of an hour—judging by my watch. When I woke up it was to the accompaniment of voices—men's voices. I looked round sleepily to see where they came from."

By this time Covington's voice had sunk to a mere whisper. "After a time I saw there were two men standing on the summit of the ridge. I can't tell you what either of them was like because each of them had his back to me. It seemed to me as I looked at them, and from the tones of their voices, that they had stopped to argue about something. One man was apparently enforcing his views upon the other—almost to the extent, I thought, of giving orders. Well, it wasn't my pigeon, I concluded, and I was just about to turn over to go to sleep again, when I heard something that made me sit up suddenly and take notice."

Covington paused for dramatic effect. "I heard your name mentioned, Guest."

A shadow fell across Guest's face. "Mine? Are you sure, Covington?"

"Dead certain. Not a glimmer of doubt. The name I heard was yours, 'Hugh Guest'. There could be no mistaking it. The smaller man of the two then said, 'What an extraordinary coincidence!' I'm sure he said that. Then the wind took his words away from me, and the next coherent word I was able to catch was 'doorstep', although I don't know what the connection was. Then the taller bloke said, 'He's at Beech Knoll—Sir Richard Ingle's place—he's been shadowed all the way. You needn't worry about the information being authentic. All you have to do is to obey the orders that are given to you. There's no coincidence about the affair, either—take that from me; it's been deliberately designed. Guest knows what he's doing down here perfectly well. You'll find that he'll be attended to all right. In the meantime, you get along to Ralph and carry out the guv'nor's wishes.'

"I was able to hear this because I had managed to crawl a bit nearer to them, but at that the two of them turned and walked away."

Guest did not seem unduly perturbed. "It's decent of you to tell me all this, Covington, but all the same, I think that you may be over-anxious, possibly, and have been inclined to scent trouble unnecessarily. The conversation may have had quite an innocent direction. These people, whoever they are, may want to see me on a perfectly reasonable every-day sort of matter. There's no earthly reason that I can see why I should hang out signals of distress."

Covington nodded. "Agreed—in a way, every time. But your uncle, Guest—this coming on top of your uncle—accumulatively it makes a difference, surely?"

"Perhaps; but there may be a dozen reasons behind it all. One in particular that I can call to mind would explain the whole business. Still, many thanks, Covington. I'll promise to keep my eyes skinned, if that will satisfy you, and I'm certainly better off for the knowledge that you've given me. Where's Ella now?"

"Gone into Trinque in the Bentley. Shopping, I believe. That was the excuse that she suggested to me when she cried off golf. More likely to interview her bookmaker, if the truth's known. She's a chip of the old block, if ever there was one. Old Ingle's always ready to bet on anything. Don't know what he'll do when Peter yields him entrance. It won't be heaven to him without a Tote double."

Guest grinned in appreciation of Covington's remark. "'Where there's a will, there's an "each way".' He'll probably run a system that will revolutionize the place. On the look-out for what he calls a decent price, he'll back the harp's second string, or something, on an increasing stake. It's astonishing what determination does for one."

Covington laughed boisterously. "Well, that's that. I'll stroll out and see if there's any sign of the daughter of the house. She might be on the way back by this time. So long, Guest, and remember what I've told you; don't forget to keep your eyes open."

"I won't," returned Guest resolutely; "don't you fear."

It was obvious that the letter which Hugh Guest look from his pocket to read and re-read was a source of worry and anxiety to him. Three or four times, after perusals of it, he rose from his chair impatiently and paced the room, to seat himself again soon afterwards. Three or four times, too, during the day he had sent for Garrett, Sir Richard's butler and general manservant, and enquired if any message had come for him by telephone, or anyhow; to receive always the same reply—which left him unsatisfied.

At a quarter to six he decided that it was time to dress for dinner. There would be no further developments that day. As he entered his bedroom a valet was standing by the bedside attending to the studs of his dress-shirt. When the man turned towards him he saw that it was not a man whom he had seen before. There had been a change in the personnel of the staff perhaps. The face of the man was entirely unfamiliar to him; there was something about it that suggested a mask. Its owner was tall, thin and cadaverous. His head was much larger than the average, with a dome-like forehead that suggested the chart of the advertising phrenologist.

He adjusted a cuff-link and then said something which made Guest catch his breath in astonishment.

"Mr. Hugh Guest?" The interrogation was definitely extraordinary. For the voice that uttered it was harsh, strange and minatory.

Guest pulled himself together so that he should face whatever might be coming. "I am Hugh Guest. . . . Yes . . . yes . . . what is it? . . . I think that you have the advantage of me."

The man smiled—a smile that held no quality of amity. "Perhaps. Yet we have something in common, I fancy."

"What do you mean?"

"This, I believe, came from you. Is it not so?"

Guest, in astonishment, took the letter from his extended hand. His eyes immediately told him the truth. Things were as he had half hoped and half feared. "Yes, yes; but what are you doing here? In this room, like this? Masquerading as a servant? For that's what it comes to, neither more nor less. Where is—"

The man addressed held up his hand. "S'sh, Mr. Guest. Walls have been said to have ears. Mention no names, please. Accept my apology also for appearing in this unexpected guise. Believe me, it would not be so were it not highly necessary. Have you the letter to which *you yourself* made reference? That, I think, if produced, will seal the matter, shall we say?"

21 | THE SPIKED LION

Guest hesitated for a moment. The position was developing as he had expected, but . . . Then his hand went to his pocket. The man took the letter and read it through coolly and carefully. A second smile equalled the first in its suggestion of hidden craft and cunning.

"Yes," he said at length, tapping the paper almost maliciously. "We will consider this as satisfactory. It is as it should be. We understand one another, as one might say."

He glanced at the door questioningly. "No one will come in, I suppose, Mr. Guest? We are safe from disturbance? The last thing that I should desire in a matter of this kind would be an interruption."

"Don't worry about that. That can be attended to very easily." Guest walked across and locked the bedroom door. "Well—my uncle; where is he?"

The man to whom he spoke spread out his hands almost obsequiously. "Safe, Mr. Guest. Quite safe, and most zealously cared for. Make your mind easy on that score. He has charged me with a message to you. You are to be patient while he is away, and to take no further action unless advised by him. He deplores, rather, the fact that you have seen fit to consult Scotland Yard. He expects to be home at Hurstfold before the next week is out. You are to rest content and just expect him."

Hugh Guest set his teeth. "That's all very well as far as it goes. But how do I know the truth of it? All the consideration seems to be on one side. What proof have I that my uncle isn't already dead? It seems to me that—"

The man whom he addressed swung round on to him with a hint of violence. "Must you be a child, and think as a child? Must you see the wires by which the marionettes are worked before you believe in them? God—the generations of Didymus flourish for all time! Well, so be it. I might have known. Come here, Mr. Guest, and look at this."

Guest, startled at first by the man's sudden fury, walked towards the bed, at the side of which stood the intruder. The latter's fingers went to the pocket of his vest. With a quick flick of the wrist he held something up for Guest to see. It was a counter, creamy in colour and square in shape.

The strange visitor blazed on: "Evolution cannot be denied; you will admit the truth of that! Argue as men will! Even in terms of animals, Mr. Guest. Take Hellenistic military history, for example. The great warhorse surely followed the invention of the cataphract or heavy-armed horse-archer. The arrow was the weapon of the long range. The elephant, possibly, tusked and ponderous, was the forerunner of our modern 'tank'. Who knows the truth of these things? But look on this picture—the sign of another animal. Your uncle has sent it to you."

Guest stared at the pearly counter, amazed, bewildered. Into what nest of grotesque mystery had his feet strayed?

"I have a surer proof of your uncle's safety here, Mr. Guest, if you care to glance at it. 'There are more things in heaven and earth, Horatio . . .'"

The fingers of the intruder went towards another vest-pocket and his eyes seemed to nod mysteriously in the direction of the window. Guest, again reminded of a flesh-like mask, looked at him with a strange sort of fascination, and then turned his head towards the window also. What was coming to him now, and from where? He was off his guard completely at the moment—forgetful of Covington's warning to him—for the first time since this extraordinary interview started.

The man's action, when it came, took him entirely by surprise. The stranger threw up the window with a quickness of movement that was startling. He pointed and then advanced on Hugh Guest. Guest moved back a pace—two paces—but it was too late to ward off the peril that came to him. He drew a deep breath—which didn't seem to be there, as it were—it lost its way and escaped from him, eluded him somehow—and the body of Hugh Guest slid gently to the floor.

The murderer turned swiftly from the dead body and departed by the way he had come. He had accomplished the task he had set himself.

Chapter V
MR. RAPHAEL SUFFERS INTERRUPTION

It was approximately a quarter past seven when Guest's absence was first noticed. On this occasion the house-party at Beech Knoll was comparatively few in number. The members shall be detailed. Sir Richard and Lady Ingle, host and hostess; Ella, the daughter of the house; Barry Covington; Hugh and Celia Guest, brother and sister; and a friend of the host, by name Slingsby Raphael, who had arrived during the latter part of that same afternoon.

This last merits some intimate description. Tall, dark—his hair was raven-black—a complexion ivory in colour, and with massive head and a most remarkable pair of eyes. At times they positively glittered; at other times they smouldered and then dulled to a dead fire. But always, whether glittering or dull, they looked through the person to whom Raphael spoke. A recent dweller in the Isle of Wight, he was clean-shaven and most slenderly built. The symmetry and athleticism of his figure were amazing; he always moved with that peculiar and arresting grace that seems to be the heritage of some. His age was difficult to gauge, if one judged by the usual external appearances. In his case, however, there had been physical influences that were unusual. He had lived for many years in North-Western China, and had the reputation of knowing more about the secret societies of the Chinese than any other living being.

The author of many books dealing with the mysticism and occultism of the East, his fantasy describing the planting of the sacred Bo tree in Ceylon by Devanampiyatissa *circa* 300 B.C. had created something like a stir from Hong Kong to Tibet, for it was given to few Westerners to understand the inner workings of the Oriental mind to the fine degree that Slingsby Raphael did.

His parentage was shrouded in mystery, but it was freely rumoured that he was a prominent member of the notorious Triad Society. On that point, however, Raphael, on the two memorable occasions that he had been questioned, had maintained a discreet silence. Discreet indeed, for he still lived, whereas his companion on each occasion, less tactful than he, had screamed horribly before entering upon eternal silence.

It was Barry Covington, fortified by his special knowledge, of course, who first called attention to Guest's defection. Raphael was speaking as only he could when Covington interrupted.

"I admit that I am orthodox," said Raphael, "when it comes to my view of Art. Art should illuminate, my dear Ella. The artist should never be allowed to degenerate into a manipulator of mechanical toys . . . clever, perhaps . . . subtle . . . but inevitably, in time, a mere second-hand dealer in emotion that should be splendid . . . in tragedies, that by all the laws of Nature should be majestically desperate. It cannot be denied that Life is violent . . . terrific in its range. . . ."

Here Raphael paused and looked into the colour of his wine. Barry Covington seized his chance.

"By the way," he blurted, "we're one short. Where's old Hugh, Celia?"

"I was just wondering the same thing," returned the girl a little anxiously. "It's so unlike Hugh to be late for dinner. For an appointment—yes—but never for 'food'."

"I'll give him a good dressing-down when he does show up," intervened Sir Richard Ingle, half jestingly and half in earnest. "Manners were different in my time, I can assure you. We were cocks of a different hackle. Never late at the starting-post. You could lay a hundred to one, at a party of this kind, without the slightest fear of losing your bet—"

"Where has Mr. Guest been this afternoon, Richard?" queried Lady Ingle. "Have you seen him about anywhere?"

The people round the table looked at one another; each seemed to seek the answer to the hostess's question in the eyes of another. Individuals surrendered their egotisms to the call of the community. Raphael seemed annoyed at the interruption which he had suffered. He was the first to throw off the mood of doubt.

"Is there any need for us to put Guest's activities under the microscope at this time of the evening?" He turned to Celia with an exaggerated gallantry. "You will forgive me, I know, my dear young lady, if I should seem unkind or ungenerous. But I am the protagonist of individual responsibility. The champion of the freedom of the 'ego'. I fail to see why the children's teeth should be set on edge because the fathers have eaten grapes that were sour. Your brother, doubtless, is a little late through some trifling cause and will be with us at any moment."

Celia smiled at him bravely. "I hope and trust so, Mr. Raphael. All the same . . ." She broke off and crumbled her bread nervously.

"All the same—what?" he asked her smilingly.

"I don't know. That's all I can think of to say. Pretty feeble, isn't it?"

"It's nearly half past seven, Daddy," contributed Ella in a business-like tone. "I can't think that Hugh would be as late as this purposely."

Sir Richard turned and beckoned to Garrett to come close to his chair. "Garrett, when did you last see young Mr. Guest?"

"About half past four, Sir Richard. Just after tea had been served. He came and spoke to me. He had been out, and when he returned he came at once to me to see if there had been any kind of telephone message for him. He had asked me that several times during the day, sir. It struck me that he was rather anxious in regard to something."

"And had there been?"

"No, Sir Richard. None at all. That was what I told him."

"Did he go out again, do you know?"

"I couldn't say, Sir Richard—I didn't see him again, sir, within the house."

"How was he dressed when he spoke to you?"

"In a grey flannel suit, Sir Richard."

Celia listened feverishly to Garrett's replies. Raphael surrendered gracefully to the mood of the moment. He realized where matters were leading. "If it will help things at all, why not see if Guest has dressed for dinner? That may clear up one of our problems. Will his bedroom tell us anything?"

"That's an idea, certainly," agreed Covington. "Will anybody come upstairs with me? No—not you, Celia. You stay down here."

The girl had half risen at Raphael's suggestion, but Barry Covington, knowing what he did, was determined to take no chances.

"Why?" she half whispered. "What are you—"

Covington patted her arm. "You stay here, Celia, and don't worry. You don't want to go dashing about for nothing. What good can you do? We'll be back in half a jiffy." He looked round to see who was to be his companion. None appeared to have accepted the invitation that he had issued.

"You go, Barry," said Lady Ingle. "Though, as you said to Celia, I really don't see what good you're doing. If Hugh isn't there, we're just as we were in the first place, still wondering *where* he is. Never mind—go along up," she concluded with resignation.

Covington obeyed orders. They heard him ascend the stairs. "Let me see, now," said Slingsby Raphael reflectively; "where was I when Covington started to scare us? Ah—I remember. I was about to demonstrate how Art should jolt us out of the channels of cynicism and prove to us that Nature has made so many things that are bright and beautiful. Each generation stands upon the shoulders of the generation that preceded it. That is indisputable. Knowledge is piled upon knowledge . . . Pelion upon Ossa . . . and yet—despite all that has been—all that has gone before us, we are only groping blindly at the beginning of things, with callous fingers and blunted thumbs."

There was a pause. He proceeded:

"The doors are ajar, perhaps—certainly not more than half open to us; the question is, therefore, how are we going to deal with the task of taking real possession and entering into the kingdom that should be our inheritance? Art, being by far Life's truest and most noble interpretation—"

Before he could complete his sentence the door opened opposite to him and Barry Covington entered. He spoke to the company generally, but it was to Celia Guest particularly that his words were primarily addressed.

"I can't get into Hugh's bedroom," he said; "the door seems to be locked on the inside."

At this statement the leaven of uneasiness that had taken hold of the room fermented into fear, but it was a tribute to the general self-control that no cry of alarm at imagined tragedy broke the silence. It was as though each individual mind was at exercise—pondering over what Barry Covington had said. Eventually Raphael made a gesture of the head towards the place where sat his host, and framed the gesture with a practical question.

"Shall we go up, Dick, you and I, with Covington?" Sir Richard looked askance at Lady Ingle and then nodded his acceptance of Raphael's suggestion. The men rose, the three of them. Celia Guest, during all this, said nothing. She looked straight across the table at Ella and clenched her hands tight.

The three men departed on their mission and came to Hugh Guest's bedroom door. As Covington had announced in the dining-room, it was locked on the inside—judging, that is, from the fact that the key was not visible. Raphael tried it. He rattled the handle. Half turning to his companion, he flung a question over his shoulder. "Did you call to him, Covington, when you came up here just now?"

Barry Covington looked doubtful and uncertain. "That's funny, you know. Now that I come to think it over, I don't believe I did."

Raphael frowned. "Why not? Surely it was the first—"

"I just didn't think of it, I suppose. I tried the door, as you tried it a minute ago . . . found it wouldn't budge, and came downstairs to tell you. I took things for granted, I think, as one does sometimes."

"What things?"

"Oh . . . I don't know. I'm not sure if I called to him or not. For God's sake don't catechize me now. What are we going to do?"

Raphael frowned again and looked at Sir Richard Ingle.

"We must break this door down," declared the latter. "There's nothing else for it. I'll lay ten to one Guest's queer or something. Help me, will you, please? You too, Barry. Come on now."

The three men put their shoulders against the door and pushed it with all their weight and might. "Put your weight just here," grunted Raphael. "This is the place where it will give . . . that should do the trick, I think."

The door slowly gave to the continued assault . . . inches at a time . . . until . . .

"My God!" said Slingsby Raphael, his voice hoarse with emotion. . . . "Down there, by the side of the bed . . . can you see it? . . . Down there . . . look!"

Ingle and Barry Covington each saw it over Raphael's shoulders. Covington gave a startled gasp. The body of Hugh Guest was lying on the floor by the bed, his back towards them, as they entered. Not a man now . . . the shell only of a man. Raphael was the first of the three discoverers to reach it. He strode quickly to the body and dropped on his knees beside it. After the slightest hesitation he put a hand somewhere on the prone form . . . and pulled it over . . . that they might see its face.

"Guest!" muttered Covington, although he had known it all the time—articulate expression of what each one of them was thinking. . . . "Guest . . . dead!"

Ingle was prompt and efficient. "I'll 'phone at once. There's a doctor quite handy . . . you two fellows stay up here. . . . I'll see that the ladies stay where they are . . . leave it to me."

Covington looked fearfully at Raphael. "How did he die . . . have you thought?"

The man addressed shook his head. "There's no weapon here. Looks like a sudden seizure of some kind to me . . . heart, perhaps, or a fit of sorts . . . can't say. . . . The doctor will tell us all we want to know when he comes. Perhaps more."

Covington shook his head and edged towards the window. "Don't move anything, Covington," said Raphael sharply . . . "You never know. There may be something in this that you and I can't see at the moment."

Covington turned quickly . . . his hands were trembling. It seemed that the shock that had come to him was overwhelming him.

*

Dr. Summerhayes answered Sir Richard Ingle's summons with quiet alacrity. His thin professional figure moved almost mechanically to the body on the floor. He knelt beside it as Raphael had done a matter of ten minutes previously. He felt the dead man's limbs . . . legs first . . . arms after that. Staring down at the body, the academic lines of his face never lost their almost expressionless reserve. After a brief period his eyes ceased to stare; he turned and gazed at the door and the window. The eyes of the three men with him followed his.

"Heart failure, Doctor?" queried Raphael in nervous eagerness.

"The heart has failed, certainly," returned Summerhayes austerely; "it generally does, you know, when death intervenes." He shook his head doubtfully, but before the action was completed he had bent his head close to the dead man's face. To his lips. To the lower parts of the nose. Then came another head-shake. Ominous this time, and more definite.

"What is the cause of death, then, Doctor Summerhayes? Is it—"

"Poison, Sir Richard. I think, by cyanide of potassium. But there is very little of the usual aroma that one finds when it is used . . . the bitter almonds, you know. Very little indeed. Nothing at all at the man's lips. I get it more from his nostrils."

He sniffed at Guest's face and closed the dead man's eyes.

"Do you mean that it's been self-administered, Doctor? Suicide?"

Summerhayes hesitated. It was evident that something troubled him, apart from the manner of the victim's death. His eyes strayed round the room again. "I gather from the broken door that he had locked himself in. You gentlemen were compelled to force an entrance—is that so?"

Raphael nodded. "Yes. We weren't able to get in any other way. The door was locked on the inside."

Summerhayes' eyes went to the lock. He seemed stirred by what he saw there. His voice, too, took on a note of strain and harsh excitement, so that its previous culture went from it. "In that case, then, Sir Richard, where is the key? Did one of you gentlemen take it out of the lock? If you did . . . I think—"

"No," blurted Covington. "I didn't. I know Sir Richard didn't."

"And I can assure you that I didn't," supplemented Raphael lightly. "I don't know why I didn't think of it before, but Guest has it on him somewhere, no doubt. Must have. Have a look, Doctor. Then there will be no mystery about it. Try his pockets."

Summerhayes returned to the body. This time he knelt down by it on one knee only. He tried the pockets, and, in turn, came to the breast pocket of the coat, on the left-hand side. Those who watched saw his eyes light a little. The reason for this was soon apparent to them. Dr. Summerhayes held up the missing key for all of them to see.

"Then Guest must have locked himself in," cried Raphael impetuously—"deliberately . . . to poison himself. He committed—"

Sir Richard and Summerhayes looked towards the window—each with intent. The doctor put into words the thought that had taken possession of each of them.

"What you say may be true, but it is as well to point out that we don't know that for certain. Couldn't the second person have been here with him and—"

"It's absolutely impossible," cried Raphael in impulsive interruption; "there isn't a foothold from that window for a cat. Look for yourselves if you don't believe me."

"He's right," conceded the host. "I know this window only too well—nobody could have made an escape that way."

The others, realizing the truth of what had been said, surveyed the situation rather hopelessly. "Everything points to suicide, then," declared Raphael. "You can't get away from it."

Again Summerhayes shook his head. "Don't you agree with me, Doctor?" urged Raphael.

"It would seem so," admitted the doctor, "when we think of the conditions—the window and the locked door; but how did he administer the poison? That's my great difficulty—explain that away. There's nothing on the floor anywhere, is there? Or rolled under the bed?"

Every inch of the floor was covered by examination; nothing could be traced of the nature indicated by Summerhayes. "I think it is a case for the police," declared the last-named gravely. "I admit, as I said, that the door being locked on the inside and the key being in the young man's pocket is most significant and almost overwhelming. . . . Also, I am forced to say from my examination that the man has been dead not more than a quarter of an hour . . . yet I am not satisfied."

He rose and dusted his knees, a resolute expression on his lean face. Raphael, grasping all that the doctor's words meant, glanced towards Sir Richard. "Surely you would be able to—"

Ingle seemed to sense what was coming, for he checked Raphael's statement. "No," he announced with quiet dignity; "Dr. Summerhayes is absolutely right in what he says must be done. It's no use us kicking against the pricks. This is a case for the police. That's a dead cert. I'll see to it at once. Perhaps you fellows would be good enough to tell the ladies what has happened. Break it as gently as you know how—Celia's just about all in, I fancy."

His distress was plain to see as he turned and made his way from the room.

Chapter VI
ANTHONY BATHURST ATTACKS

Mr. Bathurst was precise. "Do I understand that this is the *exact* spot, MacMorran? Would an X here show where the body was found? I want you to be very sure, Inspector." He gazed long and hard at a strip of green grass.

"Yes, Mr. Bathurst," replied MacMorran; "that's almost the identical place, where you're now standing."

"You know well, MacMorran, that I abominate vague impressions. If people would only treasure detail in what they hear and read, many crimes would have been solved that have gone down to history as undiscovered. The husbanding and harvesting of detail—how they count in this game of ours, MacMorran. The vital clue is always there somewhere for the observant to grasp. The all-important thread is always to be picked out, and the way to it may come from a stray word of wit, wantonness or wisdom, or from a fugitive mood of sense or nonsense, that only asks for recognition at the psychological moment."

He stared at the grass and ground. "There's disturbance here, MacMorran—look."

"Aye. I observed that, Mr. Bathurst. There was a struggle. I guess that three or four people were concerned in it. But the ground's too dry and hard for any footprints to show. Grass doesn't take 'em too well, either."

Bathurst grunted. He neither denied nor accepted MacMorran's contention. Actually he walked towards the nearest tree—a big chestnut. He gazed up at it—into its branches—wonderingly.

"Do you know, MacMorran," he said meaningly, "there's a lot about this case that's going to be damned difficult to prove."

"How do you mean, sir?"

Anthony looked at him quizzically. "Well, you can't put a tree under a microscope like you can a hair, can you? It's built on too big a scale. *N'est-ce pas?*"

MacMorran screwed up his face. "Where are you heading for, sir? I don't know that I've arrived."

"Remember my investigation of Colonel Cameron's death at Dallow Corner? That strange affair of the red leech? One of the clues that led me to the truth was a tiny smear of pink blood on a small stone near a puddle of water in an inn yard. Well, what I mean is this. You could put that pebble under a microscope, Inspector, but I'm hanged if you can do that with a tree. Who knows what horror may lurk in those branches up there?"

Bathurst extended an arm towards high heaven. "Yes, Inspector," he proceeded; "I mean it. Perhaps a tiny horror. Perhaps a huge horror. Who knows? And one might search up there for days on end . . . and fail to find the vital detail that would open up the truth."

MacMorran nodded. He felt that it was his safest course. A nod was non-committal.

"Tell me something more," continued Anthony, "for there are gaps. Who discovered Blundell's body?"

"A workman named Derbyshire engaged on repair work to the Hampton Court Bridge. A mason, working for a firm of contractors, Allan and Co. A decent sort of fellow. He wasted no time about it. Went to the police at once."

"And you eventually came along with a constable—Chatterton, wasn't it?"

"That's so. Sir Austin gave orders that I should come along. I'd been dealing with Blundell's disappearance, you see. He wanted me to take both jobs."

"H'm. Did you see the dead man's nephew when he went to the 'Yard'?"

"Guest? No, Mr. Bathurst. The Commissioner interviewed the young chap himself. I've seen him since down at Hurstfold."

"And now *he's* dead," added Bathurst quietly but pointedly, "so that we shall learn nothing from him."

MacMorran eyed him shrewdly. "You think that he knew something, then—eh, Mr. Bathurst?"

"I'm inclined to think so, MacMorran, and that they dammed his eloquence. Certainly."

"I'm not so sure."

"Why not?" Anthony's question was quick.

MacMorran seized his chance and became argumentative. "Well, this is how it strikes me. Hugh Guest came to us for help, didn't he? Reported his uncle's disappearance to the authorities, and, generally speaking, put his cards on the table. Why should anybody kill him *after* he got in touch with the 'Yard'. Before—very likely. But why *after*?"

Anthony considered MacMorran's point. "*Touché.* That's a bit of a poser, I must admit. But all the same, after some consideration I think I can find one possible explanation."

"Aye—I reckoned you would. I've never known you when you couldn't. I'd like to hear it, Mr. Bathurst."

Anthony replied to him with a certain lightness.

"I'll continue with your own simile of the cards on the table. When you play cards you don't always play with the same hand, Inspector. During the course of a game more than one hand is dealt to you. This is how I look at it. Guest may have had a card dealt to him *after* he went to Sir Austin—a card which he had never seen before and which, for some reason not clear to us at the moment, he may have decided to play entirely on his own. How's that, Inspector?"

MacMorran contemplated the idea. Also he rubbed his nose. "It's feasible, I suppose, but you've not convinced me, Mr. Bathurst. Why should Guest do that? What reason had he? It was inconsistent with his having called in help in the first place. Why should he suddenly change his tactics, as it were?"

Bathurst shrugged his shoulders. "Ah, you're going a bit too far. I don't know. We don't know. Something may have happened . . . he may have stumbled on some piece of truth unwillingly . . . not knowing, perhaps, at the time, that it *was* the link that he had been seeking. I'll grant you that the theory may be what you term 'inconsistent', but I won't concede that it's impossible or even improbable. I've made up my mind on that point."

He prodded the grass with his stick. MacMorran watched him and made no reply. Anthony allowed him no respite. He proceeded immediately:

"You know, Inspector—you haven't found a satisfactory answer to one of my *first* questions regarding this Blundell murder. A question that I put to you when we originally discussed matters at the 'Yard'. Why should a *poisoned* victim have a bruised body, a broken limb and a scratched cheek?"

MacMorran was still silent. Again Anthony attacked. "Wingfield, too, down in South Devon, poisoned, we believe, by the same person, has bruises and a broken limb . . . but no slashed face. Guest dies from the same poison as the other two . . . so we are now told, but is not bruised, maimed or slashed. But neither he nor Wingfield died beneath a tree. The Wiltshire gentleman is found in somewhat similar circumstances to Blundell, in a valley of ferns. . . . Hugh Guest himself dies in the bedroom of his host . . . with his boots on."

Anthony paced the green strip of grass. "A damned awkward problem, MacMorran, say what you will about it." He caressed his chin thoughtfully, to turn, with sudden eagerness, upon the dour Inspector watching him.

"Blundell's clothes, MacMorran? What were they like? Tell me all that you can remember about them."

MacMorran marshalled his information. "Ordinary blue serge suit, such as is worn by thousands of men all over the country, but well above the average, I'd say, in quality, cut, style and so forth. Shirt and collar of the usual kind—underclothes ditto. Shoes also. Everything, as you might say, just ordinary—not distinctive." MacMorran paused in his descriptive adventure.

"Go on," said Mr. Bathurst encouragingly. "Tell me more of this commonplace type with a stick and pipe."

"Eh—what's that you're saying—how d'ye mean?"

Anthony returned to the prosaic. "Hat—cap," he returned laconically.

"There wasn't one," returned the Inspector.

Anthony grimaced. "None at all?"

MacMorran shook his head emphatically. "That's just what I'm saying. And there's not much point in it either, if you come to work it out. It's extraordinary the number of folk nowadays that go walking bare-headed. Both young fellows and young women."

"That's perfectly true, MacMorran, so far as it goes as a general statement. But was it Blundell's habit to go abroad without a hat? You've checked up on it, of course?"

"Aye, I have that. 'Twas one of the first things I went for. But I haven't come away with a lot of what you'd call satisfaction. I'll tell you what I'm told. He would wear a hat sometimes, and sometimes he wouldn't. 'Twould depend on a number of circumstances—the weather, where he was going, who was with him, and so on. That's from his people—this Mr. Guest and his sister. The former told the Commissioner and the latter told me."

"Missing for a fortnight," quoted Bathurst. "What about the morning when he left his house in the Hayward's Heath district? Was he bare-headed then?"

"No. His niece, Miss Guest, helped me with regard to that. She is able to remember for certain that her uncle was wearing a hard felt hat when he went out that morning. That is why she is of the opinion that he was going somewhere 'important'. I'm using the same adjective that she used to me when I went down to Blundell's place in Sussex."

"H'm! Went out with a hat and is found without one."

"If you'll pardon me, Mr. Bathurst, it's not a bit of good weaving fantastic theories concerning that felt hat. The murdered man was missing from his home for about fourteen days. The good God alone knows where he went to during that period. He may have visited a hundred different places, and his hat may be in any one of 'em."

"Much more likely to have visited *one*, MacMorran, and one only, the occupant of which could join the good God in that general knowledge class of yours. Still, we're only groping, I admit. Now another line of question. Correspondence, MacMorran—in that Sussex home of Blundell's. Run across anything?"

"There wasn't a single thing, Mr. Bathurst, that would throw the faintest light upon the case. I searched everywhere. Miss Guest helped me, and her brother came from Oxford one afternoon and we all went through the missing man's papers together. All the recent correspondence was the same as his clothes—just ordinary. Mostly from people near at hand—friends, tradesmen and the like. There wasn't anything, that we were able to find, to take him out one morning on an errand that you could call 'important'."

"Nothing in the nature of a secret message or cryptogram? Hidden somewhere or *in* something? Of the excessively simple and innocent kind? Hidden, let me definitely suggest, in the most ordinary of everyday letters?"

"Not in my opinion, Mr. Bathurst," returned the Inspector with sturdy doggedness. "I'm not an authority on these matters, I know only too well, but if the stuff I looked at wasn't the real and genuine, put me down as a Dutchman."

Anthony smiled and tried again. "Servants—did you see any of them?"

MacMorran shook his head and went on to explain. "Only two—a maid and a housekeeper. It's a charming house, but on the small side. As a rule, there were only Blundell and his niece in residence there. The housekeeper's a downy old bird—foreign blood in her, I should say. Couldn't get anything out of her."

"Tight-lipped—eh?"

"Tight-lipped? I'd just say so. Wore lip-buttoners. Compared with her a clam's a hundred per cent all singing and talking."

Anthony grinned appreciatively. "Let me come back to the dead man's clothes, Inspector, for a minute. You headed me off just now, and I allowed myself to digress. Tell me this. The body was bruised, the face was slashed and a limb was broken . . . were the *clothes* torn at all?"

"Aye, they were that. The sleeve of the coat was torn. Properly ripped. There was a tear about five inches long. I reckon he got that in the same way that he got his face slashed. In the struggle. He put up a fight against odds and got the worst of it. That's all there was to it."

Anthony Bathurst rubbed his hands. "Do you know, MacMorran," he remarked almost jocularly, "I fancy that we've gained a little ground. Half an hour ago I was torn between Wiltshire and the Isle of Wight. I was inclined to move in what I will call the *sequence* of murder. That was also the Commissioner's suggestion. But what I have learned here has decided me. The scales are weighed and I have seen the manner of their balance. Beech Knoll, I believe, is the name of Sir Richard Ingle's place."

MacMorran nodded. "Aye."

"Beech Knoll," repeated Mr. Bathurst softly—it might have been to himself. . . . "I find the name distinctly attractive."

MacMorran smiled a wry smile. "Never could see much in names, myself."

Chapter VII
SLINGSBY RAPHAEL LOOKS AT PICTURES

ON THE second morning after the death of Hugh Guest, Slingsby Raphael walked through the house named Beech Knoll—the house in which Hugh Guest had died. Raphael was the prey to many thoughts and some visions. He moved with the directness of purpose. His steps were turned towards the famous Long Gallery, which filled all the upper floor of the west wing. Here were the Valhalla and the treasure-house of the Ingles. Here the portraits of bygone Ingles hung in the exquisite company of infinitely precious things which they, and their ancestors before them, had wrested from the earth.

Raphael's breath almost stopped as he stood in the gallery and gazed up at this long line of pictures. There was a catch in his throat. He worshipped beauty with an unusual passion, and would have crossed a continent for the acquisition of a beautiful thing; to him it would certainly be a joy for ever. The outward calm of Sir Richard Ingle at the tragedy that had so suddenly come upon his house surprised him. But Raphael shrewdly suspected that this calm was more or less superficial and no real index to the disturbing and alarming doubts which were agitating him within.

Slingsby Raphael had more than once publicly declared himself as an apostle of cheerful barbarity, he always maintained that the murderous impulse in humanity is by no means as rare as it is usually assumed to be. He was moderately positive in his own mind that thousands of respectable citizens, ninety-nine per cent amiable, decent and charitable, have experienced it in all its alluring simplicity at least once in their well-ordered lives. The appeal that it makes, then, seems scarcely sinful. It is tinged, however, with a quality which is difficult to define. This description shall be attempted. It is—just dangerous—and it is that element of danger with which the procedure is invested that serves as the brake upon the impulse itself. After all, argue as one may, the effects of civilization saturate our existence. The degree of saturation varies, that is all.

Raphael shivered. The Seigneurs of the Ingles were with him—in the spirit, if not in the frail flesh. Their trove and trophies were the gallery's decorations. He picked up several miniatures; their beauty was a perpetual fascination to him. Lucky man, this present Sir Richard, he contemplated. Not only had he his own estates in this gloriously lovely island, but it seemed, with the death of the present Lord Tresham almost hourly expected, that Fate would pour further treasure into his lap. Raphael held medals in his fingers now—memorials of strong, dark-featured, warrior Ingles.

On the point of replacing them in the lacquer cabinet from which they had come, he heard a light step in the passage that ran outside the gallery. The step was so light that it bordered on the furtive. He realized that interruption was almost inevitable. He turned quickly. But the door of the gallery's entrance was some distance from where he stood. Before he could reach it to command the passage, the person whose steps he had heard had gone. With a stride quickened by surprise he descended the stairs.

An uncomfortable feeling of distrust took hold of him. By impulse or instinct, he determined to find his host. Sir Richard was on the lawn in front of the music-room when Raphael came upon him, and it appeared that he had just been joined by Celia Guest. Raphael's quick pace dropped to a leisurely saunter as he came towards them. When close enough, he spoke carelessly.

"I've been in the Long Gallery. A marvellous place, Ingle. I both envy you and congratulate you. Ever been up there, Miss Guest?"

In the circumstances the words sounded like cold cruelty. But Raphael cared nothing for considerations such as these. He fought for his own, in his own way and on his own terms. If, in the fight, it happened that a woman fell in his path . . . well . . . there were at least five Chinese proverbs that he could apply with a shrug of the shoulders to the satisfaction of his personal honour. Each of the five was an exercise in cold blood, apart from the fact that one wench (to him, as to so many) was as good as another.

On this occasion, however, Sir Richard Ingle gallantly entered the breach. He stole a glance at his young companion and quickly determined how things were. "I'm going to take Celia up there myself," he said kindly; "but not just yet—a little later on. When things are—more settled, you know."

He blew his nose rather violently, and the slim figure, silk-haired and slender-ankled, looked up at him with gratitude in her grey eyes.

Sir Richard went on: "Yes, it's a marvellous place, Raphael, the Long Gallery, as you say, but the Tresham gallery is incomparably finer and grander. A classic compared with a merely good handicapper. I remember going over it with my father one afternoon when I was a boy. I fancy that it was on the occasion of my eighth birthday. Anyhow, that's of no consequence, but it was an experience that I shall never forget. You'll have to come to Tresham when I get there, Raphael, and go over it. You'll be delighted."

Raphael nodded rather coldly. "A Richard will be somewhat out of place at Tresham, won't he?"

"Yes, I suppose he will. Every one of 'em in the past who's held the title has been named Martin." He turned again to Celia. "You slip away, my dear, and find Ella. She told me that she wanted to talk to you. Then you'll feel better. You've been very brave, and I'm proud of you. Two blows in two days such as you've had would try the hardiest."

He patted the girl's hand as she started to obey him. Raphael's eyes followed her and there were both question and wonderment in them. Sir Richard continued to talk. Any subject other than *the* subject attracted him these days.

"The founder of the Tresham family was of Royal blood, you know. In the Tresham library there are shelves upon shelves of books of the family history. Chronicles—records—some early French, some early English—some even from Normandy. I doubt whether I should ever be able to drag you away. You'd revel in them, Raphael."

A curious gleam shone in the eyes of the man addressed. Apparently it was unnoticed by Sir Richard, who proceeded with serenity:

"The eldest sons of the house have always been called Martin because the first of the Treshams was interested—shall we say?—in the Abbey of St. Martin at Lacroix. The Abbey that stands there to this day."

"'Interested?'" Raphael frowned. "How—interested?"

Sir Richard shrugged his shoulders. "I don't know that it is a pretty story. I'll tell it to you, though, all the same. A certain English King was hunting in Normandy; he came to the Abbey St. Martin at Lacroix, and fell in love with the young abbess there. She was a girl, we are told, of singular beauty. For a time there was virtue that refused to yield; but the Royal desire would not be denied, and the son of the alliance was recognized by his kingly father, brought to England and given both lands and a title. The land of the King's gift was a tract by this southern sea here. Along the Hampshire border. Over there."

Sir Richard pointed across the stretch of blue water to the mainland. "The Tresham castle was built on a ridge so that it might bridle the dunes and the marshland. There is a legend that in its earliest days it was guarded by six huge lions which roamed the grounds all night. Hence the Tresham lions."

He paused and then made his last contribution. "And now it seems that all is coming to me."

"Lions as well?" Raphael laughed.

"I don't know about that."

"You will go there, of course?"

"I must. No man would be justified in turning his back on a heritage of that kind and with that history. But I shan't desert Beech Knoll entirely. I can't bring myself to do that . . . even considering the cloud that has now come over it. It's been too big a part of my life for so long. Probably I shall divide my time between Tresham and here."

"How old would the missing Tresham have been now?"

"Nicholas? Well, it's a hell of a time since I last saw him, but in the late forties, I imagine—if he's still alive. But he's not. You can bet your life on that."

"You think not?"

"No. He was wild and harum-scarum right from his boyhood days. More than that—a real bad egg. Nobody was surprised when he left the country. All I know about him is that he was reputed to have the Tresham eyebrows. There was one other piece of information, too, that he sent me gratuitously when he cleared out, that might have come in useful. But the need hasn't arisen. He was probably shot in a drunken brawl somewhere for cheating at cards or stealing somebody's liquor. I should think they would have been two of his most likely hobbies. He's dead, right enough."

Raphael smiled at Ingle's certainty. "Don't count your chickens before they leave the incubator, Richard. You never know. Ghosts of the past often rear their ugly heads at us."

Before Sir Richard could reply, a shadow was thrown across the terrace behind them. "Yes, Garrett," said Sir Richard; "what is it?"

"You'll pardon me, sir," replied the butler, "but there's a gentleman and a policeman asking to see you. The policeman's the one who was here before. The gentleman who's with him asked me to give you this card."

Sir Richard took the card from Garrett's proffered fingers. "Anthony Bathurst," he read out. "Why, that's the—"

Raphael's eyes narrowed. "We are honoured," he interrupted. "Scotland Yard must be extraordinarily interested in us to send this man Bathurst down." He paused to watch Ingle's face intently. "Do you know, Richard," he went on, "I shall be delighted to meet this Anthony Bathurst. The aristocracy of brains has always appealed to me. If only for the sake of 'clash'."

Which statement, upon careful analysis, was not unlike the expression that the same Anthony Bathurst had used a little earlier to Chief-Inspector MacMorran.

Chapter VIII
THE ASSISTANCE OF BARRY COVINGTON

GARRETT awaited his master's pleasure. Sir Richard Ingle fingered Mr. Bathurst's card for a moment or so without replying. It seemed that his thoughts were embracing the past and the future rather than the present. Even when he brought himself back by a supreme effort to the contemporary state, he trod upon the hard pebbles of personal humiliation. This continued questioning by police officers, the whole idea that Beech Knoll was under a process of investigation, irritated him beyond measure. In the past these things had only happened to other people. He had merely read about them or been told about them. Which was as it should be. At length he disciplined himself to meet the bludgeonings of Fate that he felt certain were coming to him. He addressed the passive Garrett:

"I will see both Mr. Bathurst and Sergeant Pullinger, Garrett. Bring them to me out here."

The butler retired. "Don't go, Slingsby," added Sir Richard. "I should like you to stay. You may be able to answer questions more satisfactorily than I can. By the way, while I remember to mention it, what did you think of Pullinger's interrogation of Dr. Summerhayes?"

Raphael answered with deliberation. "I put Pullinger down as having a great deal more intelligence than the usual local 'bobby'. You did the same, Richard. I know that, because I watched your face when he asked Summerhayes that question about the cyanide. But here the beggar is, looking like Charles Laughton in *Payment Deferred*."

Raphael's lips tightened. Sergeant Pullinger came on to the terrace a couple of paces in advance of Anthony Bathurst. Garrett convoyed them.

"Good morning, Sergeant," said Sir Richard.

"Good morning, sir."

Anthony stepped forward. "Good morning, Sir Richard. I must thank you for consenting to see me. My reason for troubling you is this. Sir Austin Kemble, the Commissioner of Police at New Scotland Yard, has asked me to look into the death of Mr. Hugh Guest. I expect, however, that you understood that when your butler first announced me."

Sir Richard softened a little. Things were a little more bearable. This man was a gentleman, a hundred to one on it. Somehow he hadn't expected that. You didn't associate police matters with . . . Or at least it wasn't so in the old days. He pulled himself together.

"Oh yes—good morning. This is Mr. Slingsby Raphael, a great friend of mine. You may speak as frankly to him as to me."

Mr. Bathurst bowed.

Raphael acknowledged the bow courteously. "Shall we seat ourselves? Personally I find that this stone ledge makes an irresistible appeal. On this part of the terrace one is able to enjoy the morning sunshine so thoroughly. It may be informal, but comfort is always my first consideration. You don't blame me—eh?"

"Not at all. I am entirely in agreement," returned Mr. Bathurst. "We will seat ourselves here, as you suggested. May I talk?"

"Of course. I am expecting you to. And we will listen."

"One moment, gentlemen, if you please." The interruption came from Sergeant Pullinger. His voice was curt and business-like.

"Yes. What is it, Sergeant?"

"I'd like to say just this, Sir Richard. I feel that I ought to."

"Go on. We are anxious to hear all that there is to know. Are there developments?"

"No, sir. Not what you'd call developments. But Dr. Summerhayes is even more emphatic now than before that Mr. Guest was poisoned only a short time before he was called to the body. He puts that time now as 'a few minutes'. Secondly, I've received a communication from a gentleman who, I believe, is staying here with you at the present time. A gentleman by the name of Covington. He says in his letter that he has information for me that he considers extremely important. I wrote and told him in reply that I would see him here when I came along to see you. I have your permission, I take it, Sir Richard?"

"Certainly." Ingle's tone was now definitely cold.

"Thank you, sir. When Mr. Bathurst agrees, then, I'll have those few words with this Mr. Covington."

Sir Richard caught Raphael's eye and nodded. "Very well then. Now, Mr. Bathurst, you were going to talk; perhaps you'll have better success this time."

Pullinger rubbed his nose. He could stand as much of that stuff as Sir Richard cared to hand out to him. Pullinger not only knew his job, but had considerable belief in himself. Things weren't as they used to be either; it wasn't a scrap of good the old man thinking that because he was . . . He came away from his contemplation and found himself listening to Anthony Bathurst.

"The murder of Mr. Guest—happening as it did, so soon after the murder of his uncle, Mr. John Blundell—seems to the authorities whom I represent to have assumed proportions far beyond the ordinary. I presume that you, Sir Richard, can throw no light upon the death of Mr. Blundell? You can give no hint—make no suggestion, arising from your knowledge of Hugh Guest, say—that would prove helpful to us?"

"None whatever," replied Ingle promptly. "I am not in that position. The late Mr. Blundell was a complete stranger to me. A name only. I just knew of his existence—that was all. I had never set eyes upon him."

"But you were on a different footing, doubtless, with Hugh Guest?"

"Oh, bless your heart—yes! Hugh's father was one of my oldest friends. We were boys together at, Winchester, and our friendship continued right up to Leonard Guest's death two years ago."

"I see. That brings me to a question that I must ask you. I am sure that you will realize that I consider the question an urgent one, otherwise I wouldn't dream of asking it. Did you actually *invite* Mr. Guest here on the occasion of this last visit of his?"

"Invite? Specially, do you mean?" Sir Richard's frown interested Raphael as well as Anthony Bathurst.

"Yes. Specially—on this last occasion."

"Well, putting it like that—no. Let me explain things. Guest and his sister, Miss Guest, were always welcome here. Always have been. Beech Knoll has been open house to them, as you might say. They could always come here if they wanted to. They knew that very well. When Hugh Guest wrote to me at the beginning of last week to say that he and his sister—"

"That's just what I meant, Sir Richard. What I wanted to know. The suggestion that he should come here emanated from him, then? He wrote to you?"

"Yes. That is so. He wrote to me."

"Now tell me this, Sir Richard," continued Anthony Bathurst; "was he a frequent visitor here?"

"No. Just lately—by no means. More frequent when he was a good many years younger. Used to come here a lot in his 'hols'. When was he last here?" Sir Richard reflected. "At Christmas—either four or five years ago."

"That would be a house-party, I suppose?"

"Oh—undoubtedly. Forty or fifty people would be staying here at the time. That's about our usual complement."

"On those occasions invitations would be issued, of course?"

"Naturally. As in all affairs of that kind."

"When you received Guest's letter to say that he was coming on this last occasion, were you at all surprised?"

Sir Richard fingered his chin before he ventured upon a reply. Raphael watched him intently. He thought that he could see the drift of Bathurst's questioning. Anthony Bathurst waited patiently. Eventually Sir Richard groped on the shelf of his brain and found suitable words.

"Well, to tell the truth, I was perhaps a little surprised at the first onset. I will attempt to explain my feelings when I first read his letter. He wrote to us from the Varsity, you see. Although he was in residence, it meant him getting special leave. The Trinity term doesn't end till early July. It seemed awkward . . . inconvenient." Sir Richard paused for a brief space. "But then I began to think things over. Look at them for yourself, Mr. Bathurst. There was this trouble concerning his uncle hanging over him. The man was missing. Had been missing for some days. A dreadful thing that. A wearing, worrying anxiety. That fact alone tended to place matters in the category of the abnormal. I turned it all over in my mind. The boy wanted help, perhaps . . . or advice. An old man's counsel. Who knows?"

"Do you happen to have kept this letter from Guest, Sir Richard, to which you have just referred?"

"Oh, good gracious—no! It is not my habit to retain letters of that sort. Why on earth should I? The practice merely means the accumulation of litter—and litter I positively loathe."

"Quite so," returned Bathurst. "I can't deny that. What I was trying to discover was this. Did there seem to be *anxiety* or a *keen desire* on Guest's part to come here? You admit that the idea originated with him—did he appear to be really eager to make the visit?"

Raphael listened carefully for Sir Richard's answer.

"That's a difficult question. You are asking me to tell you what was going on in another man's mind, for that's what it comes to. Always a very unsatisfactory thing to have to do."

"I am only asking you for your opinion, Sir Richard," interposed Anthony Bathurst. "That puts the question on a somewhat different footing, I think."

Ingle frowned. "I refuse to commit myself beyond this. I think Guest wanted a refuge, as it were. He was worried about his uncle. There was certainly hospitality here, and there might be help. The latter contingency was definitely on the cards. Understand my meaning?"

"Yes—and no. Viewed from one standpoint, I should have expected Guest to have devoted all his time and all his attention to the task of tracing and finding his missing relative. He couldn't have expected to find him here with you, could he? However, as you said yourself just now, Sir Richard, it is idle for us to assert with any degree of certainty the motive that had taken possession of his mind. It was known to him only, and now, alas, he will never be able to tell us. We will leave matters there for the present."

He turned away to Sergeant Pullinger, a patient listener to the last exchanges of conversation. "Perhaps it would be convenient for you to see Mr. Covington now, Sergeant Pullinger. It would suit me all right."

The sergeant sought corroboration from Sir Richard Ingle.

"I will arrange that for you immediately, Sergeant. Mr. Covington is in the library. I will tell Garrett that you would like a word with him. Though I haven't the slightest idea what he has to talk about."

Sir Richard was away and back again in the matter of a minute. "I have told my butler. He will bring Mr. Covington to you as soon as possible."

Anthony Bathurst saw the opening for which he had been waiting, and took it. "One more question, Sir Richard, before either of us may become *de trop*. When Hugh Guest wrote to you the other day, did he know if anybody else were staying with you at the time?"

Ingle looked a little puzzled. "I hadn't informed him, if that's what you mean."

"And he didn't raise the point in the letter?"

"No, Mr. Bathurst."

"Thank you, Sir Richard. That is most important."

"Here's Barry Covington," declared Ingle, "and I'm dead interested to hear what he's got to say that he can put under the heading of important. Wouldn't mind betting that he'll be an 'also ran'."

Covington, looking a little scared, came forward to the group of men awaiting him.

"Not too sure of himself. Wonders if he's done the right thing," commented Bathurst mentally. "But he's got so far and can't retrace his steps. Might prove awkward."

Garrett ushered his charge and retired again.

"Good morning, gentlemen," said Barry Covington. "Sergeant Pullinger?"

"I'm Sergeant Pullinger, Mr. Covington. Good morning. I've come to see you about that letter you wrote to me."

Covington glanced askance at the three men with them.

"That's all right, Mr. Covington. I'd rather Sir Richard were here and heard what you have to say. He knows you've written to me. I told him."

Covington accepted the situation with the best grace he could muster. "What I've got to tell you, Sergeant, falls into two divisions. Perhaps I can call them 'my suspicions' and my 'definite facts'."

As he spoke, Covington found himself wondering who the keen, grey-eyed man with the clean-shaven face was, who was watching him and listening to him so intently. Looked a useful sort of customer at most things . . . as hard as a bag of nails . . . very fit indeed, thank you. . . . Covington collected his thoughts and went on:

"First of all, I'll tell you what I suspected as opposed to what I really know. I won't beat about the bush—I'll come to it straightway. I think that Hugh Guest had discovered something about his uncle."

"You mean—concerning Mr. Blundell's disappearance?"

"Exactly. I think that he had found out something, and was definitely on the track of somebody who had harmed, or who was about to harm, his uncle. And I think, too, that up to that time he had kept his knowledge, whatever it was, very much to himself. I don't think he'd told his sister even."

"What made you think that, Mr. Covington?"

Barry Covington took the interruption with the essence of good humour. "If you'll allow me to get on with my story in my own way, Sergeant, I'll tell you that later. I should much prefer to do that, with your permission. I'll come to it, as it were, in its proper and logical sequence. That will bring me, too, to the part of my story that I designated as 'definite fact'.

"On the morning of the day that Guest was murdered I had nothing much to do, so I went for a stroll over Lashey Down." Covington's voice was lowered a little as he proceeded. He told the men who listened to him the full details of what he had previously told Hugh Guest. He went on to the finish. "Well, Guest didn't seem at all bothered about it—at least, nothing to speak of; not as much as you might have expected—and I cleared out."

Covington paused for a moment. "I never saw him again—alive, I mean."

Anthony Bathurst made a sign to Sergeant Pullinger. The latter nodded understanding.

"You say that Guest seemed anxious?"

Covington turned to this second questioner—this grey-eyed man. "No. Hardly that. I wouldn't say anxious. How shall I put it? His mind seemed *occupied*. I got the impression that there was a problem which he was tackling—single-handed in all probability. That was why I spoke to him. I wanted to help him if he would let me. It was a warning to him as well. I had heard this threat against him, and I put the two things together."

"You say that you would be unable to recognize either of these men whose conversation you overheard?"

Covington nodded. "Their voices just floated to me downwind."

"Let me check this. You say you heard 'Guest', 'doorstep', 'Sir Richard Ingle', 'Beech Knoll' and 'Ralph'—all these significant words? Is that correct?"

"That is so," returned Barry Covington.

Mr. Bathurst looked from Sergeant Pullinger to Slingsby Raphael. Neither answered the glance with speech. It was Anthony himself who eventually broke the silence.

"There are many strange features about this case, Sergeant, as you will no doubt agree, but the strangest one of all is the method of the murderer's escape. A locked door, with the key of it in the pocket of the dead man. The murderer, therefore, not having made his exit by the door, ergo must have discovered another means of escape. Which it will be our duty, Sergeant, to find out also."

He swung round on to Sir Richard Ingle. "If convenient to you, Sir Richard, I should very much like to look at Guest's bedroom. I should like you, too, to come with me."

Sir Richard acquiesced immediately. "Certainly. You may do so with pleasure. Come this way, Mr. Bathurst."

The company of men made its way indoors—to the bedroom where Hugh Guest had kept his last appointment. On the threshold Bathurst paused to examine the damaged hinges. Then he looked at the lock, on the inside and on the outside.

"The key, I suppose, was handled by several people after you say the doctor handed it over?"

Sir Richard showed signs of annoyance. "It was, I think. We were careless, I suppose, at the time. I doubt if any of us realized the importance of the thing, or thought much about what we were doing. At moments like that, values are difficult to assess. One is apt to lose the intimate touch with . . ."

He turned to Raphael for confirmation of the opinions that he was expressing. "You know what I mean, Slingsby. You can express it better than I can. You were here with us. We did the things that came to our minds."

"That is so. That is always so. It must be. Civilization and the conventions generally are forgotten in times of stress, fear or danger. One falls back on primitive instincts. I am sure that Mr. Bathurst himself would be the first to admit the truth of that."

"I know what you mean, I think." Bathurst closured the discussion rather abruptly and glanced round the room. "Where was the body when you came into the room?"

Sir Richard pointed to the floor. "Just there, at the side of the bed."

Bathurst, with his eyes, measured the distance between the bed and the window. "You've found nothing, I understand, Sergeant?"

"Nothing, sir. And while you're here, have a look outside that bedroom window."

Bathurst walked to the window and looked out. Pullinger continued his criticism. Unknowingly, he repeated the words that Raphael had used just after Guest's body had been discovered. "A cat couldn't have got away from that window-ledge, unless it had been trained years ago with Blondin."

"I happen to be fond of cats," remarked Anthony. "I never missed Louis Wain's *Annual*—and I agree with you."

He whistled softly under his breath. "Mr. Covington," he declared suddenly, "if all that we are told is true"—he paused as quickly as he had begun to speak—"you see, of course, the inevitable implication?" Barry Covington looked at him fearlessly. "I think I do. Tell me what you mean, though, so that I may see if I'm right."

"The implication to which I refer is this. The medical evidence leaves no room to doubt that Guest died but a few minutes before you gentlemen entered this room. Sergeant Pullinger assures me that the doctor will stake his medical reputation on that point. Therefore it is almost a certainty that the murderer must have been inside the room when you, Mr. Covington, came to the bedroom door the first time and knocked."

Covington nodded in appreciation of what Bathurst had said. "That's quite right. I thought that was what you meant. I can't deny the probability of it."

"The *certainty* of it, rather," amended Bathurst quietly. "You heard no sound, I suppose, when you came to the door?"

Covington shook his head. "None. Everything inside was absolutely quiet and still."

Bathurst searched for detail. "What did you do first? Knock on the door, or call to Guest?"

"Knocked—tapped on the door. Getting no answer, I spoke to Guest as one would have done had the room been occupied by him. When I was first asked about this I couldn't remember speaking at all. I didn't think that I had. My mind was all blurred. But it has come back to me since. I am clear on it. I didn't call out or shout, I just spoke in my ordinary voice. I think that I said—'Hugh, are you there?' two or three times. That was all."

"What did you do then?"

"Tried the handle of the door. Shook it and rattled it, but to no purpose. The door was locked. Then I went downstairs again to the dining-room and reported—and the others came up here with me. You know what we found."

"How do you explain it yourself, Mr. Covington? The locked door, I mean, and the key in the murdered man's pocket?"

"There is only one possible explanation, surely? That the murderer escaped by way of the window. I know that looking at it makes the idea seem perfectly ridiculous—but what else could have happened? One must deal with possibilities."

Bathurst went to the window, pushed it open and leaned out. With his right hand on the sill, the long lithe body was balanced. He craned his neck, to look upwards; and then in the reverse direction, to the ground below. Slingsby Raphael and Sir Richard Ingle watched his every movement, as though their minds were following the course of his own—as though they were confronted at the same time with the identical ramifications of the same problem.

"No footmarks below, you say, Sergeant?"

"No, Mr. Bathurst, not a mark. Nobody went *that* way. I've been over the ground most carefully."

Anthony drew in his head and closed the window again. "Motive must mean a lot here, gentlemen. Until we hit upon that, we may well describe ourselves as wanderers pure and simple, Lost adventurers, gazing at ports and cities that are always foreign. It has been established, you will remember, that both Guest and Blundell met their deaths by the same means, if not at the same hands."

He caressed the ridge of his jaw thoughtfully. Then he came, as it were, to a new idea. "Which of you gentlemen was the first to discover that Guest was dead?"

Raphael, Covington and Sir Richard looked at each other. There was uncertainty amongst them. The last-named spoke to Raphael. "It was you, Slingsby, I think, who—"

"Yes. I think you're right. I was the first to realize that Guest was beyond help. Why do you ask the question?"

"I just wanted a clear mental picture of the room here as you stood in it. Let me see if I can reconstruct it. You would be here, shall we say, Sir Richard . . . and you here, Mr. Covington . . . and you, sir, would go towards the body as it lay there . . . yes . . . I think I understand."

He walked across the room . . . considering . . . valuing . . . assessing . . . measuring. "Who went to 'phone for the police?"

"I did," replied Sir Richard promptly. "Or, rather, for the doctor. The police came later. We 'phoned for the police after we heard what Dr. Summerhayes had to tell us."

"I stayed in here with Mr. Covington," added Raphael; "told him not to . . . that we mustn't touch or move anything. Sir Richard wasn't gone for more than a couple of minutes."

"Thank you," said Mr. Bathurst. "I think I understand. All those things help me in an affair of this kind."

Chapter IX
DOCTOR SUMMERHAYES SPEAKS OUT

Doctor Arnold Summerhayes drew at his cigar with grateful appreciation of its price and quality. He had had a long and arduous day; perhaps the worst since he had taken over his present practice. The day, too, had been hot, and the doctor disliked hot weather intensely.

He looked at the time that his wrist-watch showed him. It was moderately late. More than that—it was comfortably late. The latter adverb meant more to him than the former. With ordinary luck there should be nothing that evening to disturb. Things that day, on the whole, had gone well for him; the future was beginning to look much more roseate. He had been called to Sir Richard Ingle's . . . the fact pleased him. Sir Richard was a man who counted. He went to the sideboard and took out the liqueur brandy that was his especial fancy. The portion that he was about to drink was carefully measured in the pouring out.

He had scarcely raised the glass to his lips when there came a soft tap at the door. Dr. Summerhayes raised his eyebrows in annoyance. Dr. Summerhayes frowned. "Yes? Who is it?" he called sharply.

The door opened and the man who had tapped came partly across the threshold. "You're wanted, Doctor."

Dr. Summerhayes frowned for the second time. "Who wants me? A patient? At this time of night?"

The man shook his head in denial. "No. Not a patient, Doctor. A Mr. Anthony Bathurst. A gentleman from Scotland Yard. At least, that's what he has just told me he is."

The doctor reflected. The man who had brought the message watched him carefully. "The affair at Beech Knoll, no doubt. Ah, well—I suppose I shall have to see him. I might have expected something of the kind. I can't tell him any more than I've already told the others."

He looked at the man who had brought the news. The man nodded in understanding. "Very good, Doctor. I understand. I will tell the gentleman that you will see him."

Dr. Summerhayes drank his brandy, returned to his easy-chair and awaited the coming of Anthony Lotherington Bathurst. He drew again at his eminently satisfactory cigar. "Come in, Mr. Bathurst," was his cordial invitation when Anthony was brought to him.

"Good evening, Doctor."

Summerhayes pulled up another chair. "Sit down and make yourself as comfortable as I am. Now what is it that you want of me?"

"It's extremely good of you to see me as late as this. No doubt you've had a tiring day. I know something of the exigencies of your profession. I had hoped to arrive earlier, but circumstances delayed me and prevented it. There is my card, Doctor. Your man seemed disinclined to take it. He evidently considers prevention better than cure."

Dr. Summerhayes took the card and raised his eyebrows. "You represent the Commissioner of Police, I observe. Well, I can guess what you've come about. In fact, I've almost been expecting a visit from somebody. The death at Sir Richard Ingle's—eh?"

Anthony Bathurst took the chair that Dr. Summerhayes had previously offered to him. "That's true, Doctor. If you would be so kind, I'd like you to assist me in regard to one or two matters connected with the dead man. Nobody can do that as well as you. I won't take up any more of your time than I can possibly help."

"That's good of you. We doctors are busy men—even in the country like this. I haven't been here long, but already my practice has grown considerably. Cigar?"

"Thank you."

Dr. Summerhayes exhibited the box. "Take that one, Mr. Bathurst," he said. "I pride myself on being a connoisseur of cigars—you will find it excellent. Not too new. Light? Good."

The two men settled down opposite to each other.

"Guest died of poisoning—cyanide of potassium. That's so, Doctor, is it not?"

The doctor nodded gravely.

"How administered?"

"Up the nose. Sprayed in some way, shall we say, up the nostrils."

"Thank you, Doctor. If I may say so, that is the answer which I desired. You are aware, of course, Doctor Summerhayes, that Guest is the third victim of this kind during the last few days?"

"My morning and evening papers tell me so."

Bathurst supplied details. "Blundell in the Hampton Court district, Wingfield in the South Devon, and now Guest in the Isle of Wight."

The doctor nodded. "I remember the names—now that you specify them."

"Blundell," continued Mr. Bathurst, "was Hugh Guest's uncle. I have not yet discovered any affinity either of them had with Mr. Wingfield."

"None, possibly." Summerhayes was essentially matter-of-fact.

Anthony gave him a dry smile. "You may be right in that supposition, Doctor, but you must give me a certain amount of leave to doubt it. Would you say that Guest was a healthy man, Doctor?"

"Oh, undoubtedly. There was no organic weakness anywhere. I should describe him as a very fit and athletic young man." The doctor's thin face clouded, and creases showed in his big forehead. "From an insurance company's point of view he would have been a first-class life anywhere. Many years would have passed ere his life became labour and sorrow. That fact makes this affair so extraordinarily sad. For such a young man to pass out in such a sad way . . ." Summerhayes shook his head eloquently.

Mr. Bathurst came to closer quarters. "My notes of the Guest case contain this statement, Doctor. I'll read it to you. 'When Doctor Summerhayes arrived at Beech Knoll, the murdered man had been dead but a quarter of an hour.' But Sergeant Pullinger, whom you have seen since, I believe, now states that the time that had elapsed between Guest's death and your examination of his body was 'only a few minutes'. Which is the more correct, Doctor?"

"The latter. There was no evidence whatever of *rigor mortis*." The doctor was coldly precise.

Anthony Bathurst looked up at him interrogatively. "Which means, of course, if we pursue it to its logical conclusion . . . ?"

Summerhayes nodded and placed his fingertips together. "Quite so, Mr. Bathurst. You are absolutely right. The murderer had only just escaped. I realize that just as you do. It must have been so. There is no other possibility. He could have had only seconds to spare. Had Sir Richard Ingle's party come a few minutes earlier to the bedroom door, they must have caught him *in flagrante delicto*."

"We are in agreement there, Doctor. You've cleared up a point over which I was puzzling a little. Now for the next, and perhaps most important, feature of all." Anthony paused.

Dr. Summerhayes smiled genially and encouragingly.

"And that is?"

"I allude to 'the incident of the bedroom door key,' as Holmes himself would have put it. I find that key a most intriguing factor."

"I think I know what you mean. Perhaps if I describe to you what exactly occurred in Guest's bedroom whilst I was there it will materially assist you. At any rate, it will give you a clearer idea of what happened."

Dr. Summerhayes drew his chair forward an inch or so and lowered his voice a little. "When Sir Richard Ingle 'phoned to me here and told me what had happened, I naturally went over to the house at once. As a matter of fact, between you and me, he was rather fortunate to find me in. I had just been summoned to a case over at Lashey Down, and had Sir Richard's call come a mere matter of two minutes later than it did I should have been on my way there. Luckily, however, this other case wasn't urgent and no harm was done—I was able to attend to it later on.

"When I entered Guest's bedroom I noticed, of course, how the door had been forced open. 'Hallo', I said to myself, 'suicide. Door locked on the inside to obviate any chance of being disturbed.' But the suicide theory was soon exploded. If I may be allowed to mix my metaphors, it wouldn't hold water for an instant. Nobody in the world, even in the true Maskelyne and Devant succession, could have destroyed himself by taking cyanide of potassium and then have proceeded to eliminate the evidence. Cyanide of potassium, as I've no doubt you know, Mr. Bathurst, is a compound of prussic acid and potash. The symptoms of a victim of it would be similar to those associated with poisoning by prussic acid itself—a single drop of which will cause death. The symptoms brought on by a fatal dose are rarely delayed beyond one or two minutes, and death occurs very quickly—very quickly indeed. There is only one possible way, as I view the matter, in which Guest could have committed suicide. He would have had to have a companion—confederate if you like—who, waiting till Guest was dead, took the incriminating evidence from the room with him. It's extremely far-fetched, I know, but an arrangement such as I have indicated *might* have been made."

Mr. Bathurst gave way to meditation. "Help me here, Doctor Summerhayes," he asked at length. "If I am wrong, please correct me. A sufferer from true angina pectoris obtains relief, I believe, when an attack has seized him, by crushing a capsule or glass bead containing five drops of nitrite of amyl. The bead is usually crushed between the folds of a handkerchief and the drug then inhaled. Yes?" He looked expectantly at the doctor.

"You are quite right in your assumption, Mr. Bathurst. But I don't see what that has to—"

Anthony intervened. "As a layman pure and simple, I was wondering if there were the slightest possibility of anything of that kind having occurred in this affair. Whether it was necessary for an *instrument* to have been used with the poison. The idea may sound ridiculous and fantastic to you, Doctor, as an expert in such matters, but I am bound, in my position, to explore *every* possible avenue before I can hope to reach anything like a conclusion. That is to say, before I definitely *delete* the suicide possibility in the consideration of my problem."

Dr. Summerhayes smiled—with just the suspicion of conscious superiority. "You may rest assured, Mr. Bathurst, once and for all, that nothing of the kind happened to this young man Guest. The poison was sprayed up his nostrils, in my opinion by a mechanism similar, I should think, to that used for scenting purposes. A syringe or spray of the usual type. The doctor who performed the autopsy on Blundell, this young man's uncle, came to the same opinion in that case as I came to here. I forget the name of the doctor, but I remember very well reading what I have just told you. His corroboration of my findings, entirely independent of them, as you must see, would have removed any lingering doubt that I might have entertained. Does that statement satisfy you?"

"Oh yes; splendid. It clears the air for me altogether. Now, coming back to the incident of the key—could you tell me what exactly occurred with regard to that?"

"To do that was my intention. Let me think, now. I raised the question of the key myself when I realized that the bedroom door had been forced because it had been locked on the inside. The statement may sound tautological, but I am trying to explain to you how my brain worked as I knelt by Guest's dead body. In sequence of thought, as it were, I then asked if any one of them in the bedroom had removed the key from the lock."

"One moment, Doctor." Bathurst's interruption was eager and insistent. "Who was the first man to answer that question?"

Summerhayes reflected. "I don't know that I can answer that. I'll try to, however. Let me think again." Summerhayes put his hand to his forehead, covering his eyes. "I think that young Covington replied to that question first of all. Yes—now that it comes back to me with a greater wealth of detail, I'm convinced that he did. Now what was it that he said? What were the words he used? He said that he hadn't touched the key, and he knew that Sir Richard Ingle hadn't, either."

"I wonder why he added that?" remarked Bathurst thoughtfully. "It wasn't as though—"

"I couldn't say. Let me see, what happened after that? Ah—I know! Raphael said that he hadn't removed the key and seemed to censure himself for not having given the thing a thought, as it were. He followed that up by making the suggestion that Guest had it on his person somewhere. Told me to have a look for it on Guest's body . . . 'try the man's pockets', were, I think, the words that Raphael used. I couldn't be absolutely sure on that point, but that's near enough. I went back to the body and carried out Raphael's suggestion. You know that I found the missing key. That's all that I can tell you, I think."

The doctor relaxed again.

"In which pocket did you find it?"

"In the inside breast pocket."

"Which side, Doctor?"

Summerhayes frowned. "Left."

"Left." Bathurst repeated the word after him. "Do you know, I think I would have preferred that you answered my question in that way. Thank you, Doctor."

Summerhayes shook his head doubtfully. At the moment he failed to understand this expressed preference of Mr. Bathurst.

"Sergeant Pullinger tells me that on the evening of the murder Guest had not dressed for dinner."

"That is so," confirmed Summerhayes. "His evening clothes were lying on the bed, ready to be put on. I think he must have gone to the bedroom for the purpose of dressing. They were almost the first things to catch my eye when I entered the room—the white shirt and the black clothes seemed to stand out above everything else that the room held."

Anthony rose, on the point of departure. "You've been a tremendous help to me, Doctor Summerhayes. Several features of the affair that were vague and nebulous to me when I came in are now much more clear and definite. I always find that talking over a case with one who is able to supply first-hand evidence has a great value. Definite facts are so much more valuable than individual theories."

Dr. Summerhayes smiled agreeably. "Of course. In my own sphere I have often found the same thing. The commerce of thought must mean that mental exposure is inevitable. Ideas are dragged from their hiding-places; more than that, they beget other ideas—the mind being the soil—as one can say, in which they germinate. That happens to you and to me and to everybody. Shall I have the pleasure of seeing you again, Mr. Bathurst?"

"That depends, Doctor. At this stage of the case it is impossible for me to promise. I am only just beginning to see the first few prints of the trail. I have no idea to where that trail will lead. Good night, Doctor."

Chapter X
THE LATE PROFESSOR WINGFIELD

Hurrilow is a quaint little Wiltshire village, chiefly noted for its pigs. The neighbouring village of Beckhampton is much more famous for a nobler animal. It may even be termed the darling of the Downs. Hubert Athelstan Wingfield, whose body had been found in the ferns of Sidmouth, had resided at Apperley House, which lies a distance of between two and three miles from the outskirts of Hurrilow itself.

Mr. Bathurst travelled there in a car that he was trying out for the first time—a Chrysler with several new features about it. An automatic clutch was a particular source of unalloyed pleasure to him. It was simplicity itself, which is saying something. His left foot took a holiday, except when he was forced to reverse. The journey down, therefore, was a delight. Sheep fed by brooksides, lambs ran stilted races under the rows of hedges, or curled themselves in comfort on grass that was sheltered.

In Swindon he turned to the right at the "Goddard Arms", and then left into the Devizes road. Through, the villages of Wroughton and Broad Hinton, he came to Berwick Bassett, where the externals of the church attracted him so much that he stayed his course and went inside, to be rewarded with the sight of an Early English font and Perpendicular rood-screen. Then on through Winterbourne Monkton and Avebury, Anthony Bathurst came to Beckhampton, and two miles beyond, to Hurrilow.

Judiciously placed enquiries prevented him from wasting time in the finding of Apperley House. It stood on a high swell of ground; a long, low house of crinkled white, with each end fashioned into a protruding gable. Anthony arrived at a central porch under a peaked roof and rang the bell. A step sounded within.

The door opened to reveal a maid. As was his wont, he was lucky. All was plain sailing, and within a minute Anthony stood in a long, narrow hall.

From his position near the front door he could just discern the first steps of a stairway, with old, carved end-posts. The maid beckoned him. He understood and followed her. The maid stopped and turned to him. "In this room, sir, you will find my mistress." She pushed a door open and spoke a question: "Miss Wingfield?"

Seeing her beckon again, Anthony entered. The appearance of the woman who welcomed him took him by surprise. He thought that she must be the tallest woman that he had ever seen. Judging from his own height, this woman must be at least six feet three, and gaunt and lean with it. Her voice was harsh and strident, in thorough keeping with her appearance. As Anthony entered she glowered at him. It seemed as though she desired to launch her outraged feelings at his innocent head; that she had been waiting such an opportunity, and now that it had come was determined to embrace it with both hands. Mr. Bathurst, however, returned the glare with an apparently unheeding eye.

Miss Wingfield was dressed in deep black, relieved only at her neck and wrists with touches of white.

"Well, Mr. Bathurst," she said, "what can I do for you?"

Her eyes glittered again to the accompaniment of a thin-lipped smile. Anthony affected to ignore it. "I have come, Miss Wingfield," he returned, "to ask you one or two questions regarding your brother's death. That is, of course, if you will be good enough to answer them."

Her lean face suddenly underwent a startling change. It grew hard and fierce and rigid, and the eyes were flecked again with the lights of excitement. "My brother's murder, Mr. Bathurst," came her harsh voice. "Why be squeamish? I always believe in calling things by their true names."

"And I, too, Miss Wingfield. I suppose Mrs. Wingfield—"

She cut in without compunction. "She is not here. She has gone to stay with friends in Devizes. You will realize that she is suffering terribly."

Mr. Bathurst seemed to assume contrition. "I do, Miss Wingfield. I do most profoundly. I am not surprised that she should have gone away for a while."

The gaunt grenadier bowed her head. "That is understood, then. You will not be able to see her here. What questions do you want to ask me?"

"I don't think I can do better than by making it a general one. One that will enfold many. Can you help me at all in my investigation of Mr. Wingfield's death?"

The discordant voice boomed again. "I can't. I wish to God I could. Which settles that question, Mr. Bathurst."

"Not in *any* way? *Slight*, even?" Bathurst was patiently persistent. Miss Wingfield shook her head.

"In no way whatever. I can't tell you any more than I have told the police. They have pestered my sister-in-law and me for days. They remind me of doctors. Before they can tell you anything, you have to tell them a hundred times as much. It's partly due to them that she has had to go away. If I did know anything, I should be only too pleased to tell people."

Her eyes gleamed again. "My brother left here," she continued, "on the morning of the twenty-third of April. All that his wife and I knew was that he had an important appointment, and that in the normal course of events he would be back here that same night. All that we know, beyond that, is that he waited for the little bus that runs through the villages to Salisbury. Presumably he was on his way to Salisbury station to go somewhere by train. That seems to me to be by far the biggest probability. But the conductor says that he put him down outside a public-house in Salisbury, called the 'Haunch of Venison'. That is the last news that we have been able to glean of him prior to the discovery of his body in the ferns near Sidmouth."

"He wasn't actually traced to Salisbury railway station, then?"

"No, Mr. Bathurst. Nobody at the station can remember having seen him there. Neither from passenger nor from the railway staff."

Miss Wingfield delivered herself of this latest statement with an air of finality.

"He told Mrs. Wingfield that he was keeping an *important* appointment, you say?"

"Yes. That was the word he used. But he was a man who talked little, you must understand, and we, who lived with him, knew that and rarely pressed him for details."

"Was it unusual for him to go out as he did?"

"Most." Miss Wingfield was emphatic.

"When was the last occasion it happened? Can you remember?"

Miss Wingfield set her lips. "Over a year ago. At least that."

"On that occasion did he return the same night?"

"Oh yes. I can't ever remember an occasion when he did not come back to sleep here. He was a creature of the most regular and ordinary habits."

Mr. Bathurst became eloquent. "One fact that, it seems to me, must emerge from all this is—how did this important engagement come about? Here we have an eminent man of letters, living in a comparatively secluded part of the country, suddenly leaving his home for an unknown destination. Now that appointment must have been made by *somebody*—in *some* way. And it's those two unknown quantities that we have to discover. Tell me of your brother's habits in regard to his own particular métier—the legendary inscription. According to what I have read in the Press it was a frequent occurrence for him to be consulted thereon." He looked at her enquiringly.

"That is so. Both by correspondence and sometimes even by callers here. But there has been no recent correspondence, at any rate, that we have been able to find. Neither Mrs. Wingfield nor I can remember any recent callers. That fact, however, must not be regarded as absolutely conclusive, as the interview might have taken place when we were both out. We must not ignore that possibility. I told the police as much. We go out a good deal. For instance, I play golf most afternoons, and Mrs. Wingfield is a keen motorist. So you see—"

"My difficulties are obvious," returned Mr. Bathurst. "The secrecy with which the whole business has been surrounded only points all the more to the grave issues involved."

The lean, gaunt face which looked at him seemed to grow more interested. She might have been a daughter of Lear, he thought. "That is my own idea, Mr. Bathurst—absolutely. I can think of nothing else. I've told my sister-in-law so when we've discussed it. I am convinced that my brother was the victim of a cunning and diabolical plot, just as Mr. Blundell and that poor young man, Guest, were. The plot's big too. Bigger than you and I probably dream of." She rose and towered over him, an elderly Amazon of slowly simmering fury. "Shall I tell you what was wanted of these three dead men, Mr. Bathurst? Their brains. Brains to be picked and pilfered, and then destroyed! They had brains, and their murderers hadn't. The conspiracy, whatever it was, lacked them. Contradict me if you can—or if you dare." She returned to her chair.

Mr. Bathurst was imperturbable. "Your theory satisfies me in one way, Miss Wingfield, but not in another. If you yourself look at it a trifle more closely, I think that you will see what I mean and understand my difficulty. Another question. You say that your brother was a man of methodical habit?"

"Very. Exceedingly so. I don't think that I have ever known a man more so. But why do you ask?"

"Because it is the little things that count. The sermon is in the stone. You and I have to catch a straw from somewhere that will tell us the wind's direction. Now is there any straw—any tiny fragment, even, of straw—that is floating in the air somewhere, waiting for you or me to grasp it? In that possibility, I fancy, lies our one and only chance."

Miss Wingfield nodded acquiescence slowly. "Yes—I think that your meaning is clear to me. I must rack my brains for some fugitive thought that will count for a lot, but which has so far completely eluded me. That is what you want me to do, isn't it? Am I right?"

Mr. Bathurst pressed forward in an eagerness that was undisguised. This woman was an ally after his own heart. "A straw, Miss Wingfield. Any little incident. A torn letter. An unusual phrase or a chance remark. Any deviation from the normal course of habit. An unlooked-for action. A chair moved. A book consulted. An enquiry about—"

Miss Wingfield came to quivering life and sat bolt upright in her seat. "There is just one thing, Mr. Bathurst," she said slowly. "It may be of some importance, and, on the other hand, it may not. Your mention of a book brought it back to me. But my brother was not by any means an omniverous reader. Almost without exception his reading was confined to the books dealing with his own especial interest. But an evening or so before he disappeared—it would be about April the twentieth, I should say—I saw him looking at a map. That's the only thing I can think of that—"

"A map," interrupted Bathurst; "a map of what, Miss Wingfield?"

"The Isle of Wight, Mr. Bathurst. It was an ordinary—"

Anthony Bathurst sprang to his feet and rubbed his hands. "The straw is in our hands, Miss Wingfield, and we must hold it. Thanks to you. Now tell me this—that one thought which we have resurrected may act as an inspiration to revive another. Did you hear, during these last few days, any mention from your brother of an *animal?*"

He bent down over her in eager anticipation of her reply.

Amazingly, she nodded! "Yes . . . that has come back to me too. I heard him refer once—jokingly, I should say it was—to a spiked lion."

Anthony almost held his breath. "It's the right straw too, Miss Wingfield, that you've seen in front of you and that we've grasped. Thank God for that!"

Chapter XI
SHOCK FOR SIR RICHARD INGLE

"What do you make of this, Raphael?" Sir Richard Ingle pushed a letter over to his guest. Slingsby Raphael read it critically.

>   *11, Seely Place,*
>   *London,*
>   *May 26th.*
>
> *Dear Sir Richard,*
>
> *We regret to inform you that a most unexpected development has arisen in regard to the Tresham succession. It is essential that we should interview you at your earliest possible convenience—preferably at our offices here. If this course be impracticable to you, we will, of course, make it our business to come down to see you, but both my partner and I think that the better plan would be for you to come up to town and discuss things with us. The matter that is engaging our attention could then be put before you more clearly and coherently. Please understand, though, my dear Sir Richard, that the matter is of extreme urgency. We await your immediate decision, and remain, faithfully yours,*
>
>   *Gregory Lomax,*
>   *of Lomax and Chipperfield.*

Raphael looked at his host; a train of thought had evidently started in his brain. "That's rather interesting. When did Tresham die? The day before yesterday, wasn't it?"

"It was. Why do you ask me that?"

Raphael tapped the letter meaningly with his forefinger. "My dear Richard, surely you noticed—"

"What he calls me?"

"Of course. Considering all the circumstances as we know them, why on earth doesn't he address you as Lord Tresham? That was the first thing that struck me when I read the letter."

Ingle drummed on the table with his fingertips. "There may be little or nothing in that. Just an example of force of habit. After all, he's always written to me in the past as Sir Richard Ingle, and perhaps carried on the old tradition, out of sheer routine. See what I mean?"

Raphael shook his head doubtfully. "Rather unconvincing, I think. You must be easily satisfied to be able to deceive yourself like that. Especially when one considers the tone of the letter and also the terms in which Master Gregory Lomax writes." He shook his head again, this time much more emphatically. "No, old man, there's something up the gentleman's sleeve, and it's going to come down at the critical moment—which will be the moment when Master Lomax wants it to. You mark my words. What are you going to do? Made up your mind?"

"What about, exactly?"

"This letter. Going to have him down here, or going up to town to see him as he suggests?"

Sir Richard Ingle turned the two issues over in his mind.

"I'll go up to Seely Place, I think. I don't know that I want any more disturbances down here. What we've already had have been more than enough. Both Jean and Ella are pretty well all in, although they've been deuced plucky about it all the way through, and haven't dropped the suggestion of a moan. All the same, I'm not going to say that another shock mightn't be too much for one or both of them. Especially if it were handed out by Mr. Gregory Lomax. So, on the whole, Slingsby, I think I'll trot up to Seely Place to-morrow, since my immediate decision is required. I'll send Lomax a wire at once. I'll get Garrett to see to it for me."

Hard on his departure, Barry Covington entered the room. He hung about hesitatingly before coming to the point of words. When he spoke to Raphael, it was in the form of a question.

"I don't want to seem unduly curious, or to be butting in on anything which doesn't concern me, but has Sir Richard had bad news?"

Raphael shrugged his shoulders. "Don't ask me, Covington. Why should you imagine such a thing? Also, admitting the truth of your conjecture for the sake of discussion, why should you think that our host would confide in me?"

Covington sensed hostility. He sought temporary refuge in generalities. "Oh—it's nothing. I merely thought that Sir Richard looked a little worried when he passed me just now. And as I saw no evidence of this anxiety first thing this morning, I thought, perhaps, that something unusual might have come along since. About Guest's murder, I mean."

His voice held eagerness. Raphael noticed it and remained distant and aloof. "I really don't know. Why do you ask? Are you fancying yourself as an investigator, or do you suspect anybody in particular?"

"I? Why, no. Why should I? How can I? All I know is that Guest's life was threatened and that I warned him against the danger. You heard me tell Sergeant Pullinger that. But whom I warned him against—" He broke off with a gesture of hopelessness.

Raphael smiled cynically. "I'll say this for you, Covington—when you're gyrating on thin ice you've the intelligence to realize it. Some people don't. It's a peculiarly modern tendency, that! I thought that you told Bathurst and Sergeant Pullinger just enough in that story of your doze on Lashey Down. Not a word too much—not a word too little. You were alert. You didn't let your conjectures interfere with the information you had that was based on fact."

Covington stared.

Raphael went on: "Some people in your position might have been tempted to say a great deal more. It's a rare gift to know when and where one should stop. *Must* stop. Some authors, for instance, write books that will never be read. Others write books that will never be published. But if any of them write cheques that will never be cashed—well, they're on thin ice, and the cleverer ones realize it and do their spot of skating extremely gingerly. If all eventually go well—or better—they earnestly repent and endeavour to live in love and charity with their neighbours. Cheero for now, Covington! You'll excuse me, I know. I want to have a word with Celia Guest."

He knocked the ash from his cigarette and strolled off. Covington turned to watch him. He heard Raphael's voice a short distance away, addressing Celia. The aggression had deserted it. In its place there was a warm and generous sympathy.

When, on the following morning, Sir Richard Ingle arrived in Seely Place, he remembered that it had a history of its own. He tried to recall it. It came to him that it was in a very old part of London, and as far as he was able to remember, without the opportunity for reference, was governed by a separate Act of Parliament. At least, it had been up to some few years ago— and he supposed it was the same now—that the Act had not been repealed. The gates were shut every night at nine o'clock, and one night, years ago, Sir Richard had listened to the time-old custom of the porter crying out the hours of the night. He believed he was right in thinking that it was the only place in the Metropolis where this practice had been retained. It had always been one of the most zealously guarded spots in London, where it would require a more than ordinary crook to ply drill and jemmy upon bolts and bars with much hope of ultimate success.

It is significant, when we remember his frame of mind, that Sir Richard drew comfort and a sense of security from these recollections. Upon making himself known, he was quickly shown into the private room of Messrs. Lomax and Chipperfield, to be received by Mr. Gregory Lomax, alone.

Sir Richard looked round and mentally noted his surroundings. There was positively nothing in this room calculated to arouse a man's curiosity. No matter what might happen to a woman's. The desk behind which Mr. Gregory Lomax sat was of substantial mahogany. In the bookcases there was a number of imposing-looking legal volumes, which, if the truth be adhered to, neither Gregory Lomax nor Slade Chipperfield ever consulted. Their purpose in life was to dress the room, and they achieved it. The remaining furniture was of the ordinary library pattern, upholstered in a dark sage-green. A round Chippendale table would obviously have a utilitarian purpose in the matter of four o'clock tea, whilst over the mantelpiece hung a group-picture of the judges who, years before, had controlled the famous Parnell Commission. In the room's far corner a few black deed-boxes were turned almost shamefacedly to the wall—the names of the clients concerned painted on them. Fugitives for a day or more, thought Sir Richard, as he looked at them, from the strong-room where they live their lives; even a deed-box may know the thrill of excursion, if not of entire escape.

Gregory Lomax peered at his visitor over his old-fashioned glasses. "That's right, Sir Richard," he said fussily, "sit down there."

"Cold for the time of year, don't you think? Distinct change since last week." Sir Richard Ingle tossed off the opinions like a juggler, turning to a new toy, throws away the balls with which he has finished.

"Yes. I suppose it is if you look at it from the normal standpoint. If one lets one's self be governed by the seasons as they *should* be. Personally, profiting by bitter experience, I gave up that idea long ago. I always say now that this country has two seasons only—winter and cold weather." He chuckled wheezily at his pleasantry and again peered across at his visitor. "But you haven't come to see me to talk about the weather. You are anxious to know why I wrote to you. I'm well aware of that."

He paused, giving Sir Richard the idea that he was waiting for something to be said to him. He was disappointed. The only recognition that his visitor afforded him was the very slightest suggestion of a bow. Gregory Lomax strummed nervously on his desk with his fingers. To tell the truth, he disliked, intensely, the position in which he found himself. Almost as intensely as the position that had arisen in regard to Tresham. He had hoped that his client would have given him a conversational opening and so rendered his task the easier. He ceased his five-finger exercises on the mahogany and cleared his throat ostentatiously.

"Well, Sir Richard, now that you're here, I will come to the matter upon which I wrote to you. A matter that is excessively important. I had hoped that . . ."

He rose, walked to the door of the apartment, opened it, closed it, and returned to his chair behind the roll-top desk. "I am particularly anxious that what we say should not be overheard. That is why, also, I was so uncommunicative, shall we say, in the letter that I sent to you to the Isle of Wight. You thought so, doubtless . . . h'm . . . eh?"

Sir Richard smiled. "Go on, Mr. Lomax."

The latter leaned over impressively. "Sir Richard, big things are afoot. On Monday last I received the greatest shock of my professional career. And when I remember everything, that's saying something, I can assure you."

"I suppose so."

Lomax swayed back in his chair and placed his fingertips together. "About a quarter past three on Monday afternoon, Sir Richard, my clerk brought me word that two gentlemen were downstairs and wanted to know if they could see me as soon as it was convenient. I asked Walters—that's my clerk—if he knew their names, and whether they had an appointment with either me or Mr. Chipperfield. He told me no; so, being a bit curious, and also more or less free at the time, I told him to bring them up here. Well, Sir Richard, they came up, and one of them sat where you're sitting now, and the other next to him."

He paused. Sir Richard waited for him to go on. When he proceeded, he spoke with the utmost deliberation. "Their names, Sir Richard, as they gave them to me, absolutely stunned me, or, rather, one of them did. They were Lord Tresham and Captain Forbes, the famous aviator."

Gregory Lomax, sensing the drama of the situation, paused again as he made this startling announcement. Sir Richard, stung into activity, sat bolt upright in his chair.

"Lord Tresham!" he cried in amazement. "What on earth are you talking about? Lord Tresham died in his bed at Tresham on—"

Gregory Lomax raised his hand authoritatively. *"Le roi est mort. Vive le roi."*

Sir Richard realized the meaning behind the words. He forced the issue. "In that case, then, thank you, Mr. Lomax, for the expression. I sincerely hope, with you, that I shall be spared for many years."

Lomax shook his head and accepted Ingle's challenge. "I am afraid that you misunderstand me, Sir Richard. The late Lord Tresham, to whose death you referred just now, had three sons. Martin, the eldest; Henry, the second; and Nicholas, the youngest."

"I am aware of all that," returned Ingle somewhat curtly, "seeing that my mother was a Tresham."

"Of course, of course." Mr. Lomax's tone became ingratiating. "I was just attempting to sketch the position as it is now. The deaths of Martin and Henry Tresham in 1910 and 1913, respectively, and the many years' disappearance of Nicholas Tresham, with the consequent presumption of decease, put you in the enviable position of standing next in the Tresham succession. When the late Lord Tresham passed away a few days ago, you naturally expected, out of the habitual anticipation of years, to succeed to the title. The position, however, Sir Richard, has undergone a change. More than that, from your point of view it has completely disappeared. Nicholas Tresham has returned, alive and well. Lord Tresham—as I said before—to give him his true title."

Ingle's lip curled in open cynicism. "Which is why you wrote to me?"

"Exactly, Sir Richard. What else could I do?"

Sir Richard bit his lip and shrugged his shoulders. "The whole procedure seems to me to be distinctly extraordinary. What has this man—I almost said impostor—in support of his claim?"

Gregory Lomax was obviously nettled at the remark. His tone, in reply, was cold. "That statement, Sir Richard, is not gracious; it is far from complimentary to me, and certainly unworthy of you. Do you imagine for one instant that I should have accepted Lord Tresham's statements without authentic verification of them?"

"Not for a moment, but even so—"

"Even so, what, Sir Richard?"

"The mere possession of a document is not necessarily a convincing proof that the possessor is all that he claims to be. I tell you, Mr. Lomax, I am very far from being satisfied. How is it that the gentleman whom you have mentioned failed to present himself to his father when the late Lord Tresham was alive? Or even when he lay dying? He timed his appearance very cleverly, don't you think?"

"I raised that point myself, Sir Richard, and Lord Tresham supplied me with a perfectly adequate explanation. Personally I haven't the slightest doubt of Lord Tresham's *bona-fides*. Not only has he documents that only a Tresham could possibly possess, including his own birth certificate, but he also has the historic counters—the famous mother-of-pearl counters bearing the Tresham arms, impaling Strangeways. I saw them and examined them myself. When he left Tresham, after the quarrel that he had with his father, he took them with him. Stole them, if you like, but 'convey, the wise it call'. That fact I know to be absolutely true—the late Lord Tresham told me of the incident himself soon after it occurred—all those years ago. Nicholas Tresham couldn't have deceived me over that, even if he had wished to. After all, as he himself says, they belonged to the family."

Sir Richard Ingle sat there silent. The affair was more serious than he had originally anticipated. Lomax proceeded on his essay of discomfiture.

"Moreover, Sir Richard, there is the physical evidence."

Ingle looked up at him. "The physical evidence?"

Lomax nodded to confirm his words. "One has only to look at Nicholas Tresham to see who he is. To look at him—once. Fate—er—Nature plays strange tricks. Think of the Tresham eyebrows."

Sir Richard started in his chair. He remembered his own statement to his friend Slingsby Raphael, of a few days before. "He has the Tresham eyebrows, then?"

Lomax gestured with his hands. "Beyond the slightest suspicion of a doubt. You will recall how the middle of each brow is covered with a darker shade of hair—a physical peculiarity that has persisted, so I understand, in the Tresham line for generations. Believe me, there's no mistaking it."

Sir Richard grunted non-committally. Lomax attempted to interpret the grunt. "Of course, if you still remain doubtful and unsatisfied, you are at perfect liberty to contest the claimant's position in the courts. We have the historic instance of the Tichborne claimant—Orton—as an example. But—"

He broke off and picked up his pen. Sir Richard noticed the abruptness of the pause. He sought essentials. "Well?" he queried.

Gregory Lomax finessed. He avoided the main issue. "If you wish for my advice, Sir Richard, I shall be most pleased to give it to you. Were I in your position I should accept the inevitable. I do not see that you have any reasonable alternative. I can't say any more."

Sir Richard then asked a question that caused Mr. Lomax some surprise. "How old is this Nick Tresham—or Lord Tresham, as I suppose I should say?"

Lomax referred to a file of correspondence. "Let me see now. Forty-nine on the fifteenth of November next."

"Is he? As much as that? I am a little surprised. I should have given him two or three years less than that. Still, time rolls on and one scarcely notices its passage. Especially when one has reached my age." Sir Richard fingered his moustache. "I think it would be as well, Mr. Lomax," he proceeded, "if I saw the new Lord Tresham—before his father's funeral. What do you think yourself?"

The lawyer smiled. It was a smile of self-satisfaction. "You will forgive me, Sir Richard, I am sure, for anticipating this intention of yours. It seemed to me, when I sat down and reflected on the position in its first developments, that by far the happiest thing that could possibly happen would be for you and Lord Tresham to meet and to talk things over amicably. When, therefore, I heard from you to the effect that you were coming here to-day, I arranged with Lord Tresham that he should come along half an hour after the time you fixed for your appointment. If you desired to meet him, as I felt certain you would when you heard how things stood, there were both of you ready to hand. If, on the other hand, you expressed no such desire—there was no harm done—I could see Lord Tresham on another matter to do with the estate, and neither of you would be any the wiser as to my little arrangement."

He smiled again indulgently and consulted his watch. "I have no doubt, Sir Richard," he remarked cordially, "that by this time Lord Tresham is waiting to see me. Or, rather, to see us."

CHAPTER XII
NICHOLAS—LORD TRESHAM

GREGORY Lomax leant forward to use his telephone. Sir Richard watched him interestedly.

"Is that you, Walters? Has Lord Tresham arrived?" he heard him ask.

There was a short interval before Lomax issued an order. "Thank you. That's all right, then. Bring Lord Tresham up to my private room, please. Yes—I know. As I said, that's quite in order."

Sir Richard turned towards the door, eagerly anticipating the entrance of Lord Tresham. He was not destined to wait for long. After a period of silence the door which he watched opened. A clerk stood on the threshold and announced "Lord Tresham". There entered a tall, spare, sun-burned man—with sharp face, a pronounced swing of the shoulders and an eager, alert manner. Sir Richard regarded him intently, his face rigid and his lips compressed.

Gregory Lomax rose from his chair, but a half movement from Ingle turned him from his purpose and he sank back in his chair again. Ingle looked at Tresham and addressed him with easy nonchalance.

"So you don't remember me, Nick?"

Tresham stopped short in his tracks. Then he stepped forward again, hesitant, irresolute. There was doubt in his eyes. "I'm afraid I don't. Putting it quite candidly, you have the advantage of me."

"I'm trying your memory pretty highly, I admit. It's a cool forty years, I suppose, since we met. Must be, if it's a day. I'm Dick Ingle."

Tresham's eyes flashed with pleasure. "Of course. How utterly stupid of me. I can see it now. You've worn thundering well, old man, but you're changed, you know. I expect I am too, eh?"

"Yes, somewhat. Forty years is a hell of a long time—no matter where you spend it. By the way, where have you been all this time?"

"Oh—dodging about for most of the years. In Morocco, though, most of the time."

"As far as that, eh? When did you return?"

"About six months ago. When I heard of the old man's illness I put a feeler round over here, and what I heard was good enough to bring me home. My information told me that my father couldn't possibly last long, so I came home. I knew that it would save trouble if I were on the spot when he went west."

Ingle's face was indicative of his feelings. Tresham observed the indication. He shrugged his shoulders.

"Why should I pretend a sentimentality that I don't feel? That I never felt? I had a bust with the old boy soon after I came down from Cambridge, and as far as I was concerned that ended everything. There was no love lost between us after that, I can tell you. My teeth were clenched and my fists were tingling, so I just cleared out with a chap who had been at the Varsity with me, meaning to be dead to the whole shoot of them; my crowd, I mean. Now I've come back. That's all there is to it. Satisfied?"

"You have been kept posted with family news, I suppose?"

"More or less. I knew that Martin and Henry had both 'shuffled off this mortal coil', if that's what you mean. Bad luck for them—but good for me. I realize the truth of that perfectly. None better. Well?"

"I don't quite know what to say to you, Nick. The whole thing has taken me by surprise. I only heard of it half an hour ago. Don't take me literally, but I feel that I've been well on the favourite and that a hundred to one outsider has turned up." Ingle smiled a wry smile.

Nick Tresham shrugged his shoulders.

"I suppose I'm a bit thoughtless. My life has made me so. I haven't been cradled in comfort, I can tell you. It didn't strike me at the time that I must add your name to the 'hard-luck' gallery. They say that it's an ill wind. Luck runs in cycles. My turn to-day—yours to-morrow."

"I'm afraid not. About the to-morrow, I mean. Those generalities don't always apply. Have you been down to Tresham yet?"

Tresham shook his head in emphatic denial. "No. Even I, strange though it may seem to you, Ingle, have my inherent decencies. Twenty-seven years of globe-trotting haven't eradicated *all* my better feelings. I shall attend to-morrow's funeral, naturally, but I shall preserve a modest and moderate incognito. As a matter of fact, I shall be in the company of a dear old pal—Andy Forbes. *The* Andy Forbes. You will be in the front choir of mourners, of course? You know what I mean—'Now the labourer's task is o'er'—eh? Which side do you intend to decorate—Decani or Cantoris?"

Sir Richard's cheek flushed, but otherwise he ignored this taunt of execrable taste. "In that case, Tresham, I shall see you then. If I don't hug you, or fall on your neck, you'll understand."

Tresham grinned. "Oh, that's all right, Ingle. It will be mutual. I'm not thin-skinned, I assure you. Knocking about with Dagos—rainbow-hued at that—teaches you to cultivate a thoroughly business-like and serviceable hide. You won't penetrate mine in a hurry. The elephant's my half-brother."

Gregory Lomax, silent for so long, looked anxiously from one man to the other. There was an atmosphere about this meeting that he had engineered that contained the elements of disturbance. The conversation had taken a turn that he found disconcerting. He decided, therefore, to pour oil on waters that were already beginning to simmer with trouble.

"Lord Tresham," he said with an apologetic cough. "Er—Sir Richard Ingle—the whole position is unfortunate, I admit—in a way, unfortunate for each of you—and I am deeply gratified that you two gentlemen have reached such an amicable understanding so quickly." He coughed again.

"As I've maintained for years—I couldn't have carried on the traditions of the firm of Lomax and Chipperfield, if you will allow me to say so, without that belief—'Noblesse oblige'. That counts, and must always count. I shall be at Tresham to-morrow. I hope to have the pleasure of seeing both of you."

"I shall wish you good day, then, Mr. Lomax. Many thanks for the interview. I don't think any purpose will be served by my staying longer. Good day, Lord Tresham. We shall meet again shortly, I've no doubt, excluding to-morrow's possibilities."

Sir Richard walked towards the door, but suddenly turned in his stride. "What a good job you wrote that letter to me, Nick."

Tresham flushed. "Letter? Which one?"

"Can't you remember?"

"For the life of me, I can't."

Sir Richard smiled and deliberately rubbed the back of his left leg. Nick Tresham's face cleared instantly.

"Oh, of course! I've been away so long I'd forgotten it. That idiotic business had gone clean out of my mind. But 'blood's thicker than water', eh?"

Ingle laughed understandingly. "Quite so. That has always been accepted." He bowed courteously and took his departure. Tresham, laughing lightly, turned to Lomax.

"Bit of a blow, eh? Taken part of the count. That's what comes of looking too far ahead. You never know what's coming to you in this world, and the kingdom round the corner usually turns out to be vastly different from the picture of your expectations."

Lomax agreed—with a strong suggestion of subservience. "Naturally, Lord Tresham. Very true! How right you are. Sir Richard Ingle is nettled—that was very obvious. But, after all, when you come to look at the position all round, he has many consolations. He's already a comparatively rich man, living in a most charming house, situated, I believe, in the heart of equally charming country. His disappointment should be infinitesimal compared with that of many people who might have been similarly treated. It isn't as though, too, that you were a distant member of the family whom he had never seen. You are a direct Tresham. He—an Ingle."

Nick Tresham laughed again. "He was always a bit stiffbacked, even when he was a nipper. He was an only child. Liked his own way and all that sort of thing. The result is that when the tide begins to run against him he's apt to lose his head and act impetuously."

Lomax reflected on Tresham's statement. "The tide's certainly been running against him these last few days. Besides your matter, there was that strange murder in the bedroom of his house, which the police are still investigating."

Nick Tresham answered carelessly: "Yes. A most extraordinary affair. I read about it, of course. Young fellow named Guest, wasn't it?"

"Yes. Hugh Guest. Nephew of another man who has recently been murdered—John P. Blundell."

Tresham turned interestedly. "Blundell? John Blundell?"

"Yes. You must have seen an account of that affair, too, in the papers. His body was found on the grass, under a tree, in Bushey Park."

"Yes. I think I did, now you mention it. But I don't know that I took particular notice of the murdered man's name. Blundell, eh? John Blundell? There's a coincidence there, if you only knew it."

Lomax failed to understand. "A coincidence—why?"

"Oh, nothing much. Only that I happened to be both at school and at Cambridge with a bloke named John Blundell. I fancy his second name was Pender. And, say what you like, Lomax, blood's thicker than water."

Lord Tresham looked at his lawyer and laughed softly to himself. Lomax appeared to be on the point of speaking, but changed his mind.

Chapter XIII
MR. BATHURST MINGLES WITH THE CROWD

It was obvious to the most casual observer that on the morning in question Mr. Bathurst had dressed with an abundance of care and a studied deference to the sartorial. He clad himself in the garments of civilization when it mourns, and attended the funeral of the late Lord Tresham. Chief-Inspector MacMorran, excessively grateful for something akin to a holiday with no expenditure attached, drove him down to the south coast of England where the Tresham lands lay.

The car on its journey ran by common after common all golden with gorse. The white ribbon of the road stretched out in front of it—seemingly for ever. Always beyond! Bathurst and his new chauffeur saw the dark, lush meadows of many valleys; rivers like winding white laces that rippled lazily under the breeze that stirred them, and belts of trees that had been the Creator's majestic witnesses for spans of time. The sunlight shone on the roses, but the clouds held more than a hint of the rain that was to come.

Assisted in direction by more than one pedestrian of whom enquiries were made as to locality, Mr. Bathurst, his car, and Inspector MacMorran came at length to the turning which led to Tresham church. The churchyard of Tresham lies under the hill. Stolid ploughmen of Tresham had laid the dead lord of their homeland upon one of their own farm wagons, and brought him in the cold dignity of death to the acre where his flesh would rest for ever. There, too, in the still sunlight under the blue tent of sky, stood those of Tresham blood and Tresham sinew, and those also who had called the dead man friend.

In a sparse company nearest to the grave stood the late Lord Tresham's nearest and dearest—the *"ta philtata"* of the Greeks. They were as stated—very few. The Treshams for many years had been a scattered clan, and this dead Tresham had for some long time known the bitter tang of loneliness. Wealth had been his—the tinsel and the trappings that wealth brings—but never happiness. "Better a dinner of herbs where Love is . . ."

As he lay beside his forefathers in their eternal sleep, he came nearer to the state of company than he had come during all the years of his life. Anthony Bathurst, for reasons of his own, stayed on the verge of the crowd. MacMorran remained in the lane that ran by the back of the church. The branches of the trees dipped in the wind. MacMorran watched them and listened to their music. He leant against the door of the car. Words of a hymn came to him:

> " . . . their vigil keep,
> While yet their mortal bodies sleep,
> Till from the dust they too shall rise,
> And soar triumphant to the skies."

The company of mourners slowly followed the coffin to the grave. Sir Richard Ingle, Mr. Bathurst's chief interest, be it said, stood near to the graveside, his left arm linked in the right arm of Slingsby Raphael. Ingle stood straight, dry-eyed and cold. He was no pretender, and the grey lass, sorrow, had not visited him.

The voice of the aged vicar of Tresham rose querulously and trailed into the wind. He had read St. Paul's glorious and triumphant epistle to the citizens of Corinth, without meaning and without the slightest hint of its cry of victory. He closed his book and commenced to read the words of the last offices, equally badly. His voice grew more querulous and even shrill. Clouds scudded across the sky, and the first drops came of the promised rain. The earth from a man's hand rattled on the lowered coffin. The vicar hunched himself against the lashing onslaught from the skies, and Anthony Bathurst craned his head and listened to him. The wonderful words he uttered came to Anthony over the heads of the people who had placed themselves between them: "In sure and certain hope of the Resurrection to eternal life . . . who shall change our vile body that it may be like unto His glorious body, according to the mighty working where He is able to subdue all things to Himself."

Thus it went to the last warm words of comfort: "The Grace of our Lord Jesus Christ. . . ." Some of the mourners surged forward towards the grave, others of them began to drift slowly away. Anthony Bathurst's attention became directed towards the tall man who stood between two others, the one elderly and wizened and the other of distinctly military appearance and bearing. The three men at whom he looked stepped to the edge of the grave.

For some reason born of instinct, possibly, Anthony Bathurst moved a few paces towards them. The crowd was thinning rapidly now, and it had become comparatively easy to make a smooth and comfortable way for oneself. A chance remark from the military-looking man caught Bathurst's ear and set his brain at work and his imagination racing. What in the name of heaven had happened since he had been at Lashey Down? His determination to see Sir Richard Ingle became a stronger force than ever. This latest turn of the wheel rendered it more important by far.

Making up his mind immediately, he turned quickly in the direction that he had seen Ingle and Raphael take a few minutes previously. It was vital that he should overtake them before they reached their car. He succeeded in his effort. Also, there was no need now to finesse concerning an appropriate opening. Anthony Bathurst ranged himself at Sir Richard's side. When the latter recognized the man who addressed him he gave a start of surprise.

"Mr. Bathurst? This is an unexpected meeting. I scarcely thought—"

Bathurst interposed before he could complete his sentence. "I came down in the hope of seeing you, sir. In the hope, too, of speaking to you. Those hopes have materialized."

Sir Richard frowned and half turned towards Raphael. "Quite so. But this is hardly—"

Mr. Bathurst smiled courteously. "You mean that the time and place are inopportune? For that, forgive me. To a certain extent, you see, my hands are tied. But the living, Sir Richard, have greater claims than the dead. I am sure that you would admit the truth of that."

Ingle bowed stiffly. "If you will enter my car, Mr. Bathurst, we will discuss what you have to say."

"I will tell my chauffeur to follow, then, Sir Richard. You will excuse me for one moment. It will not take more." Anthony was with MacMorran in a twinkling. "Follow up with my car, Inspector. For the time being, I'm going along in Sir Richard Ingle's car. Keep a short distance behind us, so that I can give you the tip and pick you up directly it's necessary."

The Inspector accepted the instructions and permitted himself two questions. "What's doing, sir? Anything afoot?"

Anthony Bathurst put his forefinger to his lips. "I've just heard a most extraordinary piece of news, MacMorran, and when I heard it, it certainly wasn't intended for my ear. I can tell you that."

He dashed off again, and MacMorran climbed into the car. Sir Richard waited for Bathurst to enter the other car and then pulled the door to behind him. "Sit there," he said, as the car gathered pace. "Now what have you to say to me?"

Before Bathurst could reply, Slingsby Raphael intervened from his seat opposite. "One minute, Mr. Bathurst, if you please. I should like you to answer me a question. Are you still at work on the Guest murder? Sir Richard and I would like to know that before this conversation commences. Sergeant Pullinger has formed certain opinions, we understand, and, because of them, has asked us to adopt a certain procedure. With that in view, therefore, Mr. Bathurst, and considering our position, would you be good enough to tell us where you stand?" Raphael sank back into the rich upholstery of the car. His remarkable eyes probed Mr. Bathurst's face.

Anthony smiled at them. "The Guest case is only part of my problem, sir. Just one piece of the pattern. But it *is* a part of it, and because of that the fact must be admitted. It's no use shutting one's eyes to it. At the same time, my primary object in desiring to speak to Sir Richard here, was not in *direct* relationship to the murder of Hugh Guest. You will notice that I refer to him as Sir Richard Ingle."

Ingle looked across at him intently. Anthony continued: "A few days ago I believed that he would have been Lord Tresham on the death of the man whom to-day we have seen buried. I will come to my point. May I enquire into the inner history of the Tresham succession? I will confess that it interests me considerably. That interest is not based on ordinary curiosity."

Sir Richard's reply was curt. "The late Lord Tresham had three sons. Martin, Henry, and Nicholas. It was believed that all three were dead and that I was the next-of-kin, but Nicholas, the third son, happens to be still in the land of the living, and has very naturally come forward to claim his inheritance. That's all there is to it and there's no need to make a fuss. His credentials are beyond dispute."

Anthony Bathurst looked from Sir Richard to his companion. "Hallo!" he declared; "the death of his father has served to bring him from his hiding-place, eh?"

"Where he has been hasn't necessarily been a hiding-place," remarked Raphael. "He has been abroad, we understand. In Morocco, to be exact. You can't say with justification that he has been hiding." He paused for just a second. "I pride myself on being a sportsman, and such a statement, considering the circumstances, would be manifestly unfair."

Mr. Bathurst nodded in evident acceptance of the position. He sought other information. "The new Lord Tresham had two companions at the graveside to-day. They interested me rather. An elderly man who looked like a lawyer should look, and a tall, upstanding man of middle age. This latter man was of distinctly military appearance. You may have seen them with Lord Tresham. Do you happen to know who they are?"

"Yes, I can answer that question," declared Sir Richard. "The elderly man is, as you surmised, Nicholas Tresham's lawyer, a Mr. Gregory Lomax of Seely Place, London. The other man you should know by reason of his own reputation in another sphere. It is Forbes, the aviator."

Mr. Bathurst attempted to probe deeper. "You said just now, Sir Richard, that the new Lord Tresham's credentials were beyond dispute. Those were the words you used, if my memory serve me correctly. Do I understand from that that they have been gone into thoroughly, and that you are absolutely satisfied?"

Ingle shifted in his seat a little. The question taxed his patience. "Before I answer that, I should like you to view the situation as it has developed, in proper perspective. The Tresham lawyer is the Mr. Gregory Lomax to whom I referred just now. He is a man whose reputation and—er—integrity have never been questioned. He wrote to me a few days ago, and in response to his letter, which I saw was urgent, I went to see him. He told me then of the facts concerning the succession that had recently come to light. Although I hadn't been previously informed, he had arranged a meeting between Nicholas Tresham and me at his offices. I saw Nicholas up there. Now, mind you, I hadn't set eyes on him for forty years. He was a boy of nine then."

Sir Richard stopped in his narrative. Anthony Bathurst felt his interest quicken. If only he could see into Ingle's mind. "Well, sir," he queried, "and after that? What then?"

Ingle, after a sidelong glance at Raphael, leant forward. "Mr. Bathurst," he said quietly, "do you imagine that a professional man of the standing and integrity of Lomax would accept a position, such as I have outlined to you, without tangible and irrefutable evidence thereon? Ask yourself the question seriously."

Mr. Bathurst smiled. "In the ordinary way, sir—no. But circumstances alter cases, and, thanks to a rather vivid imagination with which I have been blessed or cursed, I am able to visualize a certain set of conditions that would remove this particular case from what may be termed ordinary grooves. Granted that, we begin to move in other directions. Another thing, sir, which I am sure you will permit me to point out, you haven't quite answered the question that I asked you. Are you—apart from Mr. Gregory Lomax—entirely satisfied with things as you find them?"

Raphael intervened with a murmur of impatience. "Surely, my dear Bathurst, that is more or less immaterial? Sir Richard may be acquiescent and, at the same time, dissatisfied. Consider the position as you yourself might have found it. As he said to you a little while ago, Nick Tresham has come back to Tresham—unexpectedly perhaps—but come back nevertheless. What else remains?"

He shrugged his shoulders with a gesture that betokened finality. Somewhat to Anthony Bathurst's surprise, Ingle appeared to resent Raphael's intervention. Perhaps he was disinclined for Raphael to assume a responsibility that clearly belonged to him. On the other hand, perhaps Raphael had said one word too much. The result was that he embarked upon a more ample and more detailed explanation. He applied himself with a greater measure of directness to the query that Bathurst had put to him.

"You must understand, Bathurst, that Lomax is thoroughly satisfied with Tresham's *bona-fides*. *Ça va sans dire*. Any other possibility is unthinkable. There is no need for one to labour that feature of the issue. Putting all that on one side, however, we will come to what you evidently regard, from the direction of your questioning, as my own particular and personal point of view. It would be an idle and ridiculous boast on my part if I said that I *recognized* Nick Tresham, the man whom I had known and companioned as a boy. Candidly, if I were taxed on this one point only I should have to plead my inability . . . that I was being required to do something unreasonable . . . something that was entirely beyond me. But, and I stress the conjunction, Mr. Bathurst, very deliberately, there are certain physical tendencies belonging to the Treshams that have persisted for generations."

"I almost knew it. 'Twas ever thus." The half-whispered words were Bathurst's.

Sir Richard proceeded:

"The most marked of these is a certain peculiarity with regard to eyebrows. All the male Treshams have been given this eyebrow distinction. Nick Tresham had it as a boy—I do remember that, very well indeed; I've chaffed him about it several times—and he has it now. All other proofs, documentary and certificated, that concern Lomax, and not me, I will ignore. Every man to his own trade. The lawyer to his (he's very welcome, let me tell you) and I to mine. There you are, Mr. Bathurst. I have put things as plainly as I know how, and I have told you all that is in my mind."

"Everything, Sir Richard?" Anthony was quietly persistent.

Ingle frowned. "I think so. Why do you ask that? What are you thinking of?"

"My persistency may be disconcerting. It may even be redolent of discourtesy. But a successful investigator simply cannot mind his own business. Any more than an inspector of taxes can. I assure you that nothing is further from my intention than to be discourteous. I have two—perhaps three—murders to solve, and because of that the data that I seek must be real, definite and convincing. I am seeking that data now. Hence my passion for exactitudes." He looked both Sir Richard and Raphael straight in the eyes—Ingle first, and afterwards Raphael. Each of them sensed his eagerness.

"Well," said the former with a touch of uneasiness, "let me know what's troubling you. I may have the prescription, even though I don't feel like lodging an objection."

Anthony laughed lightly as the car swung round a corner and gave him a glimpse of his own car behind. "Oh, it's not so bad as that, sir. But there's just this. Coming back to the legal Lomax and the strictly professional part of the business—were you informed, by any chance, during the course of your interview, as to the exact nature of this Mr. Nicholas Tresham's fortifications?"

"Fortifications?" Ingle frowned and repeated the word curiously.

"Yes. The exact nature of the evidence that he was able to produce in support of his claim? I am desperately interested. I could bear to hear the truth, the whole truth, and nothing but the truth."

Ingle's frown softened into a smile. Even Raphael's face lost some of its cynicism. The former spoke first. "This is a reversal of positions. Your attitude to me, Bathurst, is very similar to my attitude to Lomax when he first broached the news; when I did feel like lodging an objection, as it were, and getting the stewards to have a look at things. Several of your questions have been replicas of my questions to him." His smile developed into a laugh. Bathurst formed the opinion that he was nervous.

"Nicholas Tresham has all the necessary documentary evidence to support his succession. There isn't the slightest doubt with regard to that. Birth certificate, private letters and papers, that could be in the hands of a Tresham only—and also the historic Tresham counters. When he left his home years ago he took the counters with him. Strictly speaking, he had no right to do such a thing. It was, at least, intelligent but non-moral anticipation. But he has brought them back with him—something like an *amende honorable*. I will repeat to you, Bathurst, in conclusion, the words that Gregory Lomax used to me. 'Personally I haven't the slightest doubt of Lord Tresham's *bona-fides*.' I find myself in the same position, Bathurst. Reluctantly, perhaps, but there, nevertheless. I am absolutely convinced that he is Nicholas Tresham. Blood's thicker than water."

He, like Raphael previously, relapsed into the comfort of the car. Bathurst, however, had scarcely listened to his last few sentences. He heard them, but the effort was mechanical. On the other hand, a word that had just fallen from the lips of Sir Richard was burning itself into his brain. The bright letters of it danced in front of him.

"Counters"—the historic Tresham counters. His mind flighted back to the day when he had stood in Sir Austin Kemble's room at New Scotland Yard. The day of the case's start when the rag had gone up. The day when MacMorran had produced the paper that told them and the world of the murder of Hubert

Athelstan Wingfield. He remembered MacMorran's appeal for instruction in the matter of Wingfield's almost unique erudition. He recalled, too, his own answer to the Inspector. "A jetton", he had explained to the knowledge-seeking MacMorran, "is a small metal plate or counter." Counter. And here was the word again. Costumed in vivid and vital dress. Bathurst took a firm grip of himself. What was to come next must be weighed and balanced meticulously. He realized only too acutely that he was, as yet, on the fringe of the problem only. What was the sinister secret that concerned these historic counters of Tresham? If this Lord Tresham held them—*had* held them—for years, why should Wingfield's body have lain in the Valley of Ferns . . . and Blundell's in Bushey Park? And then there was Hugh Guest, who had stayed with Sir Richard Ingle and died in one of his bedrooms. Such were the thoughts that raced through and flooded his brain. "Sinister." He thought of that word's etymological meaning and of its heraldic significance. The line of Tresham started with a king's lust and a bastard. Had there been . . . He checked his spate of surmise and determined to test Sir Richard Ingle. Time was getting on. He looked at his wrist-watch. They would be at the coast within ten minutes, and he would have to be quick if he were to accomplish what he desired.

"You spoke of the Tresham counters, Sir Richard. You mentioned that Nicholas Tresham had taken them with him when he left Tresham at the time of the quarrel with his father. Would you mind telling me a little more about them? What exactly are they?"

"They are amongst the most valued of Tresham possessions—chiefly from the historical point of view. Of mother-of-pearl, and rectangular in shape. Like the eyebrows, been in the family for generations! They were the gift, I believe, of an ancient Pope of Rome, Adrian IV."

Anthony Bathurst showed signs of surprise. "Nicholas Brakespear? The lone Englishman?" he queried.

"Yes. He had the Tresham arms engraved on them; it was in recognition, so I've always been told, of a great service that was rendered to him by a son of the house of Tresham."

Anthony Bathurst leant forward, an eager question on his lips. The hunt was up. "Do these counters contain an inscription on them in Latin, by any chance? In poetic form, possibly?"

To his intense disappointment, however, both Sir Richard Ingle and Slingsby Raphael shook their heads. "No, they don't," replied the former. "You've drawn a blank there. The motto of the Treshams is in old English. 'For Godde and my Kynge'. Neither does that appear on the counters."

Anthony Bathurst caressed the ridge of his jaw. It seemed to him for a second that he must start his work all over again. There was something missing here, surely. He changed his tactics.

"It appears to me," he said challengingly, "that, for all we know, everything in the possession of the new Lord Tresham may very well have been stolen."

He watched Ingle's face carefully. There was nothing on it, however, save the utmost composure.

"Dismiss the idea at once. That would be an essay into the realms of fiction. Exciting, entertaining—but absurd. If I'm satisfied and Lomax is satisfied, you must be. But here we are, I think." He looked out of the window. "You won't be coming any farther with us, I take it?"

Anthony Bathurst was forced to come to a quick decision. "No, Sir Richard. I must alight here and wait for my own car. I expect that I shall find that it won't be very far behind us. I told my chap to follow us closely. Good-bye, Sir Richard. Many thanks for all that you have told me. Good-bye to you, sir." He half opened the door of the car before finishing what he had to say. "I may come and see you again, Sir Richard," he said quietly, "within the space of the next few days. You won't mind, will you? Sir Austin Kemble may wish me to."

He slipped out of the car without further words and waited for the oncoming MacMorran. When the latter eventually arrived, Anthony Bathurst almost rivalled him in taciturnity. Whereat the son of Caledonia was by no means pleased.

Chapter XIV
WHERE HAD WINGFIELD BEEN?

Two days later Mr. Bathurst was as good as his word. With MacMorran at work on the Sussex end of the triangle, he found time to visit again the house of Sir Richard Ingle. It is not recorded either, in spite of what Mr. Bathurst had said, that Sir Austin Kemble had any knowledge of this action on Mr. Bathurst's part. Certainly he had issued no instructions on the matter. Having watched Sir Richard drive off from the house in his high-powered Daimler, Anthony chose the moments that immediately followed for the time to make his call.

As he had expected and hoped, he found himself in conversation with Garrett, the butler. The latter, with expressed regret, supplied the information that his master was not at home; he explained by how little Mr. Bathurst had missed him. Mr. Bathurst showed signs of equal regret. He even indicated annoyance. But these little inconveniences had a knack of occurring, he stated, and the only sensible thing to do when they did turn up was to make the best of them. Perhaps Garrett himself might be able to assist him on the special matter that had brought him back to Beech Knoll?

Garrett bowed to the speaker—a doyen of deference. If it were in his power—well, Mr. Bathurst could command him. He thought that the gentleman was aware of that.

Mr. Bathurst thanked him and did as Garrett suggested. The first order issued to Garrett was in the form of a question. "Garrett," he said, "you have an excellent memory, I'm sure. A man holding the post that you do would be lost without one. And 'lost', I fear, is but a mild word."

Garrett accepted the tribute with obvious pleasure. "Thank you, sir. I suppose you're right, sir. I have been in Sir Richard's service for many years, and I think I've proved myself an efficient servant. What was it that you wanted to ask me, sir?"

"Just this, Garrett. Have you ever heard of the name of Wingfield?"

Garrett opened his eyes. "In what particular connection, sir?"

"That was what I expected you to ask. I'll tell you. In connection with this house of Sir Richard Ingle's—Beech Knoll."

Garrett began to shake his head. Anthony persisted. "Has anybody named Wingfield ever been a visitor here? Either recently, or some time ago?"

Garrett's head went to one side in consideration. He pondered for some few seconds before he answered. "Well, sir, we have a number of people here in the course of the year, as you can very well guess. Sometimes at a house-party there's been as many as forty or fifty of them. For instance, a Christmas or so ago we had quite as many as that—if not more. So, as you can see, it's hard to remember the names of all of them."

He stopped. The magnitude of his task of remembrance seemed to deter him. Mr. Bathurst considered that a seasonable word would be in the nature of an encouragement.

"Many people, Garrett, situated as you are, would, I am sure, remember very few of them."

Garrett brightened visibly. "Thank you, sir. Well, looking back, to the best of my memory and ability, I can't say that anybody of the name of Wingfield has been a guest here. I think I should have been certain to recollect a name like that."

"Why?" urged Bathurst in semi-remonstrance. "Why that name in particular?"

Garrett's eyes twinkled. His moment came. "I've been to Henley several times, sir, in the old days. Saw Ten Eyck win the Diamonds. Bit of a sculler myself. Old member of the *Vesta*, sir, as it happens."

"Stout fellow," returned Mr. Bathurst; "Charon, another famous ferryman, was bright and fierce-eyed too. So your answer to my question is—'certainly not recently'?"

"That is so, sir. Certainly not recently. I'd vouch for that."

"And probably never. Eh?"

"I think that would be my answer, sir. I can't remember ever having heard the name in connection with a visitor here. Thank you, sir—although there was no need—I'm sure it's been a positive pleasure . . ."

The transference of a note bearing the Bank of England's promise having been quickly effected, Anthony judged that the time was ripe for departure. He turned his car away from the house known as Beech Knoll with his problem still churning in his mind.

The situation, so far as he could judge, was becoming desperate. The words of the tall, gaunt sister at Hurrilow couldn't possibly be ignored, he thought; and this after incessant probing. He rehearsed the vital portions of her story to him. She had seen her brother, this murdered Wingfield, just before he took his staff in hand and sought the road . . . and lay down for ever . . . all his sayings said . . . deeds all done . . . and songs all sung . . . sing it out in sun and rain. . . . So the words jangled in Anthony's brain. . . . She had seen him looking at a map of this delightful island in which he himself journeyed now. The island of the spiked lion? It was not a mere coincidence, Anthony felt sure. It couldn't be. The accumulation of circumstances was too great by all the laws of logic and reasoning. Wingfield must have come to Ingle's—the home of the third and last murder. He must have come as Hugh Guest came after him . . . and Blundell too. What could be the attraction?

Tresham itself was surely not within the picture. It was across the water—on the mainland. No map of the island would be required by any visitor to Tresham. Unless it had been a case of Tresham first and, from there, to a second and more important rendezvous. Or perhaps back to Tresham. But, if either of these contingencies were so, how could he explain that straw of salvation that the woman had tossed to him in Wingfield's house at Hurrilow? That straw of the spiked lion? Where was its home? Anthony Bathurst took a corner a trifle sharply, and as he did so, caught his breath. Here was revelation.

"My dear Watson," he murmured to himself, "I deserve to be kicked from here to that church at Tresham which lies under the hill. The father of my clan is Bartimaeus. Of all the decrepit crawling brains. . . ." He slackened speed a little to allow another car to leave the drive of a biggish house and turn into the road. It was Ingle's high-powered Daimler, that he had seen take the road just prior to his conversation with the versatile Garrett. He took care that Ingle, seated, he could see, with Barry Covington, did *not* see him.

Bathurst accelerated after the two cars had passed each other, and about a quarter of a mile along the road pulled up, to hold conversation with a rude forefather of the hamlet whose time had not yet come for sleep.

"Cold day," he sang out.

The old man straightened himself from weeding. "Aye, sir, it is that—a borrowed day."

Mr. Bathurst delved for a greater truth. "That's a new one on me. A borrowed day, did you say?"

"Aye, sir," returned the old man with the weatherbeaten face; "there's days we get given to us at times, that are borrowed, as you might say, from another month of the calendar. That's a sayin' that us countryfolk get told us early in our lives. A bit o' sun sometimes, a touch o' cold and wet it may be, at other times even snow or fog. Them's borrowed days. They come where they don't properly belong."

Mr. Bathurst smiled cordially. "Do you know, I've never heard that before. But I get the idea, and I think it's a very happy way to explain our island's weather vagaries. June, July and August must be a trio of spendthrifts. Now tell me something else—that is, of course, if you can."

The old man put a hand to his back and with the other rubbed his crinkled nose. "What is it, sir, that ye be wantin' to know?"

Anthony leaned forward out of the driving-seat. He jerked his head down the road that he had just travelled. "Have you any idea to whom that big house down there belongs?"

The furrowed face looked long-sightedly in the direction indicated. "Aye, sir. That be easy. I can tell you that, for sure. That house belongs to a Mr. Raphael. A gentleman who's just come to these parts. Great traveller, too, I do believe. Been in China and a fair number of like outlandish places. Leaving them things out, I don't know much about him. Thank ye, sir."

The old man touched his hat as the car sped away. Pocketing his unexpected profit, he resumed the trivial round. Life was better than he had thought it a few moments ago . . . a pint of beer was appreciably nearer.

Anthony's mind played incessantly with his new idea. So Slingsby Raphael lived as close to Sir Richard Ingle as this! In this same island! The separation was but a few miles. He had but recently come to live in the district. He was a great traveller—restless and wanderlusting, but had at length come to settle in a spot so remote and quiet as this peaceful, lovely little island. Was it just the desire to rest that had prompted him, or were there other deeper, darker motives underlying this change of habit and habitat?

Mr. Bathurst, driving on and on, found an inn that promised comforting hospitality, and decided to lunch on his problem. The promise of the hostelry was well fulfilled. Anthony lunched at "The Open Gate" with many degrees of satisfaction. The food provided was both well cooked and well served.

But his mental problem still remained with him. Clearer, it is true, but still—very definitely—a problem. There were two or three courses open to him he considered, and tossing away a half-smoked cigarette, he resolved to carry out two of them then and there. The third could wait.

First of all he would return to Beech Knoll and interview a certain young lady whom so far he had not seen—Celia Guest— the sister of the third man who had come by a violent death. That is, if she were still staying with the Ingles. If she had returned to Sussex, he made up his mind to follow her there. But he still clung to the hope that his luck would be in and that he could find her a mile or so away. As he drove through the gates of Beech Knoll, the ubiquitous Garrett quickly appeared to greet him. The butler had news for this visitor, which he hastened to impart.

"Sir Richard, my master, has returned, sir, and I put that question to him, sir, which you asked of me concerning a Mr. Wingfield. And my master informs me, sir, that nobody bearing that name has ever stayed here. He knows nobody of the name— neither does Lady Ingle—therefore the idea that you mooted is an impossibility. I thought you would like to know for certain, sir."

"Garrett," murmured Mr. Bathurst, "brightest and best of the sons of the morning, your worth is above rubies—I do not know what I should have done without you."

Chapter XV
CELIA MERELY WONDERS

Anthony rose from his car and descended. "Now, Garrett," he said, "I wonder if you would be good enough to do something else for me? Something quite easy this time. Would you be good enough to tell Sir Richard that I am here? That I've come back, tell him, in the hope of a little conversation with him? Thanks awfully, if you would. I'll wait here, the soul of patience, until you come back."

Within a few minutes of the envoy's departure Sir Richard came bustling out. His face was red and flustered as though he had recently indulged in much argument. Anthony, from the corner of his eye, could see the young man, Covington, moving about in the morning-room.

"Well, Bathurst?" said Ingle as he came up to his visitor, "I'm sorry I was out when you first called. What brings you here again? Are there any developments?"

"No, sir. Hardly anything to report at all. Everything's most discouraging. I've heard from Pullinger, as I arranged when I left here on the last occasion, and Inspector MacMorran from the Scotland Yard end is at work on the Blundell thread. Neither has advanced at all. We're all of us just about *in statu quo*."

Ingle rubbed his cheek with impatience. Anthony proceeded imperturbably: "When we parted after the funeral of the late Lord Tresham, you will remember that I took the liberty of inviting myself here again. Here I am." He smiled hopefully.

"Well, what can I do for you?" Sir Richard was very direct.

"I should be eternally obliged if I could have a spot of conversation with Miss Guest. I am hoping that she is still here with you. Will you arrange that for me?"

Ingle's face furrowed. Evidently the suggestion found no favour with him. "Er—do you mean privately?"

Bathurst became manifestly joyous. "Good Lord, no, sir! That is to say within reason. It need not be *à deux*, but I'm not yearning for the company of multitudes."

Sir Richard seemed to understand the position a little better. "I will tell her, Bathurst. You realize, of course, how the poor girl is? Essentially plucky, but . . . go into the morning-room and wait, will you? It will be empty by now. I'll bring Celia in to you."

He was as good as his word. Anthony gave a sympathetic hand to the slim, dark-haired girl whom Sir Richard brought to him.

"This is Mr. Anthony Bathurst."

She nodded to her host as though the proffered invitation meant little or nothing to her. He amplified his statement. "Mr. Bathurst wants to speak to you for a little while about Hugh."

She released Anthony's hand and pressed her lips together. Anthony waited. But here was no collapse. Here was no tender trembling to the edge of tears. The grief of her was made of sterner stuff. When she looked up at him her face was hard and cold, stiffened, it seemed, into a cast of set, indomitable purpose.

"I feel, Mr. Bathurst," she said with composed resignation, "that I shall disappoint you. I am living through an endless succession of horror-haunted days. I think sometimes that I have come to the end of everything."

He shook his head. "Don't you think, Miss Guest," he returned, "that 'ends' of everything are not always easily discernible—that we often mistake them?"

She shook her head. "I don't think that I understand."

He led her, as he had intended to do. "Let me try to explain out of my own experience. I am afraid that when I was a boy at Uppingham I used to divide the year into two seasons—the cricket season and the football season. And always, each year, when July came, I used to feel in the silences of high noon, as the sun lighted and warmed the brown, sweet-scented earth, that I could hear the lovely golden sands of summer running out. Such was my boyish thought, and it saddened and sickened me beyond measure. It wasn't so, because July itself had to go and August to come in its wake, but that's how it seemed to me. I could never put the thought behind me, and sometimes, even now in these after years, the same thought comes to me and stays until I drive it away. They were wonderful days, Miss Guest. All the sweet sounds of our England, at the crown of its year, would come to me and companion me. The magical whir of a mowing-machine away in the distance, the short, sharp clipping of a hedge under swift shears, or perhaps no sound at all only that wonderful soundless beating of the pulse on a hot day in July.

"In the same way, the third week in February always heralded to me the passing of wintry discontent and the incoming summer. Winter had gone for me then, if for nobody else."

He looked at her in that whimsical way of his. "So you see, Miss Guest, that sometimes what seems like the inevitable end to us is nearer even to the beginning. It's a question of personal perspective—that's all. Our scheme of life needs readjustment."

"You are trying to comfort me, Mr. Bathurst. I know that. I thank you for your kindness."

"I have no other course open to me, Miss Guest. I am your friend. I am on the side of right and justice. That is why I have come to see you here. Sir Richard has given me permission to ask you something. I should like your permission too. May I?"

Ingle looked exceedingly uncomfortable and blew his nose hard. The girl replied: "Of course. There is no need to ask me. I long to help to avenge poor Hugh. But I'm afraid that I have little assistance to give you. Please tell me how I can help you?"

"First of all, Miss Guest, make yourself thoroughly comfortable. Sit down there."

The girl did as she had been directed. Anthony, however, remained standing, one arm across the corner of the mantelpiece. There was a period of silence during which Sir Richard Ingle, on tenterhooks that were almost obvious, watched Bathurst closely. It was unlike Bathurst, he thought, to be at a loss for an opening.

"Miss Guest," remarked Anthony at length, "when your uncle, Mr. Blundell, was first missing, how did your brother seem?"

"Seem?" she repeated uncertainly. "I don't quite understand—"

"Let me put it a little differently then. How did he take it—pretty badly?"

Miss Guest attempted to explain. "Hugh first heard that uncle was missing, from *me*. He was at Oxford. I sent to him—told him all the trouble and all that I knew. Of course, he came down to Hurstfold post haste. But he was frightfully upset—I can say that with absolute certainty. But why do you ask me this, Mr. Bathurst?"

He ignored her question. "Was your brother *more* upset or *less* upset than you would have normally expected?"

She shook her head definitely. "Neither the one nor the other. He was upset. That's all I can say. I wouldn't make any statement beyond that. I shouldn't be any help to you if I did."

Mr. Bathurst was undeterred. "Thank you, Miss Guest. I'll accept that implicitly. I'll change my adjective. From 'upset' to 'surprised'. Did he seem *surprised* at your uncle's disappearance?"

"Oh, more than that, Mr. Bathurst. Much more than that. He was *shocked*. Stunned, almost, during the first few days."

Anthony persisted. "And that condition which you have just described was maintained all the time? Would you say that?"

Celia Guest was on the point of reply when she suddenly checked herself. "No, I think I see what you mean; how you want me to help you. In the first stages he was shocked, as I said. When no news of my uncle came, and Scotland Yard seemed powerless to help us, he got listless—distressed—dispirited—crushed almost. Then he changed."

Bathurst was in like a flash. "Let me help you. His depression gave way to excitement. Would that be true, Miss Guest?"

Her eyes were wide open. "Yes, that would be true—but how did you know?"

"It was hardly knowledge. I found myself *hoping* so; that was all. Now tell me, Miss Guest, what did your brother say to you when he was excited—like that? Tell me anything of which you can think. When this change came over him. What had caused it."

"But I've no idea. Not the slightest."

"He didn't confide in you at all?"

She shook her head. "Oh no, Mr. Bathurst. Hugh wasn't like that. He was frightfully obstinate and self-reliant, and—another thing—he probably didn't want to bother me. The only reason that I knew he was excited was through his wanting to come here."

Anthony Bathurst rubbed his hands. "Now that's interesting. The desire to come here, then, came upon him suddenly? He didn't consider the idea for a time, turn it over in his mind and *then* decide to act upon it?"

Celia's answer was this time most decisive, "No. He came to me one night obviously labouring under a great excitement. I could tell that from the look in his eyes. 'Celia,' he said, 'I've made up my mind to go and stop at Sir Richard Ingle's, in the Isle of Wight. You know we can go there whenever we like. That's always been an understood thing. And you must come with me.'"

"What did you say when he suggested that to you?"

"I asked him why he wanted to go there, *then* of all times, considering how we were worried concerning uncle's disappearance. I said wouldn't it be better for us to stay in Hurstfold, so that we could be on the spot in the event of anything turning up. I thought it would be a more—not exactly sensible—but *reasonable* course."

"What did he say when you said that? Did he argue it out with you?"

Celia Guest shook her head emphatically. "Oh no. Hugh was never one to argue with me. He was older than I and he always expected me to fall in with his decision or opinion, whatever it might be. What he said, he always expected me to accept as conclusive. He said that Beech Knoll was always 'open house' to us and that we would go there."

"That is quite true, Bathurst, as I told you before. Hugh certainly knew that." This contribution was from Sir Richard Ingle.

"Miss Guest," said Anthony, "did you ever definitely ask your brother his *real reason* for asking to come to this house?"

She shook her head again. "No, Mr. Bathurst. I tried to, but his manner put me off. I often worry myself, now that it's too late, and wish that I had. But it wouldn't have made a scrap of difference, I'm sure. Hugh would never have told me if he had made up his mind not to. Oh, he was like that, was Hugh. I was his little sister, you see, waiting there always to do what he told me. I can only wonder at it all."

Bathurst was silent—thinking hard. His thought came to translation. "You said, I think, that he came to you *one night* with this idea of coming to the Isle of Wight?"

"This is so, Mr. Bathurst. One evening after dinner. I remember it all so clearly."

"Where had he been that day? Out anywhere, can you remember?"

"No. He had been indoors with me all the time."

Bathurst seemed disappointed at her answer. He tried again. "What had he been doing? Anything special? Think hard, Miss Guest, if ever you thought hard."

She passed her hand over her eyes. "As far as I can remember, he had been in Uncle John's study all the morning and the better part of the afternoon. I can't recall him having gone anywhere else."

Bathurst's face grew grim and hard. "Yes . . . that might conceivably fit the case. He found it and brought it with him. . . ." He looked up. Ingle was regarding him curiously.

Anthony turned to Sir Richard with quick and ready apology. "I'm sorry, sir; I'm afraid that I was thinking aloud and that the thoughts were running away with me. It's a wretched habit from the point of view of other people."

Ingle shrugged his shoulders with a hint of irony. "It's no good sitting on a horse unless you're its master, and unless too . . ."

"Unless what, Sir Richard?" Anthony asked the question eagerly.

"Unless, too, that the horse *knows* you're its master."

Bathurst rubbed the ridge of his jaw thoughtfully. But to Sir Richard's last statement he made no immediate reply. On the contrary, he advanced to Celia Guest. "Good-bye, Miss Guest, you've been very patient with my insatiable curiosity. Thank you. But believe me, it's been in a good cause. But you know that. Au 'voir, Sir Richard. I'll remember what you've told me. I'll see you at Tresham."

At the last word Ingle turned to Celia in amazement. Tresham—why Tresham?

Chapter XVI
THE TURN OF THE SCREW

The road that Anthony now travelled he had travelled before. It may be safely presumed, therefore, from that statement, that Mr. Bathurst knew his way. When he came to the turning that he desired he made his way down it and pulled up the car in front of the first house on the right. There was a brass plate affixed to the wall, by the big gate. For the benefit of those who desired such information it read, "Arnold Summerhayes, M.B."

Mr. Bathurst descended from his car, walked up the drive and rang the bell. To his surprise he was admitted by no less a person than Summerhayes himself. Judging by the expression on the doctor's face when he realized the identity of his visitor, this condition of surprise was mutual.

"I'm afraid that you're—" He stopped and looked round rather hopelessly, as though at a loss for a word.

"Inconvenient, possibly," returned Anthony, "but surely not unwelcome? That thought would cut me to the quick. May I come in, Dr. Summerhayes?"

"Well," responded the doctor, "that you must, of course, having come, I suppose, some distance to see me. I can't very well talk to you at my front door. Come this way, Mr. Bathurst."

Anthony obeyed and followed the doctor into what was evidently the latter's consulting-room.

"Sit down, Mr. Bathurst. If you can say what you have to say in ten minutes, I should be infinitely obliged. Truth to tell, I'm in the devil of a hurry." Summerhayes looked pointedly at his watch.

"You humiliate me, you know, Doctor, when you stress so the inconvenience of my arrival."

Summerhayes laughed in apology. "Now you're putting the boot on the other foot. I'm sorry if I appear inhospitable. That would be the last thing of which I should like to be thought guilty. I assure you that I have excellent reasons for my apparent haste. I'll explain what they are after you've had your say." A smile flitted across his lean face.

Bathurst began to wonder more and more. He determined, however, to let this condition lie fallow for a time, and come, first of all, to the main point of his visit. There was no gainsaying the fact that Dr. Summerhayes had certainly given him the broadest of hints. "Something has happened, Doctor, since my last visit, which I regard as so tremendously important that I have come back to ask you two more questions concerning the murder of Hugh Guest."

Summerhayes looked puzzled. "I'm afraid that I don't quite understand. To what do you allude? I, myself, have—"

"I allude, Doctor, to the unexpected change in the position of our mutual acquaintance, Sir Richard Ingle." Bathurst watched him keenly. How had he reacted to the mention of Ingle's name?

"I'm aware of it, of course," replied Summerhayes, "but I fail to see how it concerns the poisoning of Guest—in the slightest." His tall figure fidgeted in his chair.

"We'll waive that," conceded Anthony, "willingly. I didn't expect that you would. It will save us time. Now, Doctor, let me come to my two questions. When I called upon you before, we talked about the key, the locked bedroom door and the way in which the murderer *might* and *could* have escaped. Do you remember?"

Summerhayes nodded. Anthony proceeded: "But what we *didn't* consider was the question of a *duplicate* key, Doctor. How does that possibility strike you?"

Summerhayes rubbed his chin thoughtfully. "I certainly hadn't thought of it. But it's an idea, nevertheless, that's worth consideration. It makes a big difference."

"It might explain things, eh?"

Summerhayes nodded emphatically. "Most assuredly."

"Good, then. Now for item number two. I am going to take the liberty of asking you an extremely direct and pertinent question. You examined the body of Guest . . . and you had a number of people round you while you were there. You were able to see and watch the reactions of those people because you were peculiarly placed. He had been dead for but a few minutes when you were called to him. Do you see what I mean?"

Anthony stopped. Summerhayes turned deliberately to look at him.

"That's so, isn't it, Doctor?"

"You are right, Mr. Bathurst; but I was wondering what the exact meaning was that lay behind your words. From what I've seen and heard of you, you're not the man to talk like that without having a definite object behind it." He spoke heatedly.

Anthony smiled at his vehemence. "I wouldn't contradict you. You are undeniably right, Doctor. I most certainly have."

"Let's have it, then. You can speak frankly to me. My profession accustoms me to frankness. There's no necessity to beat about the bush."

"I said just now that you had been in a position to watch certain reactions . . . of certain people. Apart from the attention that you had to give to the dead, it's just on the cards that you may have been able to give some little attention to the living."

Anthony watched him keenly for the slightest signs of response. The long, lean face of Summerhayes, however, was inscrutable. It might have been a mask for all the feeling that it revealed to the watcher. Anthony pressed him for an answer.

"Well?"

When it came, Summerhayes's voice was hard and cold. It held a quality that Anthony hadn't heard before. "No, Mr. Bathurst, you are entirely mistaken in your supposition. I observed nothing. I should have liked to have helped you—but I can't. In the way you suggest, that is."

Mr. Bathurst came to a quick decision and brought up his artillery. "Then I'll discard surmise and inference, Doctor, and ask you this question: *Whom do you suspect of the murder of Hugh Guest?*"

Summerhayes rose excitedly from his chair. The chill had gone from his voice now—it was strained and hoarse. "Mr. Bathurst," he said, "you are taking an unfair advantage of me—you must not ask me such a thing. For many reasons. Who am I to point the finger of suspicion against any one person . . . suspicion, too, that would not be based on definite facts or evidence, but on a look, a word, or even a gesture? You have no right to ask such a thing, and I must refuse to do it."

He resumed his seat, visibly affected. Mr. Bathurst shrugged his shoulders. "In that case, then, Doctor, there only remains for you to do what you hinted at just now. You were going to explain why you were in such a hurry to get away from me."

Summerhayes nodded his acceptance of Anthony's point. "And my explanation, as it happens, will come at a most appropriate moment. Mr. Bathurst, something has happened within the last twenty-four hours that has made it imperative for me to leave this practice. I am going from the Isle of Wight altogether, either to-morrow or the day after. I shall never set foot in it again. And I am going from here for two reasons. I'll make a perfectly clean breast of them. The first is, that I shall considerably profit by going. . . materially . . . which is, you will readily admit, no small consideration these days: and the second—the more important—is . . ." He paused and looked round . . . almost as though he had heard somebody else come into the room. His face held fear.

"Yes," said Mr. Bathurst softly . . . "and that second reason is . . ."

Summerhayes swung round to him almost fiercely. "What do you think it is? Because I am afraid to stay, man! Desperately afraid." The man's face twitched convulsively as he spoke the words. Bathurst refrained from interruption. He waited in patience. *In timore* there might be *veritas*. But hoping for revelation he was doomed to disappointment. Dr. Summerhayes bit his lip hard and pulled himself together.

"I don't think I ought to say any more, Mr. Bathurst. I've said enough already. Too much in all probability. If you take my advice you'll get away from the island yourself. Good-bye." He held out his hand.

Anthony realized at this moment that if he wanted any more information from Dr. Summerhayes he would be compelled to do the extracting himself. "Thank you for the hint, Doctor. It's something, at least, to be forewarned. But tell me this before you go—of *whom* are you afraid? Of *what* are you afraid?"

Summerhayes glanced round in agitation. "Don't ask me any more, for heaven's sake! I told you just now that I'd said too much. I can't tell you any more, Mr. Bathurst. I *dare* not tell you any more. Get out of the island while you can. If you stay longer it may be too late."

Anthony, seizing the psychological moment, played his ace. "And beware of the spiked lion, eh, Doctor?"

Summerhayes caught his breath. It was glaringly apparent that Anthony had hit him hard. "What do you know of the spiked lion?" The sentence came from him in a whisper.

"At the moment," returned Mr. Bathurst coolly, "very little, compared, that is, with what I'm going to know."

Summerhayes leant over towards him. "Have a care—lions have claws, Mr. Bathurst."

"So have I, Doctor . . . and I may have the chance of using them. Who knows?"

Chapter XVII
THE SPIKED LION

ANTHONY Bathurst sat at his desk in his own room. Try as he would to escape from it, he was unable to rid himself of an idea. Certain words jangled through his brain. Words from the history of that bizarre case of the great master Holmes—the case of the spectral hound. "They were the footprints, Mr. Holmes, of a gigantic hound." "And the case which I am investigating," he said to himself, "I am asked to believe in a spiked lion. A spiked lion with claws! Fantastic nonsense."

He rose and walked to the window, remembering that other idea that had come to him when he had motored near Slingsby Raphael's house in the Isle of Wight. His mind dwelt on the counters that had gone to the house of Tresham from the English Pope. Walking back to his desk, he looked again at the book of reference which lay open in front of him. This is what he read:

The Heralds' College was incorporated and endowed by Richard the Third (Crookback) in the year 1484 as a College of Arms. It was presided over by the Earl Marshal, the other members being the then Kings of Arms and the Six Heralds. Their duties were the regulation of the granting and the bearing of Coat Armour, in addition to the ordinary functions of the heralds. The first residence of the Heralds' College was in Pultency's Inn, but in the year 1554, in the reign of Queen Mary, the zealot of the old religion, that monarch granted the present site. Derby House was acquired at that time and actually stood on the site of the present College building, the original of which was destroyed during the Great Fire of London and afterwards rebuilt. Enquiries concerning all phases of heraldry may be addressed to the officer on duty in the Public Office every day between the hours of 10 a.m. and 4 p.m.

Mr. Bathurst closed the book. Help would be forthcoming if he were able to gain the precise information that he coveted. He looked at his watch. The time was right. A visit to the home of Armorial Bearings was certainly indicated. He decided not to use his car, but to walk. He was there by half past twelve. He addressed an enquiry to the officer on duty in accordance with the instructions that he had assimilated.

The official listened with an almost incredible dignity, solemnly directed him to the appropriate room, and at the same time added further information which was no doubt intended to be helpful.

109 | THE SPIKED LION

Mr. Bathurst still toyed with his idea. He tried to recall the words that Sir Richard Ingle had used to him with regard to the gift to the Treshams of those mother-of-pearl counters of Pope Adrian IV. There was neither motto nor poetic Latin on them he had said. Anthony remembered that statement for a certainty. They bore the arms only of the Treshams, and the late Hubert Athelstan Wingfield had been the author, amongst all those other distinctions, of the heraldic brochure, "The Crown of England and its former possessions—Normandy, Guienne and Aquitaine."

"Of course he had," murmured Anthony to himself semi-ecstatically; "besides his knowledge of legendary inscriptions he was an expert on matters heraldic." Eventually the book for which Anthony had requisitioned was brought to him. He turned its pages until he came to the Lion Passant; he read with avid interest:

It would be expected by most students of heraldry that the Lion Passant would be numerically plentiful if only as a polite reference and compliment to the English Royal shield. On the contrary, however, compared with the Lion Passant we find the Lion Rampant in far more popular use. The shield Gules three lions passant guardant, presumed to be the shield adopted by the Norman Kings, has one lion for Normandy, another for Guienne, and a third for Poitou or Aquitaine, three former possessions of the Crown of England.

"Here entered Professor Wingfield," communed Mr. Bathurst with himself. "Here he stepped right into the arena." Anthony read on:

But this particular coat-of-arms, be it noted, was used other than by the English Kings. The Royal lions, of course, were gold, but the other bearers of this particular shield usually showed silver lions. Some were passant and others were passant guardant. It is interesting to remember that the King of North Wales, Cadwallader ap Griffith, had this coat with his lions "armed azure". Gules two lions, in fact, was a very frequent Welsh bearing. It was attributed by some historians to Griffith ap Cynan and his descendants of the line of the King of Gwenydd. It was certainly borne of various noble families in early times, possibly even from the Planta Genista.

Sometimes the lions had blue claws. There is no lion passant barry or bendy, but the arms of the Kingdom of Friesland is two lions passant on a field semée of crosses. The lion passant, in the centre of three, appears frequently between many different heraldic devices. It is difficult to obtain authentic information on the matter, but this is probably very much more modern than the lion rampant. The lion coward should have his tail between his legs, but sometimes we find that the reguardant lion is so blazoned. This is probably more or less Scotch in origin, but it may also come from Cadvan ap Cynan as it is often to be found in the western counties and their adjoining territories. There is also yet another heraldic lion. The lions used as a bearing by the House of Tresham have a spiked collar round their neck. This lion, in all probability, came originally from France. It may be remarked, in conclusion, that lions passant are very seldom charged with badges such as occur upon lions rampant, and seldom also hold an object in their paws.

Mr. Bathurst looked up from the book and rubbed eager hands. His eyes held the light of success. At last he had run the spiked lion to earth. "But the animal is not normal, it is spiked, and remember, too, Wingfield . . ."

They were the words found on the creased piece of paper in Blundell's pocket. He was hot on the trail at last. He immediately sought further details. Details of this house of Tresham. The book into which he now delved told him much that he knew—much that had come to him during his investigation of the case. Certain other things, however, proved to be of immense interest. There was the following, for instance:

Amongst the most valued possessions of the House of Tresham is a set of rectangular mother-of-pearl counters, given to the family by Adrian IV, Pope of Rome. They bear the Tresham arms impaling Strangeways: Azure between two

THE SPIKED LION

spiked lions passant, a fesse embattled-counter-embattled. A more recent gift to the House of Tresham was an old rosewood snuffbox, believed to possess an ancient and most remarkable history. It was found in the cellar of a house in the Isle of Wight and presented to the family because of the Tresham lion that it bears on its face. A man dressed in Elizabethan style, grey trunk hose, sleeveless waistcoat and white shirt, with medici collar, is standing with a sword in his left hand, and is gazing in seeming horror at a spiked lion which is to be observed coming through the door and apparently advancing towards him. This door is green while the lion is in black and white. The box is of magnificent workmanship with varnished screwed hinges and with a lid sloping towards them. Its size is 3½ x 2½ inches. When the box was excavated it was thought by experts to have belonged to the Treshams in time past, and was, accordingly, with the Crown's consent, made over to them. The seat of the House of Tresham is situated at Tresham. . . .

Mr. Bathurst closed the book and began to think on these things . . . to think desperately hard. Right back to Nicholas Brakespear. Far enough in all conscience. It might have been worse, he commented mentally, with a twist of humour. After all, there had been a Paleozoic time, and possibly even then Treshams and Ingles had "side by side, on the ebbing tide, crawled through the ooze and slime".

He took stock again of the position. If they had wanted Wingfield, as was now eminently conceivable, why had they wanted Blundell? For the presence of Guest he could satisfactorily account . . . but why, in hell's name, Blundell? If he could manage to fit Blundell into the tracery of the pattern, true solution of the problem might be moderately close to hand.

Guest, for a certainty, had paid the penalty of knowledge. Of dangerous knowledge—two-edged—like the double-fatal yew. He had, of course, gone to Ingle's purposely. Deliberately refrained from telling his sister because of the danger that lurked there . . . or near there. But why had he held his hand that, in turn, clasped the knowledge that he could have used effectively?

Held it and allowed his enemies to murder him? After Barry Covington, too, had warned him that he was under menace.

Mr. Bathurst mused prodigiously. Who had put the screw on Dr. Summerhayes? Surely it must be somebody who possessed three things—wealth, influence, and information. And a fourth thing, too, thought Anthony—imagination. Yes, certainly imagination. Imagination, perhaps, most of all. At the same time, it was becoming increasingly clear to him that he must attack the Blundell link in the chain before he could make any appreciable headway.

Was it possible, he argued to himself, that, as he had connected Wingfield with his reputation for knowledge of the legendary inscription, instead of with that to do with heraldry, so Blundell, too, had an alternative line of approach to that of the cipher and cryptogram? That there was another trail that had so far been neglected? Anthony referred to his diary—the one that he always carried with him. What were the data that he had gleaned concerning Blundell from Sir Austin Kemble at the "Yard" on the day that he had first touched the case? Here they were: "Comparatively well-to-do and unmarried. . . ."

Anthony smiled as he remembered his first reply to this: "Father killed in an earthquake at Hong Kong. Educated Wrykyn and Luther College, Cambridge . . . recognized authority on ciphers and cryptograms . . . regarded as the English reply to Le Courvoisier . . . special job in Intelligence for the best part of the war years 1914-1918."

Anthony reflected. Here were several fields of possible explanation. Anthony essayed more meditation. Taken on the whole, he thought, it was the most intricate case that had ever fallen into his lap. The strands were so infernally twisted. One more thread, he felt, if he could but gather it, would straighten out the skein. But he was definitely bothered as to "locale". . . . Did the key to the mystery lie at Tresham or in the Isle of Wight? There was Sir Richard Ingle, to be sure. His mind began to wrestle again . . . to grapple with the problem . . . to endeavour to find light that would illumine his darkness. Wingfield . . . Blundell . . . Guest. They were the three men. Had he been wrong in

113 | THE SPIKED LION

taking the three of them singly, as it were? . . . Would he have been better advised to take them together? To look for *likeness* between them . . . to search for something which they had in common . . . and not for individual distinctions? Leaving Guest out of the picture for the time being—he was a horse of another colour—could he concentrate to advantage on Blundell and Wingfield? Had they the least little thing in common? Knowledge—any possession—any something, infinitesimal even, but belonging at the same time to each one of them? Once again his mind churned the mass of revealed and collected matter. He determined to take the two men, step by step and point by point, in every meticulous particular. Like in an English lesson in the old days at Uppingham—the analysis of a sentence or the parsing of a word.

Names—John Pender Blundell, Hubert Athelstan Wingfield. No inspiration there that he could see of any kind. Residences, respectively—Hurstfold, Sussex, Hurrilow, Wiltshire. "Pass," murmured Anthony to himself, shaking a dubious head. Ages— between forty-eight and forty-nine; forty-nine. Bathurst looked at the cardinals with the interest of sudden unexpected excitement. Hallo! Here was something that he hadn't particularly noticed before. Might be the purest of coincidences, of course— with nothing in it—but all the same, he censured himself for concentrating on the apparently bigger data, and thereby neglecting the seemingly smaller. *All* data, he had consistently advocated and argued, should be thoroughly sifted and examined, irrespective of the magnitude that they appear to present to the investigator. Here he had been false to his own creed.

Forty-nine years of age, say, each of them. Born in the same year, and at school at the same time. Exact contemporaries. That apparently insignificant fact *might* mean a lot—it *might* mean the very thread for which he was seeking. If they had been forty-nine when they were murdered, that meant, making the usual allowance that . . . "Hold hard!" whispered Anthony to himself. . . . "Forty-nine years of age. . . . Who the devil besides, in this grotesque case, was also the bearer of that identical tale of years? . . ." He was positive that there was somebody. That he had heard it somewhere. He lashed his brain. The words came to him. Ingle's words in the car, driving back from the churchyard that lay under the hill. "I hadn't seen him for forty years. He was a boy of nine at the time." Nick Tresham, too, was forty-nine. Was this revelation? Or just one of those combinations of coincidence that develop the length of its arm?

He visualized again that journey in Ingle's car when MacMorran had followed on behind. What had they discussed? As he pondered he wrote the three names idly on the diary to which he had previously referred. "Blundell", "Tresham", "Wingfield". As men will at times like this, he began to draw weirdly misshapen lines, that left the three names at all angles. Ingle had been absolutely in agreement with the strength of Tresham's credentials. Raphael, too, had insisted on that fact. Documents, the mother-of-pearl counters, the way in which the solicitor Lomax had dealt with the case, had all thoroughly satisfied Sir Richard.

"I am absolutely convinced that he is Nicholas Tresham," Ingle had said: "Blood is thicker than water."

Again Bathurst's nomadic pen traced idle words—words which he decorated with fanciful and fantastic capitals. "Blood is Thicker than Water". He made, even more ornate the "B", the "T" and the "W". Suddenly Anthony saw something that he had failed to see before. It leapt from the paper in front of him wild plucked at his eyes. B. T. W.! Blundell, Tresham, Wingfield!

"Well, I'm unutterably damned!" muttered Anthony Lotherington Bathurst. "Blood's Thicker than Water. Now, what the hell does that mean?"

Chapter XVIII
EXHUMATION

Once again Mr. Bathurst sat in the Commissioner's room at New Scotland Yard. Sir Austin Kemble at his side listened to him with many signs of attention. Every now and then he would punctuate Anthony's remarks with a nod. At length Mr. Bathurst made reference, with a wealth of intimate detail, to the piece of flesh with its evidence of pubic hair that had played so important a part in the Hilldrop Crescent murder.

"You have an extraordinary memory, my boy," commented the Commissioner; "something like myself when I was twenty years younger. On one occasion when I was—"

Anthony grinned. "Thank you, but only relatively, sir. The last time I was congratulated on my memory the donor of the tribute was a singularly callous murderer. I think that I was able to point out to him my deficiencies. It pleases me to think that he came to a nasty sticky end."

"Deficiencies?" queried Sir Austin with a frown.

"Yes, sir—deficiencies. I use the word deliberately and with malice aforethought. Have you ever read Schumann's *Gesammelte Schriften über Musik und Musiker*?"

"No; I can't say that I have. Why?"

"Read him, then, on the extraordinary memory powers of Franz Liszt. Do you know what Liszt did on one occasion? I'll tell you, then. A young composer brought him the manuscript score of a symphony for large orchestra. Liszt looked it over and returned it to him with a polite, complimentary phrase concerning its merits. Some weeks later this young composer went again to the Abbé, in the depths of despair. A fire had demolished his house and his precious score had been completely destroyed! Do you know what Liszt said to him?"

Sir Austin expressed his ignorance. Anthony went on: "He felt so sorry for the young man, and so sympathetic towards his loss, that he told him to visit him again on the next day. Now listen to the sequel. During the night the master wrote down from memory the whole score of that symphony, without missing even a single note. On the next morning he handed it to the young musician."

Anthony's eyes twinkled. "And we, sir, I think, you and I, must hand it to him."

"Remarkable," conceded Sir Austin. "Almost incredible. And where's all this leading up to?"

"To what I asked you just now, sir. I want orders granted immediately for the exhumation of the bodies of—"

The Commissioner broke in rather impatiently—"Blundell, Wingfield, and Guest, I suppose? All three of them?"

Mr. Bathurst shook his head. "No, sir. Of Blundell and Wingfield only. I am not concerned in this particular matter with the body of Guest."

"Why not?"

"He doesn't fit in, sir. Guest was murdered in the same way as they, but for a different reason. I fancy that Blundell and Wingfield were murdered for the *same* reason. I want to find out what that reason was." Anthony spoke quietly, but there was anxiety in his voice.

Sir Austin became acutely uneasy. "That's all very well, my boy, but I don't see how the exhumation is going to help you. We *know* that these two men were murdered in the same way— by *poison*. What else can you possibly find out?"

Anthony stuck doggedly to his guns. "I want to look at their bodies, sir. I want Sir Roderick Hope to look at them too, perhaps. I blame myself tremendously for not having done so before, but my excuse must be that events happened so fast and so furiously that it was a job to keep pace with everything."

Sir Austin still finessed. "What does MacMorran say about it? Have you discussed it with him?"

Anthony smiled. "Not exactly, sir. You could hardly call it a discussion. I mentioned the possibility to him, that's all."

Sir Austin tacked. "Is it absolutely necessary, Bathurst? It isn't as though the *cause* of death was in doubt. Can't you get what you want in any other way? How about seeing the two doctors? Sugden, up here, and the chap down at Sidmouth who attended the body of Wingfield. They examined the bodies, didn't they? Don't you think that if you could arrange it, it might give you the information which you require?"

Anthony held his ground. "No, sir; candidly, I don't. If I did I shouldn't have troubled you. You see, it's like this. I already know something which I haven't as yet disclosed to you. I didn't intend to tell you until I was more sure of my ground. I've been appallingly blind, but, like a new-born kitten, my eyes are beginning to open at last. I think I must be a tortoiseshell."

Sir Austin tapped the floor with his foot. "Tell me what you know," he said curtly.

"Blundell, Wingfield and the present Lord Tresham were at Cambridge together."

Sir Austin stared at the speaker. "Well, nothing particularly remarkable about that, that I can see. Oh, just a minute, I think I get you. Antecedents, eh? Some early blotted page? A skeleton in the cupboard somewhere?"

He looked at Anthony for corroboration.

"I don't know about the cupboard, but there are three skeletons in the case already. Or there will be when the worm has done his job of work."

The Commissioner was thinking. He ignored the last remark. "I'll tell *you* something now, Bathurst. I was looking at a certain Sergeant Pullinger's notes on the Guest murder. As a matter of fact, I had them sent up to me specially. Got MacMorran to arrange them for me. I wanted to look at one man's evidence particularly. Sir Richard Ingle and young Guest's father were at Winchester together! Rather a coincidence, eh? Two together, and then three together?"

Anthony nodded.

"Had you noticed it, Bathurst?"

"Yes, sir."

The Commissioner awaited developments. None came his way. Mr. Bathurst was reticent. Sir Austin assumed the offensive. "Well, getting back to this Cambridge stunt of yours, I still can't see why I should have graves dug into, coffins opened, and just to—no, my dear boy, before I give way on the point I must ask you to tell me more."

"I was just going to, sir, when you became anatomical." Anthony drew his chair an inch or so closer. "I have been down to Hurrilow again, sir—the little village at the back of the Wiltshire downs where Miss Wingfield lives. The first time I ran down there I saw his sister, Miss Wingfield, as you know. This second time I saw his wife. I asked a few questions—"

"I don't doubt that," flashed Sir Austin.

"*Touché!*" returned Anthony good-humouredly. "I'm bound to, you know, if I want to solve the problems you put in front of me. The questions I asked Mrs. Wingfield were directed to one vital point. Well, it came to this, sir. I was successful beyond my wildest dreams. I want an application made for those two exhumations."

Sir Austin turned in his chair. He rather enjoyed making Bathurst ask for things. "Tell me more. You're just getting interesting."

"Well, sir, it's a longish yarn, but I wallowed in Wingfield's ways, whims and witticisms. You know the sort of thing: tell me all about your husband, Mrs. Wingfield. The smallest details may prove to be the most important.' Much, of course, that she told me was irrelevant, but suddenly she said this: 'He had some funny little marks at the back of his left leg—in the fold, where the leg bends—right behind the kneecap. I asked him once what they were and he told me they were a sporting relic of his days at Cambridge. He laughed then and said, "Just a reminder for all time that blood's thicker than water."' Anthony became grave. "Sir Austin, those words were of blessed meaning."

"Why?"

"Why? Because Sir Richard Ingle had used the very same words to me only a few days before."

The Commissioner was still unconvinced. "It's a common phrase, Bathurst."

"I know; but it means something important here. I'm positive of it—I feel it in my bones."

Anthony was determined to say no more. The lines showed round his lips. Sir Austin would have to be content with that.

"The Sidmouth doctor who performed the p.m. made no comment on any marks behind the patella," remarked the Commissioner doubtfully.

"Would he look for them, sir? After all, why should he? There were other and (to him) more important marks on the body—bruises and things like that."

"H'm! You can always argue to suit your case, can't you?"

Anthony shrugged his shoulders. Sir Austin was quick to observe the gesture. He employed sarcasm. "Again, why exhume the body of Blundell as well as that of Wingfield? I presume that the latter's widow gave you no information about Blundell's legs?"

"I can't tell you my reason, sir. But I'm simply hoping for certain results, that's all."

The Commissioner rose from his chair and paced the room. Once . . . twice . . . thrice. His obstinacy was a force. Suddenly he turned to Anthony. "Supposing I refuse to entertain your idea? What will you do next?"

Mr. Bathurst stretched out his long legs. "Nothing, sir."

"Nothing? What do you mean?"

"That I shall be compelled to relinquish the case, sir, that's all. To turn it over to MacMorran completely."

Sir Austin surveyed him critically. He could hardly believe his ears. "Eh! What's that? Relinquish the case! You're not serious?"

"I am, sir. Perfectly serious."

Sir Austin walked to his desk with quick strides. "You get your own way, don't you? All right, then. I'll apply for the orders." He took up the telephone receiver. "Put me through to the Home Office at once."

Mr. Bathurst smiled. "So far, so good," he said to himself.

Then he heard Sir Austin's voice again. "The Commissioner of Police speaking from New Scotland Yard . . ."

The exhumation of the body of the late Hubert Athelstan Wingfield was carried out expeditiously and under conditions of extreme secrecy. Few of the inhabitants of Hurrilow saw the three vehicles drive up to the churchyard, and amongst those few, only one or two ventured upon articulate wonderment.

Sir Roderick Hope, the Crown pathologist, was not present; the Commissioner had taken Anthony's word that he would not require Sir Roderick except as a last resource.

It was approaching midnight when, under Sir Austin's directions, the coffin was removed from the grave and conveyed to a small shed that had been specially requisitioned for the purpose. It was there laid on a trestle. Silent men opened it for its human burden. Not a man in the shed spoke. Then one of the grim squad stepped back and nodded.

"Now, Doctor Sugden," said Anthony to the divisional surgeon whom the Commissioner had insisted upon bringing down with them, "the place I want you to look at is in the crease of the leg, behind the left patella."

Sugden went to his gruesome task, under the flickering light of candles. Again there was a period of complete silence. It was broken by Sugden turning quietly to Sir Austin Kemble and Anthony. "Come here, sir, please, and you, Bathurst."

The two men named stepped forward.

"The body has been in the coffin for a very short time," said Sugden, "and naturally is well preserved. Now look here. Can you see anything?" Sugden took one of the candles and held it against the back of the corpse's left leg.

"H'm! Red scratches. Scarlet marks," muttered the Commissioner. Anthony looked at them intently. Bending down, he pulled the skin tighter and taut, so that some of the looseness of the creases was lost.

"More than that, sir, if you look carefully. More than mere marks."

"H'm! Hold the candle closer, Doctor."

Sugden obeyed the Commissioner.

"See what I mean, sir?" queried Anthony. "Look down there."

There was no reply from Sir Austin.

"What about you, Doctor? Can you see what I mean?" Sugden cursed softly and scientifically at hot wax that dropped on to the knuckle of his thumb.

"Yes. I think that those marks are intended to be letters," he said. He looked more closely. "Three letters, I fancy there are, all told. Done by some form of tattooing."

Anthony made no attempt to conceal his satisfaction at Sugden's statement. "Thank you, Doctor. I agree with you. They are three letters. Could you name the three letters?"

Sir Austin had now arrived. "There's a 'B'," he said slowly.

"A 'T' and a 'W'," supplemented Sugden.

"Exactly," said Anthony with finality. "'B', 'T', and 'W', or, as Wingfield put it when alive, 'Blood's Thicker than Water'." He watched their faces for appreciation.

"Good God!" muttered Sir Austin.

"You remember my insistence on the phrase, then, sir?" flashed Anthony.

The Commissioner nodded. "Good gracious, yes. Well, I'll be hanged!"

"I hope not, sir; but I'm gaining confidence in the belief that somebody will."

Chapter XIX
BATHURST'S THEORY IS STRENGTHENED

Two days later the village of Hurstfold witnessed a similar scene to that which the Wiltshire village of Hurrilow had seen. The coffin containing the body of John Pender Blundell was taken into a little mortuary chapel used by a local undertaker, and Sugden needed no instructions from Bathurst, on this second occasion, as to what he was required to do.

"You're right, Bathurst," he said eventually; "the scarlet marks are here. In the same place as on Wingfield."

Anthony assured himself by personal inspection. "B", "T", and "W". He, Sir Austin, and Doctor Sugden drove back to town together in the Commissioner's car. Anthony was unusually silent. Sir Austin rallied him.

"My dear boy," he said, "what's come over you? Aren't you well?"

"How do you mean, sir?"

"You've proved your point; you've made me to a certain extent ashamed of my pig-headedness, and you haven't once said, 'I told you so'. You have raised yourself above the angels. It's perfectly inhuman of you—don't you think so, Sugden?"

"'Tis rather, Sir Austin. We shall have to buy him the dinkiest thing we can find in halos if he goes on like this. Yet another St. Anthony. There are already about a dozen of 'em, I believe." The Doctor turned to Anthony smilingly. "What's on your mind now, Bathurst?"

Anthony grinned back. "What's worrying me, do you mean?"

"If you like. If that's the truer term."

"Well—why should blood be thicker than water—when it applies to three men who, as far as we know, had no birth affinity whatever?"

"But does it mean that, Bathurst? Hang on a bit, man. Does it mean just what it says? Much more likely, to my way of thinking, to be a phrase used because it fitted and—er—summed up, so to speak, their three initials, 'B', 'T', and 'W'."

Sir Austin delivered himself of this opinion with commendable emphasis. Anthony looked at him curiously. "I think I agree with you, sir, as far as it goes. But the theory that you have just put forward leaves so much to be explained. Why have the marks at all? Take us three now, as we sit here in this car. You and Dr. Sugden and I. We have no blood relationship. Unless, of course, we count those little incidents in the garden of Eden. Or have we the backs of our knees tattooed with the three letters 'K', 'S', and 'B'; which trio of letters might mean merely Kemble, Sugden, and Bathurst, or, falling into line with our present case and groping for something more tangible, might come to be interpreted, 'Kippers Sell better than Bloaters', or something equally fatuous? The first of which you would at once say was distinctly fishy. There I am—back at the beginning. Why have the marks at all?"

"What's your own idea about them, Bathurst?" queried Sugden.

"How can I nurse one to my withered breast, Doctor? I've really no data *re* the marks, or, at least, it's of the thinnest. The business dates back years. *Où sont les neiges d'antan*?" He curled himself back into the corner of the car. The Commissioner frowned at the situation as he imagined he saw it.

"What do you purpose then? Without your precious data how do you intend to move? Are you going after it?"

"Surely there's an obvious indication as to that," observed Sugden.

Anthony was immediately interested. "Tell me, Doctor. Tales of fair Kashmir. I could bear to hear it all."

Sugden smiled. "Two dead men—and another man alive. The dead and the quick. Blundell and Wingfield—the dead. Tresham—the quick." He shrugged his shoulders. "Surely your line of attack for the data which is so vital to you is Tresham—Lord Tresham."

"Highly ingenious, Doctor, and thoroughly logical at the same time. But not by any means easy to carry out."

"You mean difficulty of approach?"

"Naturally. It's one thing to look at the legs of a corpse. Lord Tresham's legs, though, are an entirely different proposition."

Anthony grinned. "If I may say so, they are his own affair."

"The considerate Bathurst," murmured Sir Austin. Sugden lit his pipe; he watched the flame curl round the tobacco.

"I appreciate all that, of course. I think, however, that I might be able to help you if, in the first place, you helped me. Give me a penny for my thoughts and I'll give you a quid for your quo. I admit that you can't go to Tresham and say to the lord and master thereof, 'show a leg there'—but I'm a medical man, you know, and sometimes ways and means are open to us that aren't accessible to the ordinary citizen. I believe that there was a Watson who was also a doctor."

He puffed contentedly at his pipe. Anthony eyed him shrewdly. "What help do you want?"

"Well, tell me the line you're taking. What's your theory of the crime?"

"What do you mean, exactly?"

Sugden looked at him hard. "Will there be any more murders?"

For a few moments Anthony regarded the cigarette that he held between his fingers. "That depends. It's a difficult question to answer, you know, Doctor, offhand. You're assuming, when you ask me that, that I've solved the mystery and have all its antecedents and reactions in the hollow of my hand. Which I haven't, I assure you. By a long chalk. At the same time, being perfectly candid, I *don't* expect any more murders. Of course, circumstances might arise that would demand somebody else's removal, but they haven't arisen yet. At the moment I wouldn't care to go beyond that."

Sugden nodded. He gave Sir Austin the impression that he thoroughly appreciated Bathurst's point of view, which was more than the Commissioner himself did. Sugden spoke:

"Accepting all that, tell me this. Which is the 'key' murder of the three?"

Anthony parried the question. "Again that depends. What do you mean by 'key'?"

"I'll vary my words. Which murder has helped you most towards, shall we say, solution?"

Anthony smiled and shook his head disclaimingly.

Sugden sensed his meaning. "I see what you want me to do. Very well, I'll put it like this. Which murder is helping you most towards the truth?"

"I'll answer you that with pleasure. The murder of Hugh Guest."

"Why?"

Anthony rubbed his lip. "Because there's little doubt that Guest was on to them. Putting it bluntly, he'd struck the trail and they knew it. He was getting dangerous. So he was removed. That was what I meant just now when I said it might suit their book to effect other removals. It's on the cards that somebody else may hit the trail. We're up against people who are absolutely ruthless, you know. Witness the three murders already. They'll stick at nothing to achieve their ends."

Dr. Sugden nodded again. "I follow all that. In fact, they were my own impressions. The murder of Guest gives us a definite 'locality', you mean?"

"That's it, Doctor. You've got it."

Sugden tapped his teeth with the stem of his pipe. "And the motive, Bathurst?"

Anthony waved playful and deprecating fingers. "I'm not answering that because I'm not yet sure. I'm only just getting on the truth of that motive now. That's mainly why I wanted these two exhumations. I found Sir Austin very hard to convince of their necessity."

The Commissioner felt it was time that he took part in the discussion. "Adopting your principle of elimination, Bathurst, if we accept your theory that Guest was close to—er—successful investigations, can't we be thoroughly scientific and see where we are? Where we stand, as one may say? For instance, Guest went to stay with Sir Richard Ingle, didn't he? Why? What was his real reason? Because he was a friend of the Ingles or because he wanted to be *at* Beech Knoll—to be *near* Ingle?"

"Seems to me," said Sugden thoughtfully, "that if one person *can* be excluded from the circle of suspicion it is Sir Richard Ingle himself."

"Reasons, Doctor?" interrogated Mr. Bathurst cheerfully.

Sugden spread his hands in explanation. *"Cherchez la femme. Cherchez le bénéficiaire."*

"Meaning that Ingle comes out of it all with a great deal of real loss and no profit?"

"Well, he does, doesn't he? That's moderately obvious."

"Yes," conceded Anthony gravely; "the heritage of Tresham for which he had waited has gone elsewhere. Sir Richard Ingle must stay and end his days at Beech Knoll."

"Who else remains? There were three women in the house at the time of the murder, I believe. Guest's sister, Lady Ingle the hostess, and Ella the daughter of the house. We can surely rule all *them* out of it. Yes?"

"All right, go on then."

The Commissioner took up the parable. "Now that we're on this subject of elimination, I'll tell you something. When I looked through Pullinger's notes I thought that something emerged from them as remarkably significant."

Anthony was in like a flash. "What was that, sir?"

"The evidence of the young man Covington, who was supposed, on the strength of his own story—entirely uncorroborated by the way—to have warned Guest that he was in danger some time before he was murdered." The Commissioner paused and then proceeded: "It seemed to me that, all through, this young fellow Covington was *too* prominent by far. That there was too much spotlight on him altogether. Called attention to Guest's absence from the dinner-table, went up to Guest's bedroom door, couldn't get in, came down again, etc, etc. There was Covington always playing a leading part. And while I was thinking all this I noticed something else, something that struck me as *extremely* significant."

Anthony's eagerness spurred him to a question. "What was that, sir? Let me see if it's the identical point that made such an impression on me."

Although he would have been the last to admit the soft impeachment, Sir Austin was flattered by Bathurst's avowed interest. So flattered, indeed, that he replied immediately.

"The way in which he contradicted himself. According to Pullinger's notes he was asked, when he returned to the diningroom on the first occasion, whether he had called out to Guest, the man whom he had gone upstairs to endeavour to find. What was his answer? Something like this. I won't vouch for the exact words, speaking without the book. 'When I come to think of it, I don't believe I did.' An extraordinary admission, to my mind, for a man to make, placed in the circumstances that we know young Covington to have been. Moreover, what do we find happening afterwards? When you arrive, Bathurst, on your first visit to Ingle's place, Pullinger reports as follows. He says, in effect, this." Sir Austin paused for a moment.

"'Evidence by Barry Covington: I knocked and tapped on the bedroom door. There was no answer from within the room. So I spoke to Guest, hoping against hope that he might be in there. I didn't shout out or call loudly . . . I just said, "Are you there?"' In other words, gentlemen, nothing more or less than a complete contradiction in terms. The young man made a bad mistake and had to get out of it the best way that he could. What do you say to that, Bathurst?"

"I think, sir, that you've put an unerring finger on the most vital part of Covington's evidence. Personally I rate it of the highest importance."

"Circumstances alter cases," put in Sugden thoughtfully; "the most trifling thing may throw the whole machinery out of gear. A quick, alert mind seizes on those trifles. I'll tell you something that happened to me the other day. I couldn't help thinking at the time how mental processes vary. It's a story against myself too. Two or three weeks ago my wife was away on the Riviera. One evening I was at work in my den on a police report, when there was a ring at the front door bell. It was pretty late, and the two maids were out. They weren't due back, I suppose, for another half an hour or so. Cursing at the interruption, I answered the ring myself. A curious old bird stood on the step wearing a battered old 'topper'. I don't quite know how best to describe him."

Sugden smiled good-humouredly as he continued. "Suppose we put him down as a superior sort of 'tot-raker'—the dustman's jackal—that will do as well as anything else, I think.

"'Good evening, Doctor,' he says to me; 'any old rag or bone?' or some gibberish meaning that.

"'No,' I said curtly, on the point of closing the door. But with consummate audacity he had another go at me.

"'Any old clothes, boots, newspapers—sorry to be troubling you, Doctor, but perhaps your good lady could . . .'

"'No,' I said very curtly this time; 'my good lady could do nothing—she's away and she won't be back for at least another fortnight'."

Sugden chuckled. "What do you think the old rascal said to that?"

"I'll buy it," returned Anthony.

"'Let me take the empty bottles away then, Doctor, before she comes home.'"

Sir Austin paid tribute boisterously.

"Your point being, Doctor," said Anthony, "that this high priest of refuse collection, this golden dustman, would have brought distinction to the C.I.D.?"

"Exactly," said Sugden. "Our job in this case is to grasp the trifles—they must be there somewhere—and turn them to account."

"Returning to Ingle for a moment," put in the Commissioner; "what would you say about him, Bathurst, if you were asked? You've been to his place?"

"As a man—as a host do you mean, sir?"

"Yes; more or less like that."

"In private life I should put him down as a man who would never lose the respect of those who served him. An easy, good-tempered, good-natured, facetious companion, I should say. Not over-moody . . . on the whole equable. Free in his speech, excessively candid in the expression of his desires, hearty eater, heavy drinker, and with the best part of his heart buried in sport. Racing in particular. Loves horses, I fancy, intensely, and dogs probably only a little less. Gave me the impression that, like a horse, he would drink most comfortably out of a bucket. There you are, Sir Austin, pen-picture of Sir Richard Ingle by Anthony Lotherington Bathurst."

"Was he comfortable, Bathurst, would you say, as far as the things of this world go? No fly in the amber anywhere, I suppose? Prosperous, all right?"

"My dear Doctor," replied Anthony a little complacently, "prosperity may be the most fatal of endowments. It may fatten the body, but choke and poison the soul. And in that case—who can say the measure of Ingle's prosperity, or worth of Ingle's soul?"

"There was a third man present, I believe, when Guest was murdered," remarked Sugden, ignoring Bathurst's departure into metaphysics, "a man named Slingsby Raphael. What can you tell us about him?"

Anthony made no reply.

"Hallo?" said Sugden, "sicklied o'er with the pale cast of thought—does silence sit on Anthony Bathurst?"

The last named shook his head tentatively. "Slingsby Raphael? I find him very interesting. In fact, so much so that MacMorran's getting a line on him tomorrow for me."

"You can't eliminate him from the circle, then? It comes to that, eh?"

"Although I've very definite ideas, I certainly can't, *altogether*, Sir Austin. It does come to that." Anthony blazed into vehemence. "But where the hell does he fit, Sir Austin? Tell me that if you can.

Where the hell do any of them fit? Tell me the truth of that and I'll piece the puzzle together for you. Without it . . ."

Anthony made a gesture of resignation and relapsed into silence. The two men respected it and watched him. Suddenly they saw a curious light come into his grey eyes. Were the puzzle-pieces coming to him?

Chapter XX
ON THE TRACK

"Yet a third visit, Mr. Bathurst?" queried Sir Richard Ingle. "We are indeed honoured."

Anthony bowed to the speaker and to Slingsby Raphael, who sat with him on the same stone ledge upon which they had sat before.

"How do you come this time? As a triumphant conqueror of a ticklish problem?"

Anthony shook his head. "To think that, Sir Richard, would be, I fear, a dangerous ecstasy. I must avoid such a condition at all costs. I am still a suppliant after truth."

Raphael's eyes glinted after their habit. "Do you, know, Mr. Bathurst," he declared, "you intrigue me? Few of my own sex have been privileged to do that. But you are a gentleman of such swift subtlety. Most so-called detectives I have known have been empty-headed, fish-eyed or jelly-gutted—sometimes I have known them to be all three. You are none of these things. A lithe, various creature. Light and fierce like a flame. Impervious to set-backs and highly persevering and resolute. I can imagine that Bruce of Scotland would have used you to catch his superfluous flies. On the other hand, however, I think that I should like to see you as a lover—hear you faltering exquisite endearments in your own tongue—watch you as a merchant trafficking in the intimate and treading on tiptoe through *le pays du tendre*. You would give a woman homage, make her your most humiliated servant by avowing yourself hers and thereby touching her generosity even more than her humility. The Irish have that trait to an unusual degree. Yes, my dear Bathurst," he conceded softly, "I should like to see you as a lover. I am certain that you would intrigue me more than you do even now, and give me into the bargain rich memories that I might bequeath unto my heirs."

"Thank you. I don't know, however, that I find myself able to return the compliment."

Raphael shrugged his shoulders. "I'm humiliated myself now. Why not, pray?"

"Because of my attitude, I suppose, to a loyal woman."

"Are there any?"

"I've met one. Only one, perhaps. But one is enough. It's because of her I speak to you as I do. I can't return the compliment that you paid me because I believe that that one loyal lady is as far above my own spiritual reach as she is fatally within my material reach. In other terms, that Love—I use your own selected word, Mr. Raphael—is more of a sacrament than most of us imagine. Sometimes, to our advantage it might even be taken kneeling. I question, however, if you are able to understand that. By the way, who told you that I was Irish?"

Raphael's face flushed. "I did you the honour to look you up. Uppingham and Oxford, I believe. I must congratulate you on some of your achievements."

"Thank you again. That also is rather a coincidence. I've been looking you up. I even put a Scotland Yard man on to you. I can't congratulate you on some of yours."

Raphael's cheeks were dull red now, but Anthony turned away to address Sir Richard Ingle. "What I wanted to ask you, Sir Richard Ingle, is 'Why is blood thicker than water?' That is the question that has prompted my visit."

To Anthony's surprise, Ingle burst into a hearty and uncontrolled laugh. Raphael's face was still twisted, however, and it seemed to Anthony, as he watched him from the corner of his eye, that he did not share, by any means, Ingle's humorous point of view.

"My reception to-day," murmured Mr. Bathurst, "is certainly mixed, if nothing else. I suppose that I should be grateful for the infinite variety. I provoke cynicism in the mind of one of my hosts and risible effervescence in the other. Behold me humble, the seeker, as always, for explanation and truth. I now add incredible patience, too, to my humility."

Ingle motioned him to a seat on the ledge. Contrition showed on his face. "My dear chap, forgive me, do. I know that I laughed. But you sprang it on me rather, you know. It was like a douche of cold water to me. I was startled into some sort of action. And I laughed."

"I heard you," murmured Anthony. "Distinctly."

"My dear Slingsby," said Sir Richard, turning towards his friend and companion of that name, "can you recall that day a short time ago when you were discussing the missing Tresham with me? When you proved to be such an intelligent anticipator?"

Anthony pricked up attentive ears. So Raphael had expected this Tresham claimant to turn up! At least, he presumed that that was Ingle's meaning. Most interesting of facts.

"Only too well," returned Raphael. "I warned you, didn't I?"

"You did—and you were right. Do you remember, though, what I told you?"

"As to what, precisely?"

"What I knew of the real Nick Tresham. I said that I hadn't seen him since we were boys, but that he had the Tresham eyebrows. Can you remember anything else that I said just about then?"

"Very well," replied Raphael coolly. "I remember the sentence that you used. After you mentioned the eyebrows, you said, 'and one other piece of information that he sent me gratuitously, when he cleared out, which may come in useful'. You weren't explicit, and I remember, too, that you set me wondering what that piece of information was."

"No. I didn't tell you at the time. It was hardly necessary. I think, now that I look back upon it, that I was inclined to keep the information to myself purposely. You shall hear what it was now, however, when I pass it on to Bathurst."

Sir Richard turned to Anthony. "I suppose I must have used the expression to you on one of the occasions that you were here before. That's why you've lobbed it back to me. Is that so?"

"That will do for a reason as well as any other."

Ingle nodded. "Then I must really congratulate you, Bathurst, on a piece of most extraordinary and unusual discernment."

Anthony disclaimed the compliment. "Perhaps I was hardly fair to you in my previous reply. I must not accept bouquets under false pretences. I know more than I appeared to know. By the time I leave you, Sir Richard, I hope to know all."

Ingle laughed. "You know more, eh? Out to beat the starter. Don't mean to get hung up in the tapes when the gates go up. Well, there's no secret about any of it, as far as I'm concerned personally. Raphael and you can hear the news together. The only pity is, that it will have to be verbal. I've no document that I can show you that would have given corroboration. I did have, but I destroyed it. Don't know why exactly. Except that I had the information that the letter contained tucked away all right in my noddle, and certainly shouldn't ever forget it. So there was really no point, you see, in my keeping Tresham's letter."

He paused, and his mind seemed to flight back in reflection.

"It's a strange business altogether. When Nick Tresham bolted, taking the mother-of-pearl counters with him to remind him of England, home and beauty, he wrote me a letter. I have often wondered why. But these things are hard to explain. I sometimes think that Fate takes a hand in the game absolutely deliberately. Sticks her finger in because she knows there's a purpose in her doing so. We are made to do these things through the will of a Higher Power than ourselves."

"There is a destiny . . ." quoted Slingsby Raphael.

"Exactly. That's something of what I meant. It seems almost that Tresham had a *vision* of part, at least, of the future. That he was able, in some way that is unfathomable, to foresee the deaths of his two elder brothers, and that he, himself, despite the rigours of the adventures that he was about to give himself, knew that the heritage of Tresham would, in the fullness of time, come to him. Personally I wouldn't have rated his chance in those early days at a tinker's damn. Wouldn't have given him a quotation in the market. As I told you, Slingsby, when we first discussed the matter, I was confident that somebody a bit quicker on the draw than he was had put daylight into him, with little ceremony and less regret. As we know now, I was wrong. Still, to get to the letter that he sent me. Expect you're cursing me for being long-winded, but I'm no good at short cuts or five-furlong sprints."

Ingle's eyes twinkled, and Anthony remembered the description of him that he had given to Sir Austin.

"In this letter Tresham intimated, first of all, that he was leaving the country—destination unknown. Cabin-trunks, labelled, he said, had always produced in him a restless urge. An irresistible impulse to chuck everything stable and go a-voyaging round the world. Seeking always that kingdom that lies round the corner. At last he had succumbed to it. He pointed out that, in a certain combination of circumstances, there was the possibility that the heritage of Tresham would come to me. If he and his two brothers shuffled off and left no issue. Then he wound up, in a joking vein, by making a statement to this effect. He could always be identified, he said, apart from the peculiarity of the Tresham eyebrows. He had been at the Varsity—Cambridge— with two men with whom he had grown tremendously thick. They were known as the 'Three Musketeers'. As a matter of fact, I forget the names of the other two now. It's so long ago, for one thing, and for another, I never troubled overmuch to remember them. There was no real reason why I should. I can tell you only one thing about them. One's surname began with a 'B' and the other with a 'W.' That's easy to remember—they were the blood and the water."

Ingle chuckled at the savour of the reminiscence, and Anthony looked at him curiously.

"By a strange coincidence these three men owed each other a debt. Tresham had saved the lives of the other two men on the Cam—a punting or boating accident of some kind. I can't tell you the exact particulars because I've forgotten them. Nick Tresham was a strong swimmer, and had turned up to save them at great personal risk when everything seemed all over. The year after, they had gone to Switzerland for the summer vacation. And here these two men, by one of those tricks of Fate I spoke of, had been enabled to repay Tresham what they owed him. They were mountain-climbing together, so Tresham's story went. The usual tragedy. Bad conditions, a slip and a broken rope. They held on to Tresham literally for hours and—happily—until help came. When it did, one of them fainted from sheer exhaustion. Now mark the sequel. Nick Tresham had always been a wild, impressionable sort of chap, and the bigness of the two affairs caught and held his imagination. The two events, he said, must be marked in some way so that their memory should last for ever for all three. Nothing would satisfy him otherwise."

Sir Richard shifted his position. "All this detail he told me in the letter. The upshot of it all was that the three men were tattooed together—behind the left knee—in the crease of the leg. There was a fellow up at Luther at the time who was an expert at that kind of thing and very thick with Tresham. They were tattooed with the three initials 'B', 'T', and 'W'. There, gentlemen, now you know all that there is to know. That's the story as I had it from Nick Tresham's pen."

Sir Richard Ingle looked at his two auditors critically, but semi-humorously. From Anthony Bathurst came questions, shrewd—incisive questions.

"And because of that, Sir Richard, because of your special knowledge of this marking of these three men, you were satisfied with the present Lord Tresham's *bona fides*?"

Ingle smiled. "Of course. Can't you see it all now? I told you that I was."

"Pardon the question. How did you find it out?"

"Find out what?"

"That he had the identification marks. Did he make a point of showing them to you?" Anthony Bathurst's face showed intense eagerness.

Ingle shook his head. Both Anthony and Raphael, strangely enough, seemed creatures of disappointment. "What happened then?" asked the former, "that you are able to—"

"Well, I decided to clinch matters that day I met Tresham in the lawyer's office up in Seely Place. Towards the end of the interview I rubbed the back of my left leg so that he could see me—deliberately. Anybody who possessed the particular knowledge that I had couldn't mistake the action. Bathurst, my dear chap, he understood my meaning at once! Believe me, there wasn't the shadow of a doubt about it. The way his face showed his understanding was really remarkable. He picked up the cue almost on the beat. Not quite, but good enough. Then he said something about having been away from England a long time, and out it came—'Blood's thicker than water'. There was no argument against that, Bathurst. It was Tresham right enough."

Once again his look interrogated the faces of his two companions. "Seems conclusive to me," commented Raphael.

The situation was ripe for development.

"Sir Richard," remarked Anthony Bathurst with grave emphasis, "there is something else that I am in a position to tell you. When you hear it, make of it what you will. There have been three men murdered recently—each by cyanide of potassium, administered in some way through the nostrils. One of them, Hugh Guest, was murdered in this house of yours. His murderer has not yet been found. The other two were murdered somewhere unknown, the places have not yet been definitely located, but their bodies were discovered in Bushey Park and the Valley of Ferns, Sidmouth."

Anthony stopped. He saw that Ingle seemed mystified and that Raphael's face was turned full towards him. "Well," said the former, with a touch of jauntiness, "what has all this to do with me? About these other two murders, I mean? Guest, of course—"

"Wait, Sir Richard. The names of these two murdered men, Sir Richard, were Blundell and Wingfield. They were contemporaries at Cambridge. Of an age with Lord Tresham."

Ingle stared, as Anthony made each successive statement, while Raphael smothered an exclamation.

"Good God!" cried Ingle. "Blundell and Wingfield! It all comes back to me. I remember the names now. Before this they had held no significance for me. These are deep waters, Bathurst. Where are we?"

Anthony made a movement of broad shoulders. "Struggling slowly towards the light, Sir Richard. By degrees, it's true, but getting there all the same."

"Just a minute, though. Let's see where we are. The initials of the surnames fit the equation, I agree, but are you absolutely certain of the peculiar identity of these two men? After all, you know, you're trying to—"

"Entertain no doubt whatever, Sir Richard. I have established the truth of it. I'll tell you something in strict confidence. The bodies of Blundell and Wingfield have been exhumed. The tattoo marks of which you have just spoken are visible on them. In the exact place you indicated."

Raphael intervened. "I find your pace a little disconcerting, Bathurst. There are gaps in your story. Gaps that must be filled. Why these exhumations? Without any particular knowledge you brought off a remarkably long shot. I'm afraid that I can't—"

Anthony was unable to restrain a smile. "I'm sorry. The exhumations did take place so that these marks might be examined. I will admit that cheerfully. I obtained my information with regard to them from another quarter. But my informant was unable to tell me 'why'. Only 'of'. That is why I have come to Beech Knoll to Sir Richard here. My first question to him was, if you remember, '*Why*' is blood thicker than water?" Anthony's smile took unto itself sweetness.

"And now you know."

"And now I know. And now *we* know."

"Makes a difference, certainly," said Raphael.

"Undoubtedly," returned Anthony carelessly, "knowledge and fear are twin tyrants. When they take command they become like the God of Moses—most jealous and uneasy despots. Other gods have a thin time. Even a respectable G.P. like Dr. Summerhayes with a practice in the Isle of Wight can vouch for the truth of that."

He flicked perilously-placed ash from the end of his cigarette. There was a moment of heavy, pregnant silence. Ingle seemed surprised at the remark. Too surprised to offer comment. The eyes of Slingsby Raphael, however, came to that strange glitter that made them so remarkable. Was it the product of excitement or of some deeper, intenser quality?

"What do you mean by that, Bathurst? Why must you drag in Summerhayes?"

"For an excellent reason. Haven't you heard that the worthy doctor, under the influence of one of those restless potentates whom I mentioned just now, seeks fresh fields and pastures new?"

"My God! How do you know that?" demanded Raphael hoarsely.

"Once again—from the best of reasons. I couldn't have had a more reliable informant. He told me so himself. The dear fellow became quite communicative the last time I called upon him."

Plainly Ingle was perturbed. "Summerhayes is leaving the island now, do you mean?"

"Has already left would be nearer the truth, I should say, judging by the almost indecent haste that he exhibited during my short visit. Still, he had his good points. One must be fair and look at the thing all round. Towards the close of our little *tête-à-tête*, he became definitely altruistic. Quite touching, it was."

"Explain, please," demanded Raphael curtly.

Mr. Bathurst raised his eyebrows. "I beg your pardon."

"Oh, I'm sorry. But don't stand on ceremony now. About Summerhayes—what you have said seems to me to be extremely important."

"I should be the last man in the world to contradict you. And please don't anticipate too much. I wouldn't raise your hopes for all the King's horses, plus bodyguard. Summerhayes left the island, according to his own story, because he is desperately afraid. He as good as said, too, that he was acting under coercion. Not to put too fine a point on it, the man seemed terrified. Also, he was good enough to pass a warning on to me. That was the altruism. Hinted that I should find the island distinctly unhealthy if I remained in it."

Raphael made no reply. He stood lost in thought, with his foot on the ledge.

"What do you make of it, Bathurst?" questioned Ingle.

"Well, on the whole I think that I've changed my mind about things. Originally I formed the idea that Summerhayes had found out something—some clue that was going to prove of tremendous value—and, in a moment of indiscretion, had opened his mouth a bit too wide. Now"—he spoke very slowly—"I'm not so sure."

Raphael turned swiftly and brought his feet to the level. "Why, Bathurst? What has happened to make you change your mind?"

"My mind has become clearer, that is all. The great difficulty, as always in cases of this sort, has been to separate 'true' clues from 'false'. What may seem to be an avenue to sanity may turn out, from the point of view of success, to be nothing more than that notorious road which is paved with good intentions."

Raphael tried again. "But surely you were able to drag something from what this doctor told you—you seem to have found him in a condition that bordered on nerves, to say the least of it. The going's never better than then, when you want information from anybody. At any rate, that's always been my experience. Of whom was he afraid? Of what was he in terror?"

Mr. Bathurst answered with suavity. "He mentioned something about a spiked lion . . . with claws. Some particular nonsense of that kind. I didn't pay much attention to it."

Ingle started up from his seat. "A spiked lion? Tresham again, Raphael. What can a man like Summerhayes know about that?"

Raphael shook his head, but Anthony saw that his teeth were set and his hands clenched.

"There are two spiked lions, I believe," said Mr. Bathurst, continuing, "on the Tresham coat of arms; and somehow I fancy, from what I have been able to discover through infinite research, they have never been what may be termed *popular* amongst the Treshams. There is a family snuffbox, I understand. . . ."

"I am not a Tresham," returned Sir Richard curtly. "I'm an Ingle. Only Treshams know these secrets."

*

Late that evening Mr. Bathurst, after a long consultation with Sir Roderick Hope, the Crown pathologist, rang up Sir Austin Kemble. The call was put through to the Commissioner's private address. Sir Austin answered it in person. He listened to Anthony's query with every attention.

"I see what you're after, Bathurst. But I don't think that I can help you myself. Tattooing's never been in my line—not that kind, at least. Stay a moment, though. . . . I'll tell you what to do. Get through to the Yard again—tell them I told you to—and ask to speak to Ferdinand Urpeth. He's an authority on all matters of that sort. I doubt if there's another man in the world to touch him at it. He's made a hobby of it for years . . . written a book on the old 'Street Cries of London'. It's on the cards that he may be able to help you. At any rate, the idea's worth trying. Cheerio, my boy . . . and good luck."

As a result of his telephone conversation with Ferdinand Urpeth, Anthony sent out four letters of enquiry. They were addressed, respectively, to Adam Fernie, King Henry's Hill, N.1.; Adolf De Peyer, 12, Goldhawk Gardens, S.W.5; Serge Valdar, Grosvenor Terrace, S.W.1.; and Hadj Babayan, 5, Perivale Meadows, W.5.

These gentlemen, so said Ferdinand Urpeth, were artists with the needle.

Chapter XXI
THE YARD HAS ITS POINTS

MR. BATHURST dropped his hat on the table and beamed on Chief-Inspector MacMorran.

"Good morning, sir," returned the latter.

"MacMorran," said Mr. Bathurst, "behold me with a tankard that requires replenishment. I thirst for news—for details—for information. Don't tell me that I'm too early—that I have over-estimated your abilities. Life has enough of disappointments." He sighed approvingly.

MacMorran's eyes twinkled in appreciation. "The 'Yard' has its points, then, Mr. Bathurst, eh? When you gentlemen want information that's authentic and can be relied on."

"Have I ever denied the truth of it, MacMorran? 'Twould be the most unkindest cut of all. *Palmam qui meruit ferat.* Honour to whom honour is due. *Bon chat, bon rat.* I can't think of any others at the moment, that would be as appropriate, I mean."

The chief-inspector shook a wondering head. "We'll take it as read, Mr. Bathurst; never mind what it might have been. I'd better get you what you want, I suppose. Incidentally, you aren't too early. I haven't let you down, and I think that I shall be able to quench that thirst of yours. Let me see first of all what I have here."

MacMorran turned over some papers. "I've had one of my very best men on this. There's not a man in London who would have done better. Let me see now: Barry Covington—he's the first on the list, I think. Now what have we? Aged twenty-three. Of independent means. Educated Marlborough and Cambridge. Colours at former for hockey. Came down last year. Third Trinity. Son of Gerald Covington of Combe House, Datchet. Mother was a cousin of Lady Ingle's. Father, Member of Parliament for Kislingbury division of Wessex. Apart from that, nothing whatever known against him. Only contact with authority was when summoned at Southampton two years ago for exceeding the speed-limit. Fined ten guineas and costs. Well-known amateur actor. Member of the Cambridge University 'Footlights'. All movements, since murder of Hugh Guest, above suspicion. Carefully watched on a sudden journey that took him to Town at the end of last week, but went about his business in the most transparently open and straightforward manner."

"Jolly good," interpolated Anthony; "extracts from the Band of Hope. The new Sir Galahad. All is not lost. There is hope for the world yet. God send us more Covingtons—and there will be a ray of hope on the human horizon at last. Came the dawn. I wonder what *are* his vices. He must have some, you know."

MacMorran proceeded. "Prominent lawn-tennis player. Only just missed representing the Varsity."

"Thank you, Inspector," said Mr. Bathurst; "you've said it. You must admit that I have a genuine flair for anticipation. Spare me the rest. Who's next?"

"Captain Andrew Forbes. I have his chit here."

"Expound, then, to my open ears, MacMorran."

"Distinguished aviator. Served with considerable distinction during the Great War 1914—1918. Gained D.F.C. in 1916 for bombing raid on Turkish ammunition dump near Damascus. Severely wounded in same raid, but made marvellous recovery. Concerned, towards the end of the campaign, with rioting incident in the Blue Mosque at Cairo. Since the war, however, has formed attachments and connections that may be described as 'peculiar'. Regular frequenter of some of London's most questionable night-clubs, namely, the 'Mistletoe Bough' and the 'Purple Calf'. At times appears to be well supplied with money, at others seems to be just the reverse. Left Air Force in 1927— only flies now for recreation. Age thirty-eight, and unmarried."

"Occasionally has money, and bombed Damascus, eh?" murmured Mr. Bathurst. "Perhaps the very road even, where once walked a certain Saul of Tarsus. I wonder how many generations it would take to bridge the gap between Forbes and the Levantine. What a marvellous world it is—the Blue Mosque at Cairo, and the 'Purple Calf' not a couple of miles from here. Pretty unconventional—what? How's that for the eternally-separated twain meeting, eh, MacMorran?"

"Ah—well, I'd hardly call it that, Mr. Bathurst, and I don't think that's what Kipling meant. Here's number three on your list. Slingsby Raphael. Beyond the fact that he is a man who has travelled the world over, there is very little definite that is known of this gentleman. Several enquiries in what seemed likely to be fruitful sources produced nothing that is really worthy of record. According to rumour, may have served in the higher branches of 'Intelligence' during the Great War, but if so, his career was closely veiled and shrouded in mystery. Is reputed to have extensive knowledge of the inner workings of the Chinese 'tongs'—more than any other white man—and is rumoured also to have penetrated during the course of a most adventurous career to some of the most inaccessible monasteries of Tibet. Very wealthy and extremely active member of that exclusive society known as the Endorites—the name is believed to have been taken from that historical lady known as 'The Witch of Endor'. After living abroad for a considerable time is now residing at Vesey, on the outskirts of Trinque, in the Isle of Wight. Age—about fifty. Unmarried. Credited with being marvellously athletic and an expert in all branches of gymnastics."

"H'm," muttered Anthony; "all very interesting, don't you think, MacMorran?"

"Interesting, Mr. Bathurst, and all that, but hardly what you'd call helpful. For my own part, I can't see the slightest reason why any of these gentlemen should attach himself to a string of murders. Poison, too, of all devices."

MacMorran sniffed disdainfully—he might have admitted, had you argued with him, that death was comparatively decent when it came from dirk or claymore. But poison—up a man's nose—was beyond the pale.

"And yet, MacMorran," said Anthony, turning over the papers that the inspector had handed to him, "there are points, you know, about your man's harvesting that have vital significances. Take the case of Raphael. Lives near Trinque. An Endorite and an expert athlete. Then take the case of friend Andrew Forbes as another example. The riot in the Blue Mosque at Cairo, 'peculiar' acquaintanceships formed since the war in some of London's haunts of vice, fluctuating financial fortune *and* an accomplished airman."

MacMorran cocked to one side an interrogative head. "What the hell's the Blue Mosque at Cairo to do with it—and all? Don't tell me I've got to go chasing over there for evidence. I'm not one o' them that's got the wanderlust, by any means. I've never yet found a strange bed that was as comfortable as my own, and as for some of the stuff I've had put in front of me in times past that's supposed to have been porridge—well—it's been enough to make an honest oat—"

"Gang all awry and turn Quaker—eh?" grimaced Anthony.

MacMorran shrugged eloquent shoulders. "That's one way of putting it. Although it's not the way I should have chosen. That kind of talk wasn't encouraged where I was brought up."

Anthony laughed. "Don't worry, MacMorran. We'll get to the truth of this business without sending you either to Egypt or to view the hennaed heads of Tangiers. Now here's some information that ought to be interesting. When the late Lord Tresham was translated to the cold comfort of the grave, and we travelled there in double harness, Captain Andrew Forbes, aviator and disturber of Moslem peace, was present. He was in the company of the new Lord Tresham and his lordship's solicitor—I know this because Sir Richard Ingle, at my request, identified them for me. Now what puzzles me, MacMorran, is this—why should those people hunt in trios? Any suggestion on the point, delivered with your habitual excellence of elocution, will be enthusiastically welcomed."

"Maybe they've a motto," replied the inspector guardedly.

"The late Alfred Lester all over again, do you mean? Always merry and bright?"

"Maybe the motto's—Each for all and all for each."

Anthony eyed him curiously. "I see. 'The Musketeers', or who will stand on either hand and keep the bridge with me—eh? Do you know, MacMorran, you've given me an idea."

"And I'll be giving you something else, too, Mr. Bathurst. This time, a piece of information for *you*—worth more perhaps than a mere idea." MacMorran's face exhibited pleasure—the pleasure of anticipation.

"Behold me sympathetically receptive," murmured Anthony.

"Sir Austin Kemble, in accordance with your request, Mr. Bathurst, has had two of our best plain-clothes men in the neighbourhood of Tresham itself. That *was* your idea, wasn't it?"

"Even my natural modesty forbids me denying it, Inspector. Well, what's happened? Anything sensational? You've roused my curiosity."

"First three days—nothing to report. They've instructions, by the way, to report to the Commissioner daily. Yesterday, however, something was sent through. And this morning something else has trickled through. I've an idea, Mr. Bathurst, that each of the items that has come along will interest you."

"I shouldn't be surprised," remarked Anthony.

"In the first place, Mr. Slingsby Raphael has arrived in Tresham and is staying at the Plume of Feathers Hotel. As far as our men have been able to tell up till now, he is unaccompanied. He arrived the day before yesterday. Secondly, Doctor Summerhayes has appeared in Tresham—that's the piece of news that trickled through this morning. Up to the moment, his place of stay hasn't been reported. But it's definitely *not* the 'Plume of Feathers'. He called on Lord Tresham last night and stayed with him some time."

The inspector looked across at Anthony meaningly. "I think, Mr. Bathurst, that there's little doubt as to what has taken him to Tresham Castle. That doctor's a downy old bird."

"Unburden yourself, MacMorran. Gently but firmly. Let me see whether I'm going to agree with you."

Before coming to the point the inspector rubbed his chin. "Well, my idea's this. I think that Doctor Summerhayes *knows* something. Something that's likely to prove unhealthy for somebody else. Blackmail's a nasty exercise and the name has an unpleasant sound, but it may be lucrative—and money talks—Esperanto. You'll never put into me that this doctor would have relinquished his practice as he has done unless it has paid him well to do so. He's a cute bird and a cool card, and I reckon he's got sharp eyes. Eyes that have seen something that yours have missed."

He looked slyly at Anthony. The latter grinned in appreciation of the inspector's sally.

"Hold hard a minute, MacMorran Don't forget one thing. I don't mind you tugging my ankle in the least, but, seriously, the worthy doctor and I didn't have equal scoring opportunities. I lost the toss and had much the worse of the wicket. He walked into a bedroom to a man who had been dead for a few minutes only. I arrived after a moderate interval. When he started *his* job, what scent there was was at boiling point, I should say it could almost be heard sizzling. He *may* have spotted something—it's quite on the cards—and I agree that same something may have taken him to Tresham. I'm not going to theorize with regard to that. It would be the height of foolishness; one might hazard a dozen opinions and not hit the truth. All that you and I must be careful to remember is that Tresham has attracted, and now harbours, two more of the members of the cast."

He rose abruptly and walked to the window. "Or, in other words, my dear MacMorran, the vultures are gathering."

"Vultures—eh? That sounds like another dead body in the offing, Mr. Bathurst. Is that what you mean—wrapped up a bit?"

The only answer that came to the inspector was a movement that emanated from a pair of broad shoulders. These were all of their owner that MacMorran was able to see. They were shrugged—almost imperceptibly. Nothing daunted, the inspector continued to broadcast his opinions.

"In that case, then—and I fancy you do agree with me, Mr. Bathurst, in spite of your silence—I wouldn't be in the blackmailer's shoes for a king's ransom. I reckon I'd soon be feeling where they pinched."

"Now that's a nasty business," replied Anthony, on the half-turn, "especially when you happen to be a policeman."

Chapter XXII
SKELETON PLAN

From the very beginning of the affair, Diana Wingfield, sister of the dead Professor Wingfield, had interested Anthony Bathurst more than most women did. It may be said that his attention had been *arrested* by her. There, he said to himself, more than once, is mentality—if not intellect. In an attempt to grasp truth he had argued with himself. First of all, lightly and a little wantonly, as though the argument were of thistledown in the weight of its consequence; then stubbornly—with obstinate resistance to certain unpleasant factors; and then fiercely and aggressively—with his mind lit by the flame of reasoning.

Can it be said that the faculty of poetic thought is *invariably* antagonistic to action? Must the mind, *always*, in the process of its development, take toll of the activity of the body to which it is joined? This Diana Wingfield, with her deep voice, her Amazon height, and her suggestion of hidden physical power, occupied his thoughts continually. He remembered her look when he had asked her a certain question concerning her brother's disappearance. A strange, baffling look. Certain gestures of hers reproduced themselves to him with admirable and almost incredible fidelity. "Surely," he murmured to himself, "she should have been named Regan or Goneril."

At the same time, it must be recorded that he came to no sudden decision about her. Nights of comparative tranquillity—save for incessant mental exercise—at last gave him what he wanted and brought him—understanding—to the spur of movement. Anthony thought that he could see something slowly but surely emerging from the screen of vision, upon which he was able to trace distinct and definite lines. He saw this woman as Atropos—a gaunt, implacable, unfaltering Atropos stalking down the corridors of Time, intent upon the work that Fate had given her to do. His fancy flighted farther. His imagery increased; it seemed to him as he dwelt upon her that she must have been from the beginning; it seemed to him equally certain that she would be to the end. He quoted to himself inspired words:—"We shall rest, and faith we shall need it, lie down for an aeon or two. Till the Master of all good workmen shall set us to work anew."

But Diana Wingfield, because she would never know the need of rest, would surely go on for ever. Thus it was, out of this mixture of meditation, that Anthony Lotherington Bathurst came once again to the Wiltshire downs, to Beckhampton, and to Apperley House, Hurrilow.

Miss Wingfield played golf, he knew. That information he had had from her herself. Might she not have played—and be willing to play again—if cunningly tempted—in a greater game? She was in the garden when Anthony came to her. Her physique, even though he was prepared for it, almost shocked him when his senses took it in again. He was reminded of a certain Prince of Morocco—who had travelled no doubt through Fez, Meknes, Arzila, Casablanca, south to Marrakech. She left her roses, removed her great gloves, put down her pruning shears and waited for him as he advanced up the path towards her. Then he knew at once why he had seen her as Atropos. For the shears that she had been using were in proportion to her own measurements, and the picture upon which he had dwelt appeared clear and true in its lines and perspectives.

As she came up the path, she spoke to him. "So you honour *me* on this occasion, Mr. Bathurst?"

"I think, had I been given the opportunity, that I should have used the pronouns exactly as you did, Miss Wingfield."

She wrinkled her brows in assessment of his statement. Then her face cleared. "I see what you mean. It's very charming of you. Thanks for the compliment. You are trying to tell me that it isn't Mrs. Wingfield that you want this time—that I will do instead."

Absurd though the situation seemed, Anthony felt quite certain that this personality which confronted him, despite its attributes of character, consciousness and will, possessed a streak of jealousy—different in texture, possibly, from the ordinary, commonplace jealousies, but, nevertheless, having something in common with them. After all, he communed with himself, the expression of affection takes upon itself so many different forms. It may be rooted in admiration, desire, ambition, repression, reflex self-love, or in the eternal *caritas* of the Levantine. *Caritas aedificat.* He determined to respond to what he thought he saw most clearly in front of him, in what he considered would be the best way.

"Different people, Miss Wingfield, are able to supply us according to our different needs. That must always be so. Mrs. Wingfield, on that occasion that I came here before, furnished me with exceedingly valuable information. In addition to that, there was only she here. I wasn't fortunate enough to meet you. Perhaps I had better say that, as far as I know, you were not here. For I feel sure that had you been—"

Her rather mirthless laugh had checked him. "I should have been powerless against the temptation of revealing myself and coming to talk to you. Or, in other words, I should have succumbed to my curiosity. That's what you were about to say, isn't it?"

He laughed with her. "Hardly. Although, if it were analysed, it would probably come to mean much the same thing. Anyhow, I will make a direct statement and say that I feel certain that you were not here."

"I was not, Mr. Bathurst. You have a knack of being right, haven't you? An admirable quality, no doubt, taking the rough with the smooth; but a dangerous one at the same time. A particularly dangerous one where some women may be concerned. The qualities which belong to what I will call consistency and constancy may become mechanical; they may even become boring. I shouldn't like to think of you as an intellectual Robot. I wonder whether you have ever thought of that?"

"Miss Wingfield, the thought has positively harried me down the vista of the years. It has even disturbed my sleep o' nights. It's rather a pity, though, I sometimes think, all the same. Barabbas may have had attractions as what I may term the Independent candidate, but an alert political agent always looks confidently for that mental reversion which I believe is always alluded to in his circles as 'the swing of the pendulum'."

He had made her uneasy. She seemed to have become a little smaller; to tower over him less. "I was out when you called," she said, sullenly for her. "I was playing golf."

"That fact should make me all the more thankful that you are not playing golf now."

She shed a little more of gaunt grandeur. "As you see, I've been attending to my rose trees. I'm afraid that lately they've been rather sadly neglected. This part of the garden has always been considered to be my own especial property and under my own especial care. When there is work to be done out here, there comes a time when golf has to take second place."

Anthony smiled understanding. "I wonder how many devotees of the royal and ancient would make a confession of that kind? Very few, I fancy. May I talk to you confidentially?"

"Of course. Come to the house." She stooped and picked up the gardening gloves and pruning shears that she had previously dropped on the path.

"That almost looks as though I shall find you willing to accept my challenge, Miss Wingfield."

By the rockery she turned to him following her. "Challenge?" Annoyance tinged her voice. "I don't think that I understand you, Mr. Bathurst."

"Or that we understand each other—eh?"

They crossed the threshold of the morning-room of this long, low house. Diana Wingfield was the victim of an unusual feeling. She felt uncertain. She waved him to comfort.

"Take that chair, Mr. Bathurst. Now tell me something, please. Why do you keep coming to Hurrilow? The mystery of my brother's death has not been solved. Something tells me that it never will be solved. I am as certain of that as I am that night follows day. I wish I were as certain of some other things. This is the third time that you have been here. The first time you told me that I had given you something—a straw you called it—from which bricks might come. You led me to understand that you might make those bricks and that afterwards those bricks might build the truth. But you continue to come—and you bring nothing."

There was bitterness here, and also a quality that approximated menace. Miss Wingfield proceeded with her indictment. "I think that there's a brain behind this conspiracy that's a good deal cleverer than yours, Mr. Anthony Bathurst."

The man to whom she spoke smiled. "Very likely, Miss Wingfield. But, admitting all that, I, even with my complex of inferiority, still have a chance of getting on terms with that brain. I have an advantage—that advantage which so often falls to the lot of the careful investigator. I am aware of the criminal's existence. I can watch him. I can lay a trap for him. Sometimes the criminal doesn't possess any of these conditions."

"They've been no advantage to you in this present case," she stated with definite emphasis. "I'm certain of that. The murderer of my brother is as aware of your activity in the case as you are aware of his. Look at it for yourself, if you're foolish enough to doubt me. You were called in when Blundell's body was found; you've been here three times, and you've also been to the place in the Isle of Wight where young Guest was killed. You're positively identified with three radii from the centre of the same circle. What sort of criminal wouldn't have found out those facts?"

Anthony leaned forward towards her. "Even then, Miss Wingfield, I have a weapon in my possession that he hasn't. I have right on my side and the scales of justice and all the moral force of civilization."

"They didn't avail any of the three men who were murdered. God helps those who don't rely too much on—"

"Pardon me if I make a correction. The circumstances weren't the same. Those men may have been taken off their guard. It would be an incredible folly on my part if I allowed myself to be taken off mine. Those men were unsuspecting—we suspect. They weren't watchful—they weren't to know that watchfulness was necessary—we *are* because we *do*."

"You amaze me with your comfortable platitudes," she cried. "You speak as though you knew who this murderer was. You'll tell me next that he murdered people with spiked lions." She turned away to hide her emotion.

"But I do, Miss Wingfield," he said quietly.

She stared. "Do what? Know that he murdered people with—"

"I do know who murdered Hugh Guest, and I presume that as the mechanism used to kill Blundell and your brother was similar to that which killed Guest, I can—"

"You know who killed Guest?" she questioned, breathlessly incredulous.

"I'm almost certain that I do, Miss Wingfield. If cold logic and the science of deduction go for anything at all in the working out of this problem I must be right."

"You know *all* about it, then? All the truth of the conspiracy? *Why* they have all been killed, and for what?"

Anthony shook his head slowly. "I wouldn't say yea to all that, Miss Wingfield. It would be presumption on my part. I haven't all the threads in my hands yet. I know why Guest was killed, but I'm not fully conversant yet with the details of the stories that apply to Blundell and your brother. But I hope to be, very soon."

He rose from his chair and said something to her in a low tone. She stared again in amazement.

"Are you serious?"

He nodded. "Perfectly, Miss Wingfield. Never more so in all my life."

"But why me—why pick on me of all people? Surely, when you—" Her voice was harsh and strident.

"The idea doesn't attract you, then?"

"Do you call it attractive, yourself?"

"Perhaps 'attractive' is the wrong word. And yet—"

"And yet what?"

"There is an inducement," he said carelessly.

She looked at him, a direct glance, straight into his grey eyes. "Why do you accuse me of the possession of these things? You can't prove what you said to me just now. You are basing certain decisions on pure instinct—and you can't deny it, Mr. Bathurst. Confess now."

"Not altogether," he replied doggedly. "You gave certain things away, that was all. For instance, your big gloves came as a God-send to me. Well—which is it to be. The one or the other?"

"What is the alternative? Tell me again." She embraced sullenness.

"I told you what might happen if you refused my suggestion. I won't hide anything. I will be quite candid with you. I don't suppose for a moment that Tresham will be either a home from home or a sanatorium during the next few days. Because I don't know *all* that there is to know, I am forced to take steps to protect myself. That's all there is to it."

"But why Tresham of all places, Mr. Bathurst? How can you be certain that you are right with regard to that?"

"Because I am positive that the rag will go up on the last act of this drama on a stage *at* or *near* Tresham. Summerhayes, the doctor who was called in when Guest died, and a man named Slingsby Raphael, have both already gone there. They will remain there for some time, I think. Sir Richard Ingle, I fancy, will also be drawn there as by a magnet. And I know that I am going there, too."

"I must know more than you have told me. Why are you going there, Mr. Bathurst?"

"Because it is the home of the spiked lion, Miss Wingfield. That fantastic creature that has been used in the case so cleverly. Can you think of a better reason?"

She made no answer.

"Well?" he queried. "What is your decision?"

She drew her lips together while the struggle went on within her soul. "All right," she said at length. "I give in. But you're wrong about me, all the same. You're clever, and you find out lots of things, but in this you may have the surprise of your life."

"In that," said Mr. Bathurst quietly, "we will agree to differ. Now, listen to me. I must give you the general hang of things. Tresham Castle is situated on a ridge of ground that runs from the . . ."

Diana Wingfield listened.

CHAPTER XXIII
WATCHER AND WATCHED

MOST of the streets of Tresham are cobbled and narrow, but the road that leads up the hill to the castle is better than the others. One by one, the succeeding lords of Tresham had seen to that. After all, good roads are a necessity—in certain places, that is. The "Plume of Feathers" is a hostelry which stands right at the foot of that hill to the castle. It is not far from that churchyard at Tresham which Anthony Bathurst had visited some short time before. But, none the worse for that, it always presented a smiling face to guest, habitué and stray customer.

Slingsby Raphael, when he came to Tresham, alert and watchful, and with a special task on hand, had had no hesitation whatever in unscrewing the top of his fountain-pen and inscribing his name in the "Plume of Feathers's" visitors' book. The exterior attracted him. Its host amused and entertained him. Its cuisine satisfied him. Its propinquity to Tresham Castle delighted him. What more, therefore, could he desire?

On the second evening of his stay there, however, he received something that was in the nature of a shock. Although, perhaps, "surprise" would be the word that would describe the situation better. The meal which the ménage of the "Plume of Feathers" designated as dinner was timed for seven o'clock. A few minutes before this hour Raphael was in his room changing his suit and generally freshening himself up. On the point of buttoning his collar, he heard a soft footfall in the corridor outside which seemed to stop suddenly and immediately outside his door. Raphael paused, finger and thumb on stud, and listened. Half-turning from the mirror which he had been facing, Raphael watched the door and then the door-handle. He saw the latter object begin to turn slowly. It went round gradually in what was almost a half-circle and then twisted back again—as though the person directing it had been determined upon a certain course of action only to change his mind before that action could be completed.

Slingsby Raphael, always quick to move in affairs of this sort, took three rapid, noiseless strides across the room. An idea had struck him. Things were already afoot perhaps! If this were the person whom he had come to—He reached the door, grasped the handle, and sharply pulled the door open. But he was too late to effect anything satisfactory. When he looked out there wasn't a soul in sight; whoever had tried his door had quick ears and an active body. Taking a step forward, he looked down the length of the corridor, but neither sound nor sight rewarded him. Shaking his head dubiously, Raphael shut the door and went back inside his room. He sat down, chin in hand, and delivered himself up to a spell of intensive thinking. What did this last development mean? Which was the more likely possibility: that he himself had been spotted and that his quarry was coming forward with an offer, or that stronger measures had been determined on against him? In the consideration of each of these possibilities Raphael curled his lip in disdain. Who were these people to pit themselves against him? Against Slingsby Raphael, a member of the dread Triad Society, and an Endorite?

"Cursed presumption," he muttered to himself, with clenched hands. "It seems to me that I shall be compelled to teach them a lesson." He strolled down to the "Plume of Feathers" dining-room, therefore, with cold calculation in his heart. He would see, at any rate, the personnel of the diners—whether there were changes or additions compared with that of the previous evening. On this previous occasion that he had dined there, matters had progressed quietly. He had neither seen nor heard anything calculated to arouse his suspicion. This evening, however, his eyes were wider open than usual when he entered the dining-room. As before, he took his place at the head of one of the smaller tables that the room held. There was always a fair number of people staying at the "Plume of Feathers", and at the present time there was no exception to this rule.

Slingsby Raphael looked round the room comprehensively and wished everyone within hearing good evening. His exterior seemed to radiate good feeling. He gave the impression that he was prepared to like all his fellow-diners, and that he wished them to know it. Even the somewhat lugubrious-looking waiter, who had been awaiting the stream of diners, cheered up appreciably at the sight of Raphael's affability. He felt a sense of gratitude towards this gentleman—that very lively sense of favours to come.

The other occupants of the room who had heard it returned Raphael's salutation according to their respective lights. As far as he could see, when the meal was on the point of beginning, there were two vacant places in the room. He found himself watching curiously the man who sat directly opposite to him: a man with his two lower chins telescoping into a billowing chest. His chin proper looked proudly down at its offspring.

The lugubrious waiter arrived with the inevitable plates of soup. As he placed one of these in front of Raphael, a young lady, obviously still wearing her travelling clothes, entered the dining-room and sank with an air of subdued resignation into one of the vacant chairs. During the slight stir caused by her arrival it was natural, perhaps, that there was but little attention paid to the young man who had slipped quietly and unostentatiously into the other seat that had been unoccupied. In fact, it would be true to say that whatever attention was directed towards him came entirely from Slingsby Raphael; for an excellent reason. The young man was none other than Barry Covington.

Mr. Raphael, scenting danger and developments, finessed with the wine-list, which his cadaverous attendant had pushed towards him. "Sole à la Marguery—eh? I'll drink Lafitte," he said quietly. "Lafitte, most certainly, is indicated, that I may hold it up to the light and be charmed by its ruby radiance. Yes, waiter, Lafitte, most certainly."

Lowering the wine-list a little, he looked covertly across the room to the table where Covington was sitting. And then, at the psychological second, Raphael realized that as he was watching Covington, so Covington, not watching him, as he had been at first inclined to suspect, was watching one of the waiters. There was no mistaking it. The eyes of Barry Covington watched this waiter ceaselessly and with intimate comprehension. Wherever the man went, Barry Covington's glance went also. The man whom Covington watched was of average height and extremely well-proportioned. As he awaited the coming of the entrée, Raphael took mental stock of him. Dark, vivacious, rather coarse features, brownish eyes, hair inclined to be curly, good white, even teeth, and a mouth that was the reverse of attractive. A mouth always more open than a mouth should be; and a clear hint about it of cruelty and rapaciousness.

The courses of the dinner followed one upon the other, and as the time went on Raphael felt convinced in his mind that Barry Covington had not yet spotted him. This fact was scarcely surprising, seeing that Covington had eyes only for this waiter of his. Small commonplaces and fragments of exaggerated politeness passed between the diners. Raphael, taking little part in these exchanges, had by this time, to all appearances, given himself up devotedly to the slow and painstaking appreciation of his radiant Lafitte 1900.

But this was not so, for he was wrestling with a problem—a problem, too, to which he was unable to supply the right answer. The presence of Covington here was likely to interfere seriously with his plans. That fact stood out clearly defined. He had always thought him to be a young meddlesome fool, and now he was damned sure of it. Suddenly, however, Raphael brought himself up with a jerk. Surely there was a contingency here that he hadn't considered! He looked up, to find Barry Covington's waiter's eye fixed upon him. Raphael came to a quick decision. From which, he thought, he might kill two birds with one stone.

Raising his left hand, he beckoned to the man to come to him. Somewhat surprised by a gesture that came from the other side of the dining-room, the waiter obeyed the summons.

"You called me, sir?"

Mr. Raphael nodded curtly, and at the same time attempted to add to the physical inventory of the man that he had already commenced to prepare. Before he replied, he took in all that he could of the man's expression and outward bearing.

"Yes, I called you. Would you be good enough to open that window that was behind you where you were standing—just a few inches? That one over there. It's insufferably hot in here." He put a finger between collar and neck. "And I can't mix my dinner with a Turkish bath. Some people can, I know. But I can't—never could—never learnt the habit."

The waiter glided swiftly away and gave Mr. Raphael those inches of cooler air. But not before Mr. Raphael had had time to notice certain things. Indications, perhaps, rather than definite inferences. The dress-suit that the man was wearing had been made by an absolutely first-class tailor—there could be no argument about that. Raphael's knowledge of the sartorial told him the fact immediately. Also, there was a button missing from the cuff of the right-hand sleeve. Despite this deficiency, however, the quality stood out for all to see. Moreover, it had been made for the man who wore it. In this respect alone, Slingsby Raphael decided, as he glanced round the room at the various waiters, it was—in this gallery—unique. He realized, too, a moment later, that his brief interview with the waiter had had one of its two desired effects. It had drawn Barry Covington's attention towards him.

Covington's eyes flashed a look of surprised recognition across the room. On the whole, Raphael was puzzled at the turn that things had taken. Once again he fell to surmise. Covington had made no attempt to evade him, it was true—which fact might, or might not, mean that Covington was playing with fire; on the other hand, it was futility to speculate, because it might mean anything. The meal came to an end.

At the first possible and convenient moment, Covington came to Raphael's side. "My dear chap," he said, with outstretched hand, "what on earth are you doing here?"

Raphael looked him straight between the eyes. "Come to think of it—that is the identical question which I was about to ask you."

Covington at once showed signs of acute uneasiness. "I suppose I asked for that, but I'd rather not answer here, if you don't mind. You see—it's not altogether—"

Raphael interrupted him. "Yet you expected me to answer your question. I'm afraid you young Englishmen don't practise what you're so fond of preaching."

Covington nodded, still uneasy. "Sorry, and all that. Expect I seem all sorts of a snivelling cad, but you don't understand—that's all. I've got something pretty big on. Where can we talk? Any idea?"

Raphael, ever a disciple of open warfare, determined on a bold stroke. "Do you happen to be aware," he asked quietly, "that, at this precise moment, you and I are the subjects of a little—shall we call it?—espionage? Don't look round, please."

Covington played up well. He lit a cigarette with a perfectly steady hand. Not a muscle of his head or eyes moved. "From whom?" he asked, with an almost ominous quietness, as he blew out the flame of the match.

"One of the waiters. A chap that was over your side of the room. Is he expecting a tip or something?"

Barry Covington shook his head hurriedly. "No, no. It's not that. I think it's because I've come to speak to you. It's made him suspicious of us. Which brings me back to where we were just now. Where can we talk? In the lounge? Or is it too crowded, do you think? They'll be bringing the coffee out there in a moment or so."

"It was pretty congested last night," replied Raphael. "On one occasion an ace of spades was perilously close to my ear. What about coming upstairs to my room? I'm on the second floor—number twenty-five."

"Righto. That ought to do splendidly. I'm on the floor above you. We'll go up in the lift. Come on."

The two men came to Raphael's bedroom. "Take that big basket-chair, Covington," said Raphael, "and I'll sit on the bed. Comfortable?"

"Oh yes, thanks. I want to talk to you. I want to tell you something."

Raphael raised an imperative hand. "Before you start to do that, Covington, let us understand each other. No man ever hated a misunderstanding more than I do. When people pit their wits and brains against Slingsby Raphael, it's as well that they should learn certain things right at the very start. I like them to know that it is both dangerous and unprofitable to play with fire. Will you forgive me if I recall to your memory those historic words recorded by M. de Marsac? 'You had better steal the King's crown jewel—he is weak; or the Guise's last plot—he is generous at times; or Navarre's last sweetheart—he is as easy as an old shoe. You had better do all those together, I tell you, than touch one of Turenne's ewe-lambs. Unless your aim be, you fool, to be broken on the wheel.' In this respect, my dear Monsieur Covington, please regard me in the light of the Vicomte de Turenne. I have no doubt that, if necessary, I should have little difficulty in finding a convenient wheel."

He paused, and then muttered softly, "Mon Dieu, yes!"

Covington looked a little puzzled. It appeared that he understood neither remarks nor attitude.

Raphael embellished his point. "You do not understand me, Mr. Covington. I can see that. I will endeavour to make myself more clear. Why did you attempt to enter this room just before dinner?"

At the direct accusation, Covington flushed to the roots of his hair. Then he laughed nervously. "Good lord!" he replied. "I wondered what on earth you were getting at. I was beginning to have cold shivers down my spine. I'm most awfully sorry about that, and must apologize for the little *faux pas* here and now. Fact of the matter was this. I didn't come up in the lift; it was full up. I walked upstairs and thought that I was farther up than I actually was. Mistook the second floor for the third. Quite easy to do that, you know. They're as like as the proverbial two peas. My room on the floor above is in exactly the same relative position as this one is. So you see how it happened. I'm most profoundly sorry for the mistake and can only congratulate myself on the fact that I found out I was wrong before I had irreparably committed myself. Pictured an outraged dame all floppy on the bed from shock. I scooted away like merry hell, I can tell you."

Covington paused and mopped a wet forehead with a handkerchief. Raphael watched him keenly, almost as cat to mouse. Barry Covington rattled on, at his ease now, seemingly.

"Now what I particularly wanted to tell you before you began to lecture me, was this. I've found out something. Something about that murder at Ingle's place. That waiter whom you say you saw watching us just now, in the dining-room, is one of the men I heard threatening poor Hugh Guest when I lay half asleep on Lashey Down. I recognized his voice, and when I heard it again I decided to follow him. I'd nothing much to do, my time was pretty well my own. I've followed him to Tresham, as you see. I'm absolutely positive I'm right. You've turned up absolutely at the crucial moment. Now the question is—what are we going to do? Shall we—"

Barry Covington stopped. He wasn't sure whether Slingsby Raphael was listening to him. Noticing, however, the expression on Raphael's face, he proceeded.

Chapter XXIV
MR. BATHURST DELVES INTO THE PAST

THE Commissioner of Police listened to Mr. Anthony Lotherington Bathurst. When what Mr. Bathurst had to say had become history, he executed a half-turn in his chair and listened to Chief-Inspector MacMorran. After a period devoted to a considered examination of the two statements, he delivered judgment.

"According to your theory, then, Bathurst, this conspiracy may be said to have been aimed at what we will call the Tresham succession. H'm? That the idea?"

"In a way, sir—yes."

Sir Austin was quick to pounce on Anthony's indecision. "What do you mean by that? Aren't you satisfied?"

Bathurst rose and paced the room. Once, twice, three times. They watched him silently. They knew him of old. Suddenly he turned to them. "No, sir, I'm not. I can't deny that I'm puzzled by at least one aspect of the case. I can't make a certain piece fit."

"What's your worst trouble?"

Anthony gave himself up to a moment's meditation. "This man who joined the cast as Lord Tresham, and whom we are now calling Lord Tresham. I can't altogether—"

The Commissioner was quick to interrupt. "You can't get away from two vitally important facts, my dear boy. Look at it how you will. This man has been accepted by Lomax, the solicitor, and also by Sir Richard Ingle, his blood relation. If they're satisfied—particularly Ingle—seeing how he was placed—"

Anthony smiled. "I know that very well, sir. But our friend could have stolen the counters—and any documents that he may possess—and faked, so it seems to me, what we will call the *physical* evidences."

"But how could he *know* about them? That's the point you can't get away from. How could he know, for instance, about the three letters behind Tresham's knee?"

Anthony flicked the ash from his cigarette. "I think the answer to those questions is comparatively simple."

"Well—what is the answer?"

"There are two—surely."

"Well?"

"Blundell and Wingfield," said Mr. Bathurst quietly. "Their bodies," proceeded Anthony, "had certain marks on them, as we know, which the murderer or murderers regarded as necessary to fake. Anyhow, that's how I see the pattern of our problem. The marks on Blundell and Wingfield *had* to be on the body of the pseudo Tresham. In case of accidents. They couldn't risk *not* having them there. They had learnt that fact somewhere, somehow and somewhen."

"But why Blundell *and* Wingfield? Why wasn't one body enough for their purpose? I can't for the life of me see any sense in killing *two* people when one would have been—"

"From that point of view, can there ever be sense in killing anybody, sir? Especially in this country. Looked at with cold, dispassionate judgment, murder is the most foolish of all crimes. British justice never forgets it—never forgives it. Once a man lifts his hand in murder, he's more or less finished. Everybody's hand is then turned against him. As to your question concerning the bodies, I can only suggest this. That the murderer wanted to make sure that the tattooing on each of the bodies was exactly the same—as regards detail, I mean. This Tresham *must* be an impostor. It is the only possible solution as far as I can see. Otherwise, why all this chain of crime?"

MacMorran intervened. "Accepting all that, Mr. Bathurst, and I'm not denying that the way you put it makes it appear extremely feasible, there's still a point that I, for one, can't get a proper grasp of."

"What's that, Inspector?"

"Why, just this. You say that the murderer, whoever he may happen to be—got his claws into Blundell and Wingfield purposely. That they were necessary, shall we say, to his plan. That's what you meant, isn't it? Well, that being so, he must have known about Blundell and Wingfield *beforehand*. Must have known their secret before he got hold of them. Otherwise why should he want them? Are you seeing what I'm meaning?"

The Commissioner nodded vigorously.

"I must congratulate you on your question, MacMorran," replied Anthony. "I've had to face the same difficulty that's confronting you, and I don't know now that I've answered it in the right manner. The solution, though, may lie in the difference between 'general' and 'particular'. There's a definite possibility there, I admit. On the other hand, there may be a deeper and more deliberate significance somewhere."

He paused and seemed to shake himself free of something. "But let's hear what the inspector has to tell us with regard to those pre-war years at Cambridge. When Blundell and Co. were at work on bugs and drugs. Have you traced the man I wanted, MacMorran?"

The inspector went across to a table and picked up a docket. He smiled as he turned to the others. "Aye, Mr. Bathurst, I have that. Taking all things into consideration, it didn't turn out to be too difficult. A long time had elapsed, it's true, but at the same time we had something pretty definite to go on. You've given me more ticklish tasks than, this one. It wasn't as though the chap's hobby was fishin' or stamp collectin'—tattooin's a bit different. Doctor Valentine, who is the present director of the FitzWilliam Museum and Marlay Curator at Cambridge, was at the University when those other people were there, and remembers them all fairly well. The name of the fellow you're wantin', Mr. Bathurst, is Eddington. He was up at Luther College. The eminent doctor recalls that this man Eddington was a contemporary of Tresham, Blundell and Wingfield, and that there was a rumour extant at the time that he was a marvellously clever hand with the tattoo needle. There was a barmaid at one of the pubs there who let him perform on her. She was sacked, but that didn't worry her. She went in for politics as a substitute; joined the Labour Party and is an M.P. now."

"Excellent, my dear MacMorran. You have surpassed yourself. Continue, please, with details of this Comrade Eddington."

The inspector flushed with pleasure at Mr. Bathurst's eulogy. "Well, this young man Eddington went abroad some time afterwards in the companionship of Nicholas Tresham. To be heard of afterwards in Morocco. At Marrakech, I believe, to be exact as regards locality. With the outbreak of hostilities in 1914, Eddington came away from whatever place he was in, and enlisted."

"One minute, MacMorran, please," interposed Anthony. "Is there any record, do you know, of Nicholas Tresham having enlisted with him?"

"As far as I can tell you at the moment, Mr. Bathurst, none."

"Thank you, MacMorran. Go on, please."

"There isn't much more for me to tell you. I'm on the last chapter, as you might say. Eddington was badly wounded at Gaza and was taken into a C.C.S. for immediate treatment. But there was little or no hope for him from the very first. A shell had exploded quite close to him, blowing off both an arm and a leg and inflicting severe facial injuries. He lingered for some little time and eventually passed out." MacMorran replaced the paper within the docket. "That's the sum total of my news concerning this man Eddington, Mr. Bathurst. It can't very well go any farther, though, can it?"

The grey eyes of Anthony Bathurst seemed to look across that room into nothingness. "So, Eddington, the tattoo artist, died in a British casualty clearing station, did he?" He turned to Sir Austin Kemble with an eye that now held interest. "Doesn't that strike you as significant, sir?"

Before the Commissioner could reply, however, Anthony Bathurst was back again to MacMorran. "Can you get me exact details and dates with regard to Eddington's death, Inspector? Locale, year, etc., etc. I shall be eternally obliged if you can."

MacMorran nodded acquiescence. Sir Austin looked curiously at Anthony. "You think that Eddington, knowing what he did about three people, gave something away? In delirium, perhaps? That's the idea isn't it, Bathurst?"

"I'm coquetting with the theory, Sir Austin, but it's Tresham that's bothering me. Tresham, probably, spent years with Eddington. Eddington's all very well as far as he goes. Which isn't very far, you know, considering everything. The point that's worrying me—where is Tresham *himself*, as I said? *Where's Tresham?* Does he touch the circle anywhere?"

"That's easily answered," returned Sir Austin didactically.

Anthony regarded him critically. "How would you answer it then, sir?"

"He's dead, of course! Died years before, in all probability. Eddington knew it. Was with him when he died, no doubt. Got hold of his papers and of those infernal counters. Realized their worth—their extrinsic worth. Knew all about the spiked lion—knew about everything, I should say. Then, when his turn came to hand his checks in, gave the whole bag of tricks away to somebody, and that somebody is the man whom we have to find. Eddington blew the gaff! Unintentionally, perhaps, but blew it all the same."

"It's quite possible, sir, I agree. But it's all conjecture—and at this stage of an investigation I don't like conjecture. I could bear to discover a great deal more *fact*."

"Facts aren't easy to get hold of sometimes, Bathurst. When you can't get 'em you're bound to work on what you have—theories and conjectures. To a hungry man half a roll is better than a bag of flour."

Anthony Bathurst shook his head. "When I get those dates and details from MacMorran here, that I asked him for just now, I am hopeful that I may be able to see a little more light. Till then, I'm determined to keep an open mind on more than one aspect of the case. You'll get to work on them at once, won't you, Inspector?"

"Rely on me, Mr. Bathurst."

Anthony became reminiscent. "The great tragedy of the affair is that Hugh Guest took nobody into his confidence. He elected to see the thing through off his own bat and, as we know

now, went to his death. A chance word to his sister, even, might have proved enough to have turned the scale in our favour."

As Anthony finished speaking, Sir Austin's telephone became an instrument of insistent sound. The Commissioner hastened to interpret. "Yes? What's that? Oh yes . . . send him up here at once, by all means. For Mr. Bathurst, you say? . . . Yes, yes . . . that's quite right . . . to my private room . . . he's with me at the present time."

Sir Austin replaced the receiver. "There's a telegraph boy downstairs for you, Bathurst. I've told them to send him straight up here. Something important, do you think?"

"I shouldn't be surprised, Sir Austin. As a matter of fact, I've been expecting a message for some little time. However, if we possess our souls in patience we shall know all about it in a very few minutes."

He answered the tap at the door that followed almost immediately. "There are four telegrams here, Sir Austin. Wait just a moment, will you, my boy, in case I want you again?"

Anthony came back to the middle of the room. "We'll take them seriatim, sir." He grinned. "If that's possible." Opening the first telegram, he read it aloud.

"Appointment referred to made but not kept. Reason given illness. Serge Valdar."

Anthony opened the second telegram and repeated the previous performance.

"For our use, the kindly fruits of the earth so that in due time we may enjoy them. Adam."

Anthony rubbed his chin.

Sir Austin looked at him blankly. MacMorran smiled his dry, twisted smile. "Aye," he said, "Mr. Bathurst likes bein' a wee bit cryptic."

"We will pass on to telegram number three," said Anthony, "and murmur a thanksgiving for our Litany." He opened the third telegram.

"To Anthony L. Bathurst, New Scotland Yard, London. Please come at once to Tresham Castle for most important consultation. Wire train if necessary and car will meet you. Tresham."

"Hallo, sir," said Anthony. "Things are moving, what! Our friend calling himself Tresham has hauled down the skull and crossbones and is now flying signals of distress, and at the same time, I suppose, paying me something like a compliment."

The Commissioner fell to consideration. "What are you going to do? Are you going down there?"

"*Festina lente*, Sir Austin. Let us see what telegram number four has to say before I answer that question."

He tore open the envelope of the fourth telegram.

"Since visiting Tresham Castle Doctor Arnold Summerhayes has disappeared. All enquiries so far made have failed to trace him. Police informed. Many-breasted Ephesus."

MacMorran was in like a rapier thrust. "Aye, I'm not surprised. The chicks are coming home to roost just as I've been expectin'. Are you rememberin' my words to you, Mr. Bathurst, about not carin' to be in the shoes of the blackmailer? Somebody's given the worthy doctor a dose of medicine that he won't get over in this life. I wish I were as sure of a thousand Jimmy O'Goblins as I am of that! Blundell, Wingfield, Guest, and now Doctor Summerhayes! That makes four."

The Commissioner went to the table where Anthony had laid the four telegrams and picked them up. "Well, Bathurst," he interrogated, "what's the position now? In the light of all this, do you intend to go to Tresham?"

"Seems indicated, don't you think? There certainly seems room for further investigation."

"I suppose you're right. How about taking MacMorran down there with you?"

"The noble lord doesn't ask for that, sir. I don't think it would be a diplomatic move to run the risk of upsetting him.

Personally, of course, so far as individual taste and company go, I should be more than delighted to have the inspector. But—"

"But what, Bathurst?"

"I sometimes think, sir, that the presence of a 'pukka' detective, right on the spot, as it were, cramps people's style. Tends to shut them up a good deal—give them a 'blue-point' complex. Besides, there are a couple of plain-clothes men in the area already. It amounts to this, sir. The more people are allowed to talk, and the more they are permitted to go about their daily business openly and actively, all the better for us bungling amateurs."

He grinned and slapped the inspector on the back. "What do you think of that, MacMorran? Not bad, what?"

"I reckon you've had your lips close to that Blarney Stone, Mr. Bathurst. If you haven't, then I'm no judge of anything. I'll be there at Tresham, though, if you're ever wantin' me."

"Thanks, MacMorran. I know that—none better. It's damned good of you. Now I want a word with that telegraph boy."

Sir Austin Kemble examined the four telegrams more closely. "I say, Bathurst," he declared, upon the latter's return. "Who are these unknown correspondents of yours in the Tresham locality? Who's this man Adam, for instance? Any relation to Eve's first husband?"

Anthony's smile lit up his face. "The identical bloke, Sir Austin. The first man of all time. Sire of Cain and Abel. Lived goodness knows how many years B.C. I was lucky to be able to press him into service. It all came about from an advertisement that I saw in a local paper. And I was lucky also to get into such happy touch with Serge Valdar."

Sir Austin was still unsatisfied. "And this other telegram, Bathurst? Who's—"

Anthony came suddenly from levity to gravity. "Don't ask me any more questions at the moment, sir, please."

Chapter XXV
DOCTOR SUMMERHAYES REMEMBERS AN OBLIGATION

ANTHONY Bathurst alighted from his car, referred to a letter that he took from a pocket, glanced at his wrist-watch, and walked straight into a telephone-booth that stood at the cross-roads. He asked for a number. After a period of waiting, he heard the voice of his *vis-à-vis* and joyfully pressed button "A". He spoke words into the mouthpiece. He then listened gravely to the replies which came to his ear.

"Now, tell me this? Where was Summerhayes staying before he disappeared?" he asked anxiously. "Have you managed to find that out?"

The answer came with prompt emphasis. "At the little inn opposite the station. The 'Golden Hoop' it's called. It is known that he went to Tresham Castle on the second evening of his stay in Tresham. He told the landlord that he was going up there. He never came back to the 'Golden Hoop'. The landlord—a man named Tosswill—has informed the police."

"What do the police say about it—do you know? Have they any theory that will hold water?"

"The police seem convinced that the doctor has met with foul play. They live, I believe, in almost hourly anticipation of finding his dead body somewhere. The river has been dragged—but with no success."

"By the station, you say, this 'Golden Hoop'?"

"Yes—a little rambling sort of place. But there are two extremes here, it seems, which makes choice limited. It's either that or the 'Plume of Feathers', which borders on the magnificent—a sort of 'Grand Babylon'. You want to be there to appreciate that."

"How are the other matters progressing? Those of your own department? Satisfactorily?"

"Splendidly. I've been able to keep a watchful eye nearly all the time. Luckily the man's under my nose a good deal. Don't know whether it will be like it always. Seems too good to hope. Still—sufficient for the day."

"Have you seen any sign of the lion?" Anthony listened eagerly for the reply.

It came slowly and deliberately. "Inside, eh?" he returned. "Inside the house itself?" He listened again.

"How did you manage that?" he eventually asked. He nodded acceptance of what he was told and then issued a warning. "For God's sake be careful! Don't let there be the slightest suspicion. If you do, God knows what will happen. I've thought things over very carefully during the last few days, and I'm out to do a bold thing—the boldest perhaps that I've ever yet undertaken. Nothing venture—you know—and all that. But I'm walking right into the midst of it . . . in answer to a telegram that I've had sent to me. Not so bad—eh?" He laughed. "What's that? All right then— if you put it like that—right into the lion's' den. You'll know when I'm there, though. Listen: I want to arrange something with you. This, most important. . ." Mr. Bathurst's voice sank to the merest whisper.

"Now, is that understood?" he asked at length. "Shall I repeat it?" He waited. "Right. You've seen my car and you'll know it again. Don't forget I'm going to have a look at the 'Golden Hoop' before I put my nose inside the castle. Now, to take no chances, I'll repeat what I said about the inside business. If the worst come to the worst . . . and I need your assistance . . . I'll communicate with you in the way that I suggested, but I'm relying generally on your intuition and initiative. . . . That's the lot . . . and cheer-o for the present."

Anthony replaced the receiver, stood for a second in contemplation, and then closed the door of the kiosk quietly behind him.

Samuel Tosswill, licensee of the "Golden Hoop", surveyed the tall, grey-eyed stranger who faced him, with undisguised interest. Ordinarily, life was dull at the "Golden Hoop". Then his glance dropped to the card with which this same stranger had presented him. The attachment of Sir Austin Kemble's name, with appropriate designation, worked wonders. He wiped his hands ostentatiously upon his apron and gave Mr. Bathurst cordial invitation.

"Come in, sir. Come into the sitting-room, sir, and sit yourself down. You're very welcome. And have a glass of refreshment, too. Ale, sir? Very good, sir. You've come about that poor doctor, sir, who's disappeared? I've no doubt on it."

Anthony expressed assent. He followed this up with a question. Tosswill put a tankard of ale on the table and made rapid reply.

"No, sir. The good doctor was a complete stranger to me. Ab-so-lute-ly. I had never set eyes on him before, and I think too, from one or two questions that he put to me, that he was a stranger in these parts himself."

"He told you he was going to the castle, I believe, when he left here on that last occasion?"

"Yes, sir. Told me he'd been invited up there by no less a person than Lord Tresham himself. Said that was the real reason for his havin' come to Tresham. Seemed almighty pleased about it, too. Almost chuckling he was when he told me. Like a dog with two tails."

"You expected him to come back, of course?"

"Naturally. He didn't say naught about *not* comin' back."

Mr. Bathurst became more practical. "What did he leave behind here?"

"He left naught behind him. But there, again, he hadn't much with him when he came. So he couldn't very well, could he? In the way of luggage and personal property, as you might say. Reckon he'd got all he required in a small suitcase that he was a-carryin' when he first came in. Just a toothbrush, I guess, and razor and somethin' to sleep in. But he didn't have no spare wardrobe as you'd call it."

"You've no objection, I take it, to my seeing his room?"

"Not a bit, sir. Come along upstairs now and give it a good lookin' over. The local police have had a go at it before you. They came down here soon after I sent word up that he was missin'."

The two men ascended an old-fashioned staircase. Anthony had to duck his head more than once to avoid certain contacts.

"Here's the bedroom the doctor had, sir. This one facin' you. And pretty bare I'll think you'll be findin' it."

Tosswill's vatication was only too true. Summerhayes had gone—leaving no trace. Bathurst's search yielded nothing at all. He turned to his host.

"It looks to me," he said, "as though the doctor intended sleeping one night in Tresham Castle at least. Otherwise, why should he take *all* his personal things with him? Don't you think so yourself?"

Tosswill nodded his agreement. "Aye. That's as may be. But he never settled his bill with me, you know. He meant to come back here all right. There's no manner of doubt about that. He wasn't the sort to swindle an honest workin' man. I reckon I'm judge enough of character to know that."

Anthony smiled at the man's certainty and at the foundation upon which he averred it to be built. "What have the police learnt at Tresham?" he asked. "Have you any idea?"

"Aye. I had a bit of a chat with Sergeant Wookey. I've known him since he was a nipper no higher than that, so I reckon, I can talk to him pretty freely. Lord Tresham said the doctor had been up there on the evening that he left here, but had gone away again. He said he didn't know where he'd gone so he couldn't tell them any more." Tosswill adorned his statement with adequate gestures.

Anthony reflected. "I wonder if he gave a reason for Summerhayes going up there to see him. Seems rather strange to me—all of it—this doctor arriving here, putting up with you and then going off to the castle to see Lord Tresham himself. Going up by what he calls invitation, too."

Tosswill led the way downstairs. A postman had entered the bar. He handed a letter to the landlord. The latter opened the envelope and then felt in his pocket for necessary spectacles. He peered at the letter almost frowningly.

"Now, dang me, if this isn't what them writin' chaps call the long arm of coincidence. This is from Doctor Summerhayes himself." He became material and assessed values. "Let me see now. Postal orders, amountin' in total to two quid—that's very generous of him, because his bill didn't come to as much as that—and a letter. Let's see what he's got to say for himself."

Tosswill began to read the letter with slow deliberation. He then passed it to Anthony Bathurst. There was no address shown. Also, it was terse and distinctly to the point.

Herewith find postal orders value two pounds in settlement of my outstanding account. I shall not return.
Yours faithfully,
Arnold Summerhayes.

Mr. Bathurst handed it back to Tosswill. "Doesn't waste words on explanation, does he? May I glance at the envelope?"

Tosswill complied.

"Thanks." Anthony's interest lay in the postmark. It was Tresham. He pointed out the fact to Tosswill.

"Tresham, you see. Local postmark. Posted this morning, too."

Tosswill's eyes were wide open. "So the good doctor's not very far away after all. Well, now, if that don't beat cock-fightin'. Reckon I've got something more to tell Sergeant Wookey. I guess he'll prick up his ears when he hears word of these."

He indicated the two postal orders. "Do you want anything more, sir?" he questioned.

"I think not, Mr. Tosswill. A good deal of our uncertainty is clearing away. This letter that you have just received has altered the situation considerably."

Tosswill laughed heartily. Things were certainly going better for him. "There's no gainsayin' that, sir. I thought the good gentleman was dead." He tapped the letter meaningly. "But if he wrote this, he can't be. He must be alive and well and not far from here—shows how you can jump to wrong conclusions—and, as you say, it makes a rare lot of difference." Tosswill scratched his head. The hues of to-morrow's dawn would be more roseate.

"Yes," said Mr. Bathurst as he took his departure—"*if* he wrote it."

He turned his car in the direction of Tresham Castle. When he came to the churchyard under the hill, and to the "Plume of Feathers" opposite to it, he stopped again. Mr. Bathurst has always contended, when discussing the science of deduction, that no avenue which may bring success should be left unattended.

Chapter XXVI
ALL ROADS LEAD TO PHILIPPI

To tell the reader the truth, Anthony Bathurst stopped his car outside the "Plume of Feathers" for *two* reasons. One—that he had nurtured the intention to stop there ever since he had come to Tresham; and two—which was perhaps the more important—he saw Slingsby Raphael and Sir Richard Ingle in close conversation on the steps of the hotel.

Anthony stopped his car, as has been said, descended and approached them with obvious cordiality. The two men ceased their conversation and waited for him.

"I told you that we should meet at Philippi, Sir Richard. Substituting Tresham territorially, that is, sir."

Sir Richard and Raphael each shook hands with him. Neither exuded enthusiasm. Then the latter shrugged his shoulders. "One might be inclined to imagine all sorts of things," he declared cynically, "if one paid attention to signs and portents. First Summerhayes, then our young comrade Covington, then you, Richard, and now our friend Bathurst. Tresham must have magnetic attractions."

Anthony smiled at the thrust. Raphael always roused within him the elements of hostility. He couldn't help thinking that Raphael brought about this condition deliberately.

"And yet there is not one rendezvous, but two rendezvous."

"What do you mean?"

"Surely there must have been others who have met similarly, before us, Mr. Raphael? In the not so dim and distant past?"

Raphael's marvellous eyes glinted. "Is that so? I wonder if I understand you?"

Anthony imitated Raphael's gesture of a moment or so before. He shrugged his shoulders. "If not here, in the Isle of Wight, shall we say? Blundell, Wingfield, and—"

"And who?"

"The man who murdered them. Who else?"

Ingle gasped his astonishment at Mr. Bathurst's calculated statement. Raphael nodded what Anthony thought was meant to be corroboration of his own theory. His words, when they came, confirmed the idea.

"We do understand each other, Bathurst, after all. I was just a little, shall we say, uncertain? It's as well, I think, that we do."

Anthony decided upon a policy of supreme frankness. "All the same, I don't think my coming to Tresham has the same origin as yours."

"If we get down to essentials I rather think it has." Raphael's face was set as he made this almost contradictory statement.

"Which, being interpreted . . . ?"

"Curiosity, inquisitiveness! The desire to know things—to find things out. To use your own words—the habitual defence of the crime-investigator against the justifiable charge of Paul Pry-ism—'to arrive at the truth'. Why don't you admit it? *I* do. I'm curious. So are you, if you're sincere."

"And yet, in a way," murmured Anthony, "you do me an injustice. Your indictment is not altogether fair. I have come to Tresham by invitation."

"By invitation?" queried Raphael.

"Yes," returned Anthony sweetly. "I was invited, even as I am told a certain Dr. Summerhayes was. There is more than a faint familiarity between our two positions. Indeed, there is a distinct likeness. Our host, in each instance, is none other than Lord Tresham himself. In other words, we twain have been called to the castle. Perhaps, too, I shall disappear. Who can tell?"

Ingle interposed impatiently. "Do you mean to tell me in all seriousness, Bathurst, that Nick Tresham himself has invited you down here?"

Anthony Bathurst fished in his pocket for a telegram. "There is nothing like first-hand evidence. Read that for yourself, Sir Richard."

Sir Richard Ingle read the words of the telegram from Tresham that had gone to Scotland Yard.

"Fairly conclusive, is it not, sir?"

Sir Richard grunted non-committally. "What trouble has come to Tresham now, Richard?" asked Slingsby Raphael.

Ingle shook his head. "I can't put a name to anything definite. I lunched with him yesterday, as you know. I had to see him on some most pressing family matters. Beyond the fact that his manner seemed a shade excited and nervy, and that he was perhaps a trifle off his food, I could see little amiss with him. He was very decent to me all the time that I was there. In fact, an altogether admirable host, and that despite the fact that one or two things which I was forced to put before him were deucedly unpalatable."

"He hinted at nothing, then, that would explain his desire for a consultation with Bathurst?" Again Raphael put the question.

"No. At nothing whatever."

A strange light danced in Raphael's eyes. There was no doubt that he was pursuing an idea. "You are still convinced that he is the man he claims to be? Harbour no doubts?"

Anthony Bathurst listened eagerly for the reply.

"None at all. I am quite sure. If I had possessed any lingering doubts, yesterday afternoon would have cleared them away very effectively."

"Why? What happened yesterday afternoon?" pressed Raphael.

"Well, as you may guess from what I've already told you, Tresham Castle is a wonderful place. From almost every point of view. One of the latest additions is a magnificent swimming-pool tucked away in the utmost sequestration in a corner of the grounds. I don't think I've ever clapped eyes on a finer. After a light lunch, Nick Tresham suggested a cooler—it was infernally hot in the afternoon, as you probably remember. I can tell you I welcomed the idea. So we had a splash about together."

"Well?" queried Raphael.

Anthony, of course, knew what was coming, and he could have sworn that Slingsby Raphael knew too.

"You can guess the rest," returned Sir Richard with easy nonchalance. "You don't need to be a Rouletabille."

Raphael nodded and came to the point. "Blood's thicker than water."

Anthony interposed at once. "Pardon me, Sir Richard, if I butt in here, but did Lord Tresham call attention to that fact?"

"Which fact?"

Anthony smiled. "The fact that you have just mentioned—concerning those relative thicknesses."

"He did—but purely jokingly. There was no discussion on the point. Anyhow, once again I'm satisfied with all of it and I bear him no ill-will—please remember that. Goodness gracious, it's a sorry state of affairs if Englishmen can't be good losers!"

"I loathe him, if you want to know," retorted Raphael grimly; "if only for the fact that I envy him excessively."

"I envy him, too, I think," said Anthony softly; "but not perhaps in the same direction."

Raphael turned slowly to the speaker. "For what do you envy him?" he asked curiously.

"For one of two things," replied Mr. Bathurst: "either audacity or whimsicality—I am not yet quite sure which."

Raphael laughed softly. "Then I have an advantage over you there, Bathurst, because I am very sure of the foundation of my envy."

Chapter XXVII
INSIDE THE CASTLE (AFTERNOON)

ANTHONY Bathurst's car took the hill to Tresham Castle. When he reached the crest he was amazed at the extent of the lands and estate. It was indeed a goodly heritage that had come to Nicholas Tresham. For one thing alone it must mean employment of the best kind for hundreds. Men, women, and the children of those men and women, rendered service to their temporal lord. Anthony stopped his ear at the lodge. But neither lodge-keeper nor lodge-keeper's agent emerged therefrom to interrogate him and set him upon his further way. Instead, one of the gardeners came from his work on the box-hedge that skirted the drive and advanced towards Anthony's car.

He was a tall man of such magnificent physique that he compelled Anthony's instant admiration.

Putting a hand on the door of the car, he enquired Mr. Bathurst's imminent desires. Anthony's brain functioned in two directions. He made inward comment: "You can pack a tidy wallop in that gossamer fist of yours"; and audible utterance that was more conventional: "Can you tell me, please, if Lord Tresham is in residence at the castle?" The gardener nodded affirmation.

"Yes, sir. Drive straight on, sir. Until the drive turns slightly to the left. Then go straight on again—you will see your way in front of you."

Anthony thanked his informant, sounded his horn twice and obeyed instructions. There were many more men at work on the gardens of Tresham. He counted at least a dozen whom he passed on this short journey.

A footman, almost as tall as the hedger had been, came to meet him on the threshold.

"Lord Tresham," enquired Mr. Bathurst softly; "is he in? I have been told that he is."

The majestic personage to whom he had addressed the question looked first at Mr. Bathurst's car and then at Mr. Bathurst himself. A slight wrinkling of his nose was to be observed. He was a man who had his own measurement of personal worth and social prestige. Anthony declares to this day, in fact, that had his car been a Baby Austin, he would have been flung into boiling oil on the spot. The personage dropped his chin a little and descended into speech.

"Have you an appointment with his lordship, may I ask?"

"Most certainly," replied Anthony. "My name is Bathurst. Anthony Bathurst. I was led to believe that Lord Tresham was positively pining to see me."

The footman ignored the pleasantry. The verb, though, is much too mild and ingenuous. He spurned the witticism from him—by facial play, by body movement and by general gesture. It was a baseness with which Tresham could not traffic. His chin, therefore, decided to resume its normal position.

"For what time was the appointment . . . sir?" The titular address was belated and puny—born prematurely of parsimony and regret.

"There," said Anthony, "you touch me on my weakest spot. Alas, I cannot answer as to time. Let me say, rather, in reply to your question, that it would be as well if I were hastened into Lord Tresham's presence. Immediately upon my arrival here, bearers should have met me at the gates and carried me into the august arena."

The footman appeared to attempt to assess accurately the exact worth of Anthony's answer.

"I have a telegram here," continued Mr. Bathurst, patting his pocket with a gesture of affection, "which, besides demanding my presence, contains the adverbial phrase 'at once', and the adjective 'important'."

"In that case, then, sir," announced the footman, "will you please enter . . . and I will acquaint his lordship of your arrival."

"You are kindness itself," murmured Mr. Bathurst. "I knew it from the first."

Anthony came to a lounge hall. The footman had brought him there. The footman desired him to wait. Anthony obeyed. Facing him, as he stood there, was something which almost took his breath away. A magnificent piece of interior decoration. No less than a painting in oils of a lion, standing on all fours and confronting the onlookers. Round the beast's neck was a kind of ruffed or spiked collar. Although he had been prepared to see it, Anthony held his breath as he regarded it. The eyes and nostrils almost shimmered with light and life, and the tufted tail seemed to hold the secret of movement. "The Spiked Lion"? The picture was not framed or hung, as pictures are ordinarily. It had been let into the side of a staircase, as a centre-piece almost, of the general design.

Beneath it was a blue divan with blue cushions. At each side of this divan was a stand holding a superb fern. Above the picture of the lion ran the curved baluster of the broad and spacious staircase which led from the lounge hall to the upper rooms. The walls of the apartment were shaded in the pale purple of the delphinium. The ceiling was lavender, and the floor covered with a bronze-purple linoleum, with insets of green comprising the background. Leaf sprays of anaglypta, painted white, made an effective and pleasing contrast against the blue walls. The chairs were upholstered in quince-green corduroy, which shaded most delicately with the prevailing tints of blue.

Lord Tresham did not keep his visitor waiting very long. When he entered he was accompanied by a man whom Anthony had seen before. At the funeral of the late Lord Tresham. Captain Andrew Forbes.

Tresham's face wore an unmistakable frown.

"He's rattled," communed Anthony with himself. "Forbes is here as support. The situation becomes extraordinarily eloquent."

"Good afternoon. What is the meaning of this intrusion?" Nick Tresham's demand was cold.

Mr. Bathurst's frown matched his.

"I beg your pardon," he said curtly. "I'm afraid that I don't quite understand you. Did I hear you say 'intrusion'?" The grey eyes of him were inscrutable.

"Yes, that is the word I used. You heard it all right. Don't pretend that you didn't."

"What the devil does the Johnny want?" demanded Captain Forbes, on the verge of truculence. "And who the hell is he, anyway? Forcing his way in here."

Anthony was coolness personified. "This is a most extraordinary reception that you're giving me, you know. The standard of English hospitality, concerning which so much ink has been spilled and paper spoilt, appears to be on the decline. I will endeavour, though, to clear up any misunderstanding that there may be. I am Anthony Bathurst. Please look at that."

Anthony handed over his visiting-card.

Forbes burst in again. "Even so, what the hell are you doing here? Your usual job of Mr. Bloody Nosey Parker?"

Anthony scratched his cheek. "I think you must be referring to the Gloucestershire Parkers. I am sorry to disappoint you, Captain Forbes, but I can't claim any relationship with them. In the meantime . . ."

Nick Tresham himself seemed to become a little more reasonable.

"Cut out the rough stuff, Andy. At any rate, till we see where we are." He turned to Bathurst. "I have your name and your card, Mr. Bathurst. Even so, I am still mystified. You see, I don't know why you are here. Surely there must be a mistake somewhere?"

"I assure you that I share your mystification. Not, though, as to why I am here. My mystification concerns the manner of my reception now that I *am* here. 'Pon my soul, it's as warm-hearted as the Spanish Inquisition. Perhaps you would care to see my justification?"

Tresham looked completely puzzled as Anthony handed him the telegram. He unfolded it with uncertain fingers.

"I did not wire the time of my train to you," proceeded Mr. Bathurst, "as you suggested I might, because I came by road."

The explanation seemed to accomplish little or nothing. Nick Tresham read the words of the message, rubbed his chin in wonderment and beckoned across to a sullen Captain Forbes.

"Come here, Andy. Read that."

Forbes came across and took the flimsy piece of paper.

"Well?"

Forbes shook his head.

Tresham unbent. "Say what you like, Andy, we owe this gentleman a most handsome apology."

"That's of little consequence, as I see the affair. What's behind it all? That's what—"

Tresham silenced him with a wave of the hand. "Mr. Bathurst," he said courteously, "you must forgive me for what, in the circumstances, must have seemed abominable rudeness on my part. But, you see, you and I have been at cross-purposes all the time. Neither of us is really to blame. The explanation lies here. This telegram is a hoax."

He handed back the piece of paper.

Anthony frowned again. He expressed incredulity. "Do you mind if I sit down—while you explain matters?" He anticipated his host's permission and continued. "You were about to say—"

"I don't know that I'm in a position to explain," returned Tresham with less geniality. "All I can say to you, with any certainty, is that you've been hoaxed. That telegram's been faked. It's a dud. You've been brought down here by a trick."

The ghost of a smile played round Tresham's mouth. It found a fellow round the lips of Forbes.

"Do I take it, then," asked Anthony softly, seeing these smiles, "that you disclaim the authorship of this telegram that bears your name?"

"You've got it in one, my dear chap. You've been the victim of a practical joke. Neither more nor less. Rather a pity, now you come to think, that you didn't wire back here when you first received it. Then we should have been able to put you wise about it."

Tresham's smile developed into a soft laugh.

"All I can do then," declared Anthony, "is to await your observation on the matter."

Tresham stared. Anthony continued, still softly: "It has been sent from here, you know. Have another look at it for yourself. It's been sent from Tresham right enough."

"What's the point in that?" demanded Forbes aggressively.

Anthony shrugged expressive shoulders. "Well, just this. If Lord Tresham here didn't have it sent . . . and you didn't send it . . . or have it sent . . . who did? The field of selection is comparatively small, surely?"

"I guess I don't cut ice at double acrostics," returned Forbes, "for you, or for anybody. Get out of here while the going's good."

Anthony Bathurst rose. He drew himself to his full height. For now he saw his plan clearly in front of him.

"Captain Forbes," he said, "to certain ears, that might sound something like advice." His tone grew silkier. "At the same time, to my ears, it contains just the hint of a threat. I don't care for threats . . . never have done, particularly . . . and I don't happen to be delirious or dying . . . like Eddington."

There came a period of dead silence. Forbes broke it. He advanced to Anthony slowly, step by step. His face was distorted by passion. "And what the hell do you know about Eddington?"

Anthony was imperturbable. "Not a lot. Cambridge man, I believe. Luther. Died in a British C.C.S. somewhere near Gaza. Decent fellow, I've always been told—liked a tankard of good beer and had a nice kind face."

"And what has all that muck got to do with us?"

There was a contemptuous smile on the face of Forbes as he put the question.

It caused Mr. Bathurst some uneasiness.

"Be quiet, Andy, please. Let me deal with this gentleman."

Tresham's voice was quiet and restrained, but it held also, to an acute ear, the peculiar vibration of emotion.

"Shucks! You of all people know he's wasting his time, if anybody does," growled Forbes, turning away disgustedly.

The smile of contempt that had been on his face was transferred to Tresham's.

Anthony waited patiently for developments; he was not quite so sure of his ground as he had been. Had he missed anything? Tresham was speaking.

"I think that I'm out of my depth. What was your point in referring to this man Eddington? I confess that I am at a complete loss to understand you. I fail to see how he could have been a contemporary of yours."

Anthony hesitated before coming to the reply.

His eyes looked up . . . straight into those of the spiked lion. God . . . what was that? He caught his breath. Had he stumbled upon another secret of the Treshams? Almost immediately he realized that he was in terrible danger. The two men with him were watching him intently, he knew. Had they observed that he had seen and understood? Or did . . . Another second and he might be near betrayal of himself. He *must* achieve control and self-mastery; it was vitally imperative that he should get a thorough grip of himself. As the result of a stupendous effort he succeeded. Turning away from the lion's picture, he found careless words with which to answer Nicholas Tresham's last question.

"Captain Forbes, at least, seems to be no stranger to my friend Eddington. His face is a transparent index to the truth of what I say."

Anthony could almost hear the beating of his own heart.

Forbes came back and caught Tresham by the arm.

"He's talking through his hat, we know, but this bird knows too much." He turned on Anthony. "A little knowledge can be a most dangerous possession, Mr. Bathurst. And you'll soon know the truth of that."

His right hand went like lightning to his hip pocket. Despite his quickness, Anthony was quicker. They faced each other, each with the right hand hidden from sight. Anthony, though, was handicapped because he knew his double danger. One false step on his part, and disaster would be inevitable. Five seconds ticked by—taut, tense, and torturing. On the sixth, a well-known voice sounded behind him.

"We appear to be somewhat *de trop*, my dear Nicholas. Believe me, it arises from ignorance rather than from intention. It's my mother's fault, really, you know."

The voice was Sir Richard Ingle's, and he was companioned by Slingsby Raphael.

Anthony, of the thankful heart, seized the shining second.

"Don't apologize, Sir Richard. As a matter of fact, your arrival, if you only knew, couldn't have been more opportune. For I was on the point of departure, although not sure of my route. Good day, gentlemen all."

Mr. Bathurst made a comprehensive bow and strolled complacently from the room and towards his waiting car. What he had seen and heard had provided him with much food for thought.

Chapter XXVIII
INSIDE THE CASTLE (NIGHT)

It was approaching darkness when Anthony returned to Tresham Castle. He ran the car deliberately past the gates—having first hooted twice. At a convenient part of the road he turned, took the car under the dusky comfort of an overhanging hedge and alighted. Then he looked to the welfare of a revolver that he placed carefully in a side-pocket. There was little moon. Heavy dark clouds that raced up, one behind the other, flotilla of the sky, had almost obliterated it. There was rain in the wind already, and probably much more of it to come before morning broke.

Three times he looked at his watch. It was late. Somewhat later than he had intended it to be for what he desired to do. Suddenly he heard the hoot of another car. It seemed to come from inside the grounds. It was the signal for which Anthony had been waiting. Turning up the collar of his jacket, and pulling down the brim of his hat, he crept under the shadow of the hedge and strode onwards, until he reached the high wall of Tresham. This wall was not one to present insuperable difficulties to him. Lithe and lean, he scaled it, at the comparatively trivial expense of a barked shin, and found himself within the Tresham grounds.

It had already become much darker. Anthony could have hugged himself at the thought, for his luck was in. No conditions could have suited him and his purpose better. Comparative darkness . . . no moon . . . and rain to come. Taking his torch from his pocket, he flashed it once, twice, thrice . . . four times. To his intense pleasure his flashes were immediately answered. His way was clear now, and the disposition of his forces in accordance with his desires.

Again he looked at the illuminated dial of his watch. Not so bad after all. If his calculations were anything like correct, the coast should be moderately clear for, at the very least, another quarter of an hour yet.

With an almost uncanny certainty of direction, he came to a door that his quick eye had spotted during the afternoon. Anthony felt in the breast-pocket of his coat; the tool that he took from it had once been the property of a gentleman named "Flame" Lampard, who had figured prominently in an affair that has since been designated as the case of "The Triple Bite". It had formed part of Lampard's housebreaking kit, and inasmuch as the rightful owner would have no opportunity of using it for some years, Anthony was about to use it himself, for the first time.

Although unskilled in the use of the centre-bit and crowbar, he wielded Lampard's tool so effectively that the door he attacked quickly yielded him entrance. Mr. Bathurst's bump of locality was rather more than moderately useful, and, as he had anticipated, the door that he had forced opened on to a long corridor that ran, roughly, along the west wing of the castle. If he followed straight along it, he argued to himself, it must bring him to a more or less central situation.

Half a minute's rapid and noiseless travelling, past several closed doors, found him outside another door. From the interior of the room it guarded came the sound of many voices. The realization of this thought brought him two sensations: satisfaction, that his calculations had been accurate—and a knowledge that the position that he now occupied had a distinct tendency towards unhealthiness. Obviously, it would not do for him to remain where he was a second longer than was absolutely necessary. At any moment the room might be vacated. He must get to his destination without further delay. That fact was most certainly indicated.

Keeping close to the shadow of the wall, Anthony made more silent progress. Then, to his intense delight, the corridor took an unexpected turn, and he could see in front of him the pale purple walls of the apartment where he had been that afternoon with Lord Tresham and Captain Forbes. It was in darkness, save for the subdued glow of a standard lamp that stood almost at the foot of the staircase. What he had to do now had to be done quickly.

Crossing at once to the picture of the spiked lion, and feeling inordinately grateful for the state of comparative darkness that the room enjoyed, he looked up at the lion intently. What he saw there evidently pleased him. He gave a quick nod that seemed to express assent, made what appeared to be a mental measurement, turned and began to tiptoe up the staircase. In doubt for a second or so as to whether to put out the light that came from the lamp, he decided to leave things as they were. The soft light, he considered, would help him. That was positive. And it might not hinder him from any other point of view. Once or twice he stopped on the staircase and listened. There was no sound yet of returning voices.

When he came to the eleventh stair of ascent he stopped, and his head showed over the banister. Quickly withdrawing it, he used his torch on the surface of the stair. He could see nothing. There wasn't the slightest indication that the stair was anything but normal. Ah well—to-morrow was also a day—and there was a twelfth stair ready for examination. He used the torch again, flashing it on the stair and also on the side of the staircase itself. Nothing! Not a mark on the wood anywhere, of any kind. Anthony grew impatient—matters were becoming desperate. Surely he hadn't been deceived by the picture of the spiked lion? He cudgelled his brains. The place *must* be here or hereabouts. The entrance would be nowhere else . . . there *was* nowhere else where it could be.

He turned a little and assessed again the distance that he had travelled up the staircase. He counted the stairs for the second time. Eight . . . nine . . . ten . . . eleven . . . twelve. Thirteen? That was an idea certainly . . . the appropriate stair for sinister happenings . . . another gruesome jest at the expense of Iscariot. He knelt on the twelfth stair and flashed the torch on the thirteenth. Nothing again! At that sickening moment he heard a door open somewhere in the near distance—a distance too near to be pleasant—and the murmur of voices in conversation. The voices came nearer . . . the murmur grew louder . . . more distinct. He could even hear some of the things that were being said. If he were to move, he must move immediately. A thought came to him. What about the side of the staircase, hard by the thirteenth stair? Merciful heaven! He had been right, after all. There was a protuberance in the wood . . . something in the nature of a knot or raised stud. To use it was a dreadful risk, he knew perfectly well, but there are times in life when one must take one's risks . . . and Anthony took one now. Maybe he was forced to . . . to stay on the stairs where he was would be to court instant and certain discovery and possible disaster.

He pressed the raised stud, hard, with his right-hand thumb. A panel slid open in front of him easily and smoothly. . . . There was a cavity . . . large enough to admit a man's body. He extinguished his torch and wriggled through the opening. The panel swung to again at the insistence of his hand.

In the nick of time. He breathed freely again. Moreover, he knew exactly where he was. Although in the dark, he determined not to use the torch . . . he was uncertain as to the effect that the light might have. He soon came to the conclusion that there was ample room in the cavity for two men. He wondered how long the hiding-place had been there. Had it been originally a priest's hole, or had it been constructed during more recent years? The picture of the spiked lion had been let into the wall at the side of the staircase. He was immediately behind the spiked lion, he knew.

He held up a hand and felt in front of him . . . with the utmost care and vigilance. Then, after a moment's consideration, he went on his knees . . . still feeling above him. He pressed his eyes . . . ever so gently . . . against the back of the picture. Suddenly his heart almost stood still with excitement. There were two "somethings" against his eyes that were not so smooth as the rest of the surface. Bringing up his hands, slowly and carefully, he caressed these parts with the daintiest of touches. Cajoled them, as it were, with the intimacy of finger-contact . . . this way . . . that way . . . coaxingly . . . up . . . down. A certain movement of his fingers . . . it is doubtful whether he can remember it with exactitude . . . and he felt those two roughnesses give way, and *move*. Simultaneously, he placed his eyes in the exact places where his fingertips had been and looked down into the, apartment below him . . . the room of the pale purple walls.

He could see distinctly. There were four people there. Four men. The men whom he expected to see there. No more and no less. Tresham himself, Captain Andrew Forbes, Slingsby Raphael and Sir Richard Ingle. A door opened and a man entered carrying a tray.

"Coffee," said Anthony to himself—strangely elated . . . "coffee in the lounge after dinner. I timed my arrival beautifully—a triumph of psychology."

"Black or white, sir," he whispered to himself . . . "of course you're saying it, old scout . . . I can almost see your lips moving . . . all the same, I wish I were wearing knee-pads. This floor's cursed hard."

Then another idea came to him. Was it probable that this hiding-place would have been constructed and used for the purpose of espionage only? Surely such an ingenious weapon—considering the times through which it had passed—would be turned to offence as well as defence? If that were so—and he felt certain that he was right—there would be another indication somewhere. His attention, however, was arrested by a movement on the part of Raphael. How he watched the man who called himself Tresham! Anthony could see Raphael's eyes . . . cat watching mouse business. Ingle was speaking.

"Well . . . that's the position, Nick. You can take it or leave it, of course. It's entirely a matter for you and nobody else. But you've been top dog for some weeks now, so you mustn't grudge me the chance of getting my own back a bit. I take it we're both sportsmen. Good losers—what?"

Tresham laughed in response. A low laugh that didn't sound exactly pleasant. "Your mater was smart over that, Dick. Damned smart. That particular piece of land, especially; any other piece would scarcely have mattered two hoots."

"You forget something, Nick . . . surely?"

"What's that?"

"The mater was a Tresham . . . they're all more or less cunning. At any rate they've always a thunderin' good idea as to which side their bread's buttered on."

Raphael extended a hand. "Now . . . now. Let me fly to the Tresham defence—inadequate though the assistance may seem to be. I know more of them and more about them than you might reasonably think. Efficiency and business ability are often miscalled by harder and uglier names . . . especially by those who don't possess the qualities. Lack of qualities breeds jealousy. Jealousy breeds envy. Envy breeds hatred and malice. I don't mean that Dick here is like that for a moment . . . but sour grapes not only put teeth on edge, but are responsible for a great deal of evil thinking, lying and slandering."

Ingle laughed good-humouredly, and put his coffee-cup on a low stool. "Ah well—talking won't alter matters. Nick's heard my offer and it's up to him now. I can assure him that I shan't come down as much as a fiver. We ought to be going, Raphael."

"I agree with you. We ought."

Tresham made a signal to the manservant. The man understood and left the apartment. "I'm having your car brought round here, Dick," said Tresham; "that'll save you a couple of minutes."

It was at that moment that Anthony's hair almost stood on end and his fingers curled round his revolver. There was a soft step on the stair outside his hiding-place . . . descending . . . not ascending. Instantaneously he knew its meaning. It was the contingency that he had feared . . . that he knew might happen . . . that he had deliberately risked happening!

Motionless, he held his breath. The step stopped on a stair just outside the concealed panel. He heard an excessively quiet, low cough. There was no time now for fresh plans to be made . . . conflict now was inevitable. He braced himself for the shock of clash . . . and breathed again . . . for the steps went away . . . upstairs this time.

Anthony now was on the sharp horns of an acute dilemma. Should he stay where he was or quit instantly? If the latter— where to? Once again his luck held. Sir Richard Ingle and

Raphael were on the very point of departure; to Anthony's intense delight, when they went, Tresham and Captain Forbes, speeding the parting guests, followed them out of the room.

He got up from his knees, adjusted the two openings behind the picture of the lion and slipped quickly from his hiding-place. Once again, there was no time for him to weigh decisions. Of easy access from the room that the four men had just left there was an ante-room. It had originally formed part of the Tresham tapestried chamber and there was a tradition that the sixth Henry had once slept within it. It was on the opposite side of the apartment to that room which had been used by the manservant to bring in the coffee, and on that account nearer to the staircase upon which Anthony was crouching. There was this one doubt, however—Would the door of it be open?

He made a quick, almost silent, dash down the stairs and towards it . . . grasped the handle of the door . . . thank God the door was open! Mr. Bathurst slipped inside the room . . . just as Lord Tresham and Captain Forbes returned. With the door kept just ajar . . . he could both see them and hear them.

CHAPTER XXIX
THE SHOT FROM NOWHERE

"That Ingle's a confounded old bore," growled Forbes, as he seated himself. "Waggles a wonderful jawbone. 'Pon my soul, I thought the blighter was never going. Raphael would have cleared out ages ago if it hadn't been for him." He paused, seemingly uneasy. "Don't forget, old man, that you and I have something to discuss before we toddle up to Uncle Ned."

Tresham remained cool and nonchalant. "Which is . . . ?"

"Oh—don't fence, you old devil! Summerhayes put it pretty plainly to you, didn't he? I don't think that I can put it any more plainly."

"You know how I dealt with Summerhayes, don't you, Andy? If I'm forced to do it again, believe me—"

Forbes interrupted him with an ugly laugh. "You'll try the same game on with me—eh? That's what you mean, isn't it?" He shrugged his shoulders. "Ah—well—threats won't frighten me. You'll have to put up something more convincing than threats, Stephen. Beg pardon, *Nick*."

Tresham flicked the ash from his cigarette. His hand was as steady as a rock. Forbes noticed this and extracted no comfort therefrom. Anthony, behind the door, watched and listened eagerly. So there was a Stephen in the cast now?

"That's better," returned Tresham; "don't call me that—I'm not sure that I oughtn't to insist on your calling me 'your lordship'."

"Oh—come off the high horse, do! You give me a pain in the neck."

Despite the bravado, there was an anxious note in Forbes' tone, although he did his best to conceal it. Tresham leant over to his companion and spoke calmly and deliberately.

"Do you remember what I told Summerhayes before the—er—end of our interview? I made myself perfectly clear to him, didn't I? Was it my fault what happened afterwards? He thought he knew a few things that would frighten me. Thought he'd feather his nest very comfortably. My dear Forbes, if I wasn't afraid of tackling the worthy doctor, I'm certainly not afraid of you, or anything that you may threaten to do."

"Not *threaten* to do. Do."

"Pooh—who would believe your cock-and-bull story when you had told it? Besides—Lomax is satisfied and Dick Ingle, my excellent cousin, is satisfied. My dear fellow, you're properly in the dirt. Be careful I don't push you in any further."

Forbes looked more ugly than ever. "There's one person though, who isn't satisfied. Don't forget that. Perhaps you're not quite so safe as you imagine you are."

"Oh—and who's this one person, may I ask, on whom you set such a store?"

"The man who was here this afternoon . . . Anthony Bathurst."

Tresham laughed contemptuously. "Now tell me the one about the three bears. I fear him, my dear Forbes, as I fear you . . . and as I feared Summerhayes. That is to say—not at all."

Anthony smiled at the words, and as he did so something right away from the two men whom he watched caught his eye. What he saw set all his nerves tingling . . . the spiked lion was in action again!

Forbes moved uneasily. "I'm not in mourning over the departure of Summerhayes. Far from it. I'm ready to admit the fact. Besides, 'two' gives a better dividend than 'three'. That's how I've learnt to look at things."

Tresham looked at him—straight between the eyes. "Get that idea out of your head, Forbes, once and for all. Right now! As far as you're concerned . . . there's going to be no dividend. Or, in the words of the inimitable and immortal Phil May, 'there ain't goin' to be no core'. I'm Lord Tresham of Tresham in the county of Hants . . . and you . . . well, we'll call you a soldier of fortune who's backed a favourite that's come unstuck. I know some people who'd call you something else . . . something much worse if you'd care to know." Tresham stuck out an uncompromising jaw.

Forbes chewed his underlip. Here was plain speaking indeed. He decided to adopt different methods. "Lord Tresham—eh? That's the line you're going to take? Don't you forget something?"

"What's that?"

"Blundell and Wingfield . . . and young Guest."

"No—I don't think so. There again, it would be just your story against mine. Also, you couldn't attempt to incriminate me without putting a very pretty noose round what is, after all, a distinctly ugly neck."

He laughed again, almost challengingly. "No—take my advice—leave Tresham to me—and retain for yourself a pleasant reminiscence of what has been a most agreeable adventure. And adventure, my dear Forbes, as we agreed long years ago, is the spice of life. Be content with the struggle—for the struggle's sake. Leave the spoils to a better man than yourself. After all, the real opportunity might never have come at all. Think of that. As it was, you had to wait—"

"Fifteen years," cried Forbes bitterly; "but, my God, we waited for them together! Don't you forget that, you dirty double-crosser."

"You speak as though you were all that mattered," returned Tresham. "Don't be so damned ridiculous. You're like a child crying for what he can't have. Who knocks the chessboard to pieces because he is losing the game. My father—beg pardon, the late Lord Tresham—might have lived to be eighty, instead of seventy. Much comfort that would have brought you. Captain Andrew Forbes—faithful unto death! What a charming picture you'd make! God, Forbes, you're better at poker than patience!"

Something seemed to snap and Forbes realized with sharp bitterness that Tresham had brought him to the very edge of things. "That's your last word, then?" he said, white-faced and trembling.

"Oh—I wouldn't go so far as to say that. It might be an exaggeration. Besides, I rather pride myself on my elocution. And 'last' sounds so dreadfully and definitely final. But if you mean am I going to—"

Tresham rose, took another cigarette from the silver box on the table, and stood at his full height to light it. As the hungry flame of the match caught the tobacco, there came the sharp crack of a revolver. Tresham crumpled helplessly and slid heavily to the floor. His hands plucked hopelessly at his chest ... and the red blood began to stain and shame the white of his shirt. The spiked lion was about to claim another Tresham!

Chapter XXX
THE ARREST

Forbes stared at his companion with amazement. He looked round the room, trying to discover who had fired the shot.

"The staircase," he muttered to himself, looking behind him, "that was the direction it came from."

He gazed at the stairs fearfully. Then his better nature asserted itself and he went to the fallen Tresham.

Kneeling by his side, he attempted to staunch the flow of blood from the wound with his handkerchief.

Before Anthony could come to help him, however, Mr. Bathurst had another duty to perform. He went to the window of the tapestried chamber, pushed it open, and flashed his torch across the dark space that lay beyond. Receiving his appropriate answer, he flung open the ante-room door. The picture of the spiked lion told him what he wanted to know.

By this time Tresham's manservant had also arrived upon the scene. Forbes was peremptory. "A doctor, quick, man! Go and 'phone the nearest you know of. There's been an accident to your master."

The man, inarticulate, understood the order and ran quickly from the room. Anthony advanced to the dying man. "Can I be of any assistance?"

Neither man seemed surprised to see him. Tresham shook his head with a faint smile . . . game to the last.

"I'm finished, Bathurst." The words came with difficulty. "But I'd give a hell of a lot to know the name of the swine who got me." The blood welled to his lips as Forbes turned accusingly to Anthony. Tresham shook his head again . . . more slowly this time.

"No, you're wrong, Andy! Wrong as usual. No sense of judgment. Your old trouble. Bathurst isn't that kind. Can't you see that, you damned old fool? It's from the lion—" Again words refused to come.

Forbes seemed bewildered. "The lion? Then who—"

Anthony looked straight at the questioning Forbes, and put a finger to his lips. "Wait," he whispered, "if you want to see the end."

He had hardly spoken, when three people entered. The manservant, whom Forbes had sent out for help, the gardener, whom Anthony had met when first he had entered the grounds of Tresham, and Chief-Inspector MacMorran.

Forbes, from his kneeling position, looked up at the new arrivals with undisguised disapproval. Before he could speak, however, the servant stepped forward.

"I have 'phoned for Doctor Emerson, sir. He's the nearest doctor to here. I told him as much as I could of what had happened. He will be here as quickly as he can."

"Thank you, Gibson. That will do for now. You can go."

"Who are these people?" continued Forbes to Anthony; "why are they here? Can't a man die—"

The dying man rallied a little. "They've come to honour a dying Tresham. Let them be, Forbes. Why should I die alone ... like a commoner?" His courage forced a smile on to his lips.

Anthony caught MacMorran's eye. An almost imperceptible nod passed between them. Quietly and unobtrusively, the inspector moved to the foot of the staircase. Convulsive coughs, each bringing blood, began to come from the figure propped against Forbes' knee. Anthony dropped on his knee to help. Forbes was on the point of pursuing his previous question when Gibson's voice was heard again—a short distance off.

"This way, Doctor, please."

Dr. Emerson entered ... almost as the dying man's head dropped on to his chest. Emerson was quick and efficient. He went to the dying man ... ministered to him. Then he looked at the others and shook his head slowly.

"No hope. I can do nothing. A few minutes ... only ... gentlemen. He cannot possibly last longer than that. Shot through the lungs."

The end came almost as he finished speaking. Anthony covered the dead man's face. "Your brother is only partly avenged, Miss Wingfield," he said, turning to the tall gardener and speaking with stern resolution, "but that knowledge should give you a certain satisfaction. Also, you will oblige me if you will come and stand at the foot of this staircase. I can't take any more chances, you know."

Diana Wingfield looked at him—testing his worth as it were. ... Their eyes met and challenged ... and then she slowly obeyed him.

MacMorran, after dismissing Gibson and the doctor, came forward and stood by her side. Anthony whispered words in his ear. Forbes watched the proceedings with amazement.

"It will have to be one on each side, you see," said Mr. Bathurst softly, "that gives us a tremendous advantage."

"We may want it," he added grimly. He and the inspector crept up the staircase. There was scarcely a sound as they ascended.

When the two men reached the twelfth stair, Anthony motioned to MacMorran to go higher. The inspector went to the fourteenth stair, lay at full length at the side of the sliding panel and drew a revolver. Anthony, also lying at full length, his left elbow leaning on the twelfth stair, his left hand holding a levelled revolver, reached forward, and with the fingers of his right hand felt for the wooden stud in the staircase side that worked the panel of the spiked lion.

He found the raised knob, and for the second time that night pressed it hard with his thumb. The panel slid open, as smoothly and easily as on the previous occasion. For the space of about five seconds there was an almost indescribable silence, tense and nerve-shattering. The watchers below could have cried out in the emotion of suspense. Then there came a slight movement from inside the cavity. The figure that had lurked within moved forward a little towards the opening . . . startled . . . wondering . . . apprehensive.

Suddenly—one from each side—and without a word being spoken, Anthony Bathurst and Inspector MacMorran flung themselves upon the crouching form. There was a short, sharp scuffle. But the odds of two to one, added to the element of surprise, were too great for the man who had hidden behind the panel. He rolled over on the stairs, Bathurst and MacMorran on top of him . . . pressing his shoulders down . . . his hands powerless to use the revolver that he had drawn on the dead man in the room below.

THE SPIKED LION

A sudden jerk of Anthony's elbow shot the weapon flying from the murderer's hand. "Quick, Inspector," cried Anthony, "now's your chance!"

MacMorran planted a skilfully wielded kneecap under the man's chin that knocked him half senseless, and, with Anthony's help, snapped the handcuffs on his wrists.

"There you are, MacMorran," said Anthony, "there's your man . . . murderer of John Blundell, Professor Wingfield, and Hugh Guest. Doctor Arnold Summerhayes, late of Lashey, in the Isle of Wight. Bring him downstairs, will you?"

MacMorran prodded his prisoner in the back. The three men came downstairs, the prisoner between the other two, sullen and defiant. They advanced into the middle of the room. Captain Forbes, dazed and wondering, wondered still more when MacMorran stepped forward quickly and handcuffed him also. The inspector's words of arrest, however, brought him to his senses and he understood . . . only too well.

"You can also, Inspector," said Mr. Bathurst, "add to your charge against the first prisoner the wilful murder of Nicholas, Lord Tresham."

Summerhayes turned to the speaker, hatred burning in his eyes. "Then that's where you slip up, Mr. Smart Alec. The dirty double-crosser that lies in front of us there was no more Lord Tresham than I am. And he got no more than rough justice when he got what I gave him. So you can cut that charge out. If you want to know his real name, it was Stephen King. Tresham died years ago in a British C.C.S. out East . . . a Turkish shell had got his number on it. One of England's bloody heroes—I don't think."

His voice was hoarse and seethed with menace. MacMorran was reminded of Blundell's creased piece of paper . . . "The crackling voice".

But Anthony was speaking . . . replying to the murderer. "And that's where you slip up, my dear Doctor. Singularly enough, it was Eddington who died from that Turkish shell and not Nicholas Tresham. He was in the next bed answering to the name of Stephen King. And it's taken all these years for you to find that out. Rather a bad break for both you and Captain Forbes, right from the beginning—what? Ah, well—the way of transgressors is hard—even though blood may be thicker than water."

He motioned to MacMorran and turned to Diana Wingfield. "My car's outside, Miss Wingfield. The Inspector will see to these people. Will you please come along? And there's one other thing I should like to say to you . . . can I ever thank you enough?"

Chapter XXXI
MR. BATHURST AND RECONSTRUCTION

"The most remarkable case," said Anthony, "that I have ever been called upon to handle. I can assert that, I think, without the slightest fear of contradiction. Help yourself, sir. And you, Sir Austin. What about you, MacMorran—isn't your glass empty yet?"

Lord Tresham, *né* Ingle, took advantage of the invitation. Anthony pushed the tantalus towards him. The new Tresham filled his glass and then pushed the whisky over to the inspector.

"Goes back twenty-seven years, you say?" said Sir Austin.

"The Scotch? Oh, you mean the case? Yes. To the University of Cambridge. I don't think, though, that I need start from there. I think I'll lead off from the death of Philip Eddington near Gaza. The Eddington—don't forget—who had tattooed the three men at Cambridge and who for many years had been Nick Tresham's inseparable companion. The man about whom you had told me—although you didn't know his name." This last remark to Lord Tresham.

"They had gone abroad together, and when war broke out in 1914 had left Morocco, where they were, to join up, Eddington under his own name, Tresham in an assumed name—King. The shell which first wounded and eventually killed Eddington had wounded Tresham also; not badly, I imagine, but a little— shall we say?—facially. Eddington, besides being wounded in the face, had lost his arm and his left leg. Don't forget that I'm conjecturing, a lot . . . a lot, too, that we shall probably never know. Anyhow—"

"Just a moment," intervened Tresham; "how did you find out—"

"All in good time, sir, if you don't mind. I'll tell the bare story first and then follow up with the details of my investigation and deductions." He smiled. "That suit you?"

"I'm sorry. I understand. Please go on."

"I am certain that Eddington and Nicholas were casualties together—probably in the next bed to each other. One was dying; the other had, I think, a wounded forehead. I'll tell you why I think that a little later on. Near them—in the next bed to Eddington—was another wounded man: Captain Andrew Forbes, D.F.C. And the medical attendant on these three wounded gentlemen was a certain Doctor Arnold Summerhayes. There's little doubt about any of these last statements. Before he died Eddington became delirious. Forbes, the doctor, and Tresham (alias King) heard his delirium. By a strange freak, his mind, I should say, was reacting all the time to his associations with Tresham, Blundell, and Wingfield. The tattooing of the three men that he had done all those years before, 'blood's thicker than water', the marks behind the left knee, the flight from England with Tresham, the counters that Nicholas had stolen from his father . . . Tresham . . . Tresham . . . Tresham Castle . . . the spiked lion . . . all that he had learned from Nick concerning Tresham . . . its heritage . . . and its heir . . . the next in succession . . . his many years' absence from Tresham.

"Summerhayes, a wrong 'un right through and always on the look-out for the main chance, listened avariciously . . . so did Forbes . . . and Nick Tresham himself, hidden under the identity of Stephen King, saw them, overheard them talking when they probably thought he was asleep . . . *and realized in a flash of intuition what they were thinking* . . . that Eddington was none other than the heir to the Treshams. Eddington died, with Forbes and Summerhayes still hugging the idea . . . and its possibilities! Tresham, ever ready for new sensations and adventures, attached himself to them and fanned the flames of their fancy. Corroborated what they were thinking... confirmed the idea with which they were coquetting. Told them that they had got hold of Eddington's secret—previously only *he* had known. Told them—a master-stroke this—of certain things that Eddington had left behind... in *his* care. Produced them... the mother-of-pearl counters, Tresham's birth certificate... other documents that he naturally possessed. Described the peculiar eyebrows (and their history) that he said Eddington had had before he was wounded."

"One minute, Bathurst, please. Surely you've forgotten something there." Sir Austin had interrupted. "Tresham, or King as he then called himself, had the eyebrows himself! Couldn't the two men see—"

Anthony smiled. "That was my reason, sir, for saying that I thought Tresham had been wounded in the forehead. Because of the wounds the feature that you mention was not plainly apparent."

"I see. Proceed, please."

"Well, the plot was hatched... just in embryo, one might say, for Lord Tresham was still alive... might live years... and did—Nick Tresham, the cool and callous devil that he was, laughing at his fellow conspirators all the time. For it suited his book splendidly. At least, that's how I explain what happened. Details began to be discussed. Nick himself, by reason of his height—Eddington was tall—and by reason, too, of his intimate knowledge of Eddington from many years of companionship, was chosen as the substitute. They three alone knew that the Tresham heir had been gathered to his fathers! When the time came they would profit hugely. But there were difficulties, and here, I think, was where the plot suited the book of Nick Tresham."

Anthony paused to light a cigarette. His three hearers were hanging on his words.

"The main difficulties, as I see them, lay in the marks of the tattooer. Eddington's delirium had told them that Blundell, Wingfield, and Tresham had been marked behind the left knee. But how marked? They didn't know. Eddington's leg had been blown to pieces. Tresham knew that fact all right. They dared not risk an heir minus these tell-tale signs, because their existence might be known to many. Summerhayes and Forbes discussed it together time and again. However, there was no hurry, they had years for the maturing of the plan, and the matter was probably left over, I should say, by agreement, until the old Lord Tresham began to ail. This news leaked through to them and then the vultures gathered. The details of the scheme were discussed with greater care. I will sketch them for you as I imagine they were arranged . . . and first of all, I will come to the suiting of Nick Tresham's book, as I called it just now."

"I'm blessed if I follow you," said Richard, Lord Tresham.

"I'll endeavour to make myself as clear as possible, then. Summerhayes, I feel sure, was the mastermind of the conspiracy. Nick Tresham, of course, held a more or less watching brief. He could afford to, with a sleeveful of laughs. Summerhayes played his first card. Blundell and Wingfield must be got hold of in some way, and then, when they had yielded the vital information that they carried on their bodies . . . must be removed. This scheme had Nick's entire approval. I can well imagine that he rubbed his hands when he first heard the plan broached."

Anthony turned to Tresham. "Perhaps you can help me here, sir. Was there any scandal at all, do you know, when Nick Tresham was at Cambridge? Any, I mean, in which he *might* have been implicated rather seriously?"

The new Lord Tresham rubbed his chin contemplatively. He repeated Anthony's words. "In which he might have been implicated rather seriously? That's asking me a good deal, isn't it? But I can tell you this. A man hanged himself in his rooms after a card-party in Nick Tresham's rooms—but it was a clear case of suicide as far as I can remember. At the time there was no doubt as to the verdict. As far as I know, no real suspicion ever attached itself to Nick. That's the only affair that I can think of."

Anthony was all interest immediately. "Were Blundell and Wingfield at the card-party in question?"

"I couldn't answer that, after all this lapse of time, but I should say it's highly probable. Where Tresham was, they were—usually. *'Les Trois Mousquetaires'*, you know."

Anthony nodded. "I see. Well, I'm aware that I'm drawing a bow at a venture, but I'm going to suggest that in that story we have the real reason why Tresham left the country with Eddington. That Blundell and Wingfield knew the truth of this so-called suicide . . . that it was much more like murder. So that when Nick Tresham heard the first plans being mooted for the deletion of these two men—a removal, also, which would give him his real and rightful inheritance—he had no objection whatever to offer. On the contrary, however, he found the idea vastly refreshing. It removed from his path two men who knew too much. They had kept silence for years, it is true—bargained with him, perhaps, the price of the bargain being his flight abroad—but circumstances alter cases and it would be distinctly more comfortable for him to avoid all risk of their talking tongues."

Anthony lifted his glass to his lips.

"Well, we've reached what may be termed the turning point in the scheme. The news has reached the three conspirators that the old lord has but a few months to live. They commence to assemble the flats and set the stage. Summerhayes settles down in a practice near Lashey, so that he may be as close to Sir Richard Ingle, here, as possible."

Anthony turned to Sir Richard. "You were the heir, you see, with Nick Tresham out of the way, so it would be as well to be in a position to watch you, if necessary. Many a vital point might be picked up in this way. Tresham and Forbes took up residence with the doctor. Blundell and Wingfield then became their next problem. How to get hold of them? The old man was dying . . . the substitute heir, as Summerhayes and Forbes thought, must be equipped . . . must be made *ready* to be produced . . . for the time of his being wanted might arrive now at any moment. There was little time that could be safely cut to waste. Now Nick Tresham, of course, knew Blundell and Wingfield pretty well. Knew their habits. Knew their foibles. Knew their inclinations. Each of them had a definite, and, if I may use the word, *peculiar*, avenue of approach. Blundell was a recognized authority on ciphers and cryptograms. Wingfield was just as famous for his knowledge of legendary inscriptions and his intimate touch with heraldry. They decided to attempt to trap these two men by dangling their own special baits in front of them. Cunningly worded correspondence, I would confidently assert, was prepared and sent to Blundell and Wingfield, containing much that influenced their curiosity, much that was furtive and secretive. The plot worked almost magically . . . it developed. . . . The mother-of-pearl counters with the spiked lion became *special* bait, and both Wingfield and Blundell, caught and held on the spurs of their all-absorbing hobbies, and pledged to the utmost secrecy, left Hurrilow in Wiltshire and Hurstfold in Sussex for the house of Doctor Summerhayes in the Isle of Wight. It is comparatively easy to guess what happened when they arrived there. Nick Tresham, naturally, was kept in the background. Neither of them ever set eyes on him. For a time the pretence of the enquiries was kept up—information was sought from them . . . their respective reputations were flattered to the full. When all the information necessary was obtained, the gloves came off, and Wingfield and Blundell were removed by the agency of Summerhayes's special apparatus. The same one, no doubt, that Inspector MacMorran found in his case the day after he was arrested. By the way, you must get MacMorran to show it to you, Lord Tresham. An ingenious affair, with a mechanism, as I anticipated, after the manner of a scent-spray."

Anthony Bathurst resumed the thread of the main explanation.

"The bodies of the murdered men were disposed of by Captain Forbes, the distinguished aviator. They were taken from the house of Summerhayes. . . . One was dropped in Bushey Park and the other near Sidmouth, in Devonshire. Each under cover of darkness. The greater the distance between them, the more perplexing the case became from the standpoint of police investigation. The two men had served their primary purpose and delivered up their message . . . 'blood's thicker than water'. But there came, at this juncture, an entirely unexpected development. I refer to the entrance into the tragic arena of Hugh Guest."

Sir Austin interposed with a question. "Are you conjecturing here, Bathurst, or speaking from knowledge?"

"Well, it's conjecture, really, Sir Austin, but it's so absolutely certain that the conjecture becomes almost as good as actual knowledge. I have interviewed Celia Guest, his sister, remember. Hugh Guest was Blundell's nephew, and when his uncle disappeared he was sent for, and, not content with enlisting the services of the 'Yard'—started 'sleuthing' on his own account. He found a letter, in his uncle's library—between the leaves of a book, shall we say? . . . or stuffed away somewhere. This letter puzzled him. It was from Summerhayes . . . it had the man's address . . . and although the terms of it may have appeared innocent enough superficially, Guest determined to follow it up. The locality was convenient. The address was close to the house of his father's old friend—he could stay at Beech Knoll and have every convenience to pursue the affair. But he made two grave mistakes. He communicated with this Summerhayes, of Lashey, and also kept his own counsel in regard to the details of what he was doing. Summerhayes immediately scented danger. He made an appointment with Guest. Asked him, I should say, to bring Blundell's letter with him. It was all done most cleverly and most cunningly, no doubt. The doctor kept this appointment that they had made in an unusual locality . . . in Guest's bedroom at Beech Knoll! He entered by a trick of audacity, the details of which we shall never know; and when he had recovered his letter—the letter that incriminated him and his associates—Hugh Guest travelled the same journey that two men had travelled before him, and joined John Blundell and Professor Wingfield."

Chapter XXXII
THE SCIENCE OF DEDUCTION

Anthony turned to his circle of listeners with a smile of whimsicality. "That's the point from which I began to make progress, gentlemen. I was faced with a problem that suggested in its main features one of my earliest cases. I refer to the case of the singular hiding-place of the famous black pearls of Lorraine. It has been handed down by my commentator under the title of the *Black Twenty-Two*. In that case, there was a piece of evidence that was deliberately *imposed* by the murderer upon the minds of two other people. These two people were prepared to swear quite honestly that, upon their entrance to a room, a certain pair of french doors was shut, whereas the doors were open, and were shut *after* their arrival.

"In the case of the death of Hugh Guest, we were up against a missing key; that turned out afterwards to be on the body of the dead man, who couldn't, by any reasonable stretch of imagination, have committed suicide. Apart from the possible existence of a duplicate key, how had the murderer got away from this room with a locked door if Guest retained the key in his pocket? Escape in any other direction than the door was impossible, unthinkable. I immediately, therefore, asked myself the question: *Had the murderer brought the key back with him and placed it in the dead man's pocket?* I thus had my first circle of suspicion in front of me already. Raphael, Covington, Doctor Summerhayes, and, if you will pardon me, sir, you, Lord Tresham—as Sir Richard Ingle. But Barry Covington I decided to eliminate as soon as I had time to consider the evidence with any care."

"Why?" flashed the Commissioner. "You asked MacMorran—"

"I'll tell you why, sir. Because of the two stories that he told me about his knocking on Guest's bedroom door. One amounted to an almost flat contradiction of the other. You pointed that fact out to me yourself, sir, if you remember."

"I do," returned Sir Austin. "It struck me as highly suspicious."

"I know it did. You told me so. But, after consideration, I decided that it pointed in the opposite direction. I argued that no guilty man would have made such an appalling mistake. Surely the first thing he would have done would have been to have his story 'pat'? Covington first stated that when he went upstairs to the bedroom he didn't call to Guest; then he said that he *had* called. It was simply an instance of the frailty of memory in a time of stress. At any rate, influenced by something else, I ruled him out of my guilty circle for the time being, and subsequent events proved that I was right.

"The 'something else' was this. I was convinced that Guest had gone to the island to be 'on the spot'. No—not in the Chicago sense. But he *didn't know that Covington was at Beech Knoll*. I learned that by enquiry. So Covington could hardly have been his quarry. I was left with Sir Richard Ingle (as he was then), Raphael, who lived close at hand, and Doctor Summerhayes. My 'four', you see, had begun to look much more like 'three'. I determined to let the question of motive slide for a time and have a second look at our medical friend. I was intrigued by what I found when I called upon him. Not only was he packing up, but he even attempted to frighten me in terms of 'knowledge'—he was aware of the spiked lion—the first reference to which we had found on the fragment of creased paper in Blundell's pocket. What I learned from Summerhayes on this occasion, added to what he had previously told me, set me definitely on the track. The little thing again, Sir Austin, the tiny thread that means so much. He had admitted upon being questioned that the missing key had been in Guest's *left hand* breast pocket."

Anthony looked up quizzically. "Anything significant strike any of you in regard to that?"

No reply came. The three listeners were silent. Mr. Bathurst went on.

"The left-hand side, gentlemen, is the 'heart' side. I told myself that it would have been the easiest thing in the world for a doctor, key in hand, to have made the pretence of examining the dead man's heart *(one of the first things a doctor would do)*, and to drop the key at the same time in the breast-pocket."

"Excellent, Mr. Bathurst," contributed MacMorran. "I take my hat off to you for that."

"Thanks, Inspector." He grinned. "It's nice to know that somebody appreciates me. I shall begin to believe next that everybody's loved by someone, a fragment of philosophy that I've denied for years. Well, there I am, having a good look at friend Summerhayes, and beginning to have a better look at 'motive'. Don't forget, too, that being called in when Guest was dead gave Summerhayes the chance of establishing a false alibi. He was able to fix the time of death.

The inquiries that I had made concerning Raphael and Covington brought me nothing to cause me to alter my opinion. It was pretty obvious to me now that we touched the Tresham succession. We had the reappearance of Nick Tresham at a propitious moment. He had been unheard of for years, and I found out that this spiked lion was a part of the Tresham coat-of-arms. So it was the Tresham succession they were after, right enough; that fact was, by now, plainly indicated. Also, I was intrigued by the proximity of Captain Forbes—an aviator. For I had long ago deduced an aeroplane. Blundell's body had fallen through a tree and his face had been scratched by a broken branch. So I bracketed Forbes with Summerhayes and the pairing pleased me.

"But why had they gone for Blundell and Wingfield? Where did they come in? For a long time I laboured to no purpose, and wasted an appalling amount of time. Hammered at the attractive. . . . ciphers and heraldic inscriptions . . . and missed the simple and unostentatious . . . just the plain fact that Blundell, Wingfield, and Tresham were the same age and had been at Cambridge together. Not something *particular* or *peculiar* about each individual, you see, *but, on the direct contrary, something they had in common.* Well, you know how I cottoned on to it. The exhumations and what they told us. That this Tresham claimant had to be 'prepared', so that, if challenged, he could substantiate his claim. At the same time, I couldn't forget that both Lomax, the solicitor, and Sir Richard here, were absolutely satisfied with him. I resolved to take a long shot. When the conspirators discovered what the marks were that Blundell and Wingfield carried, the claimant would have to obtain them too; his leg would need decoration. The chances were, I argued, that they would have to be produced properly by a skilled tattoo artist, so I got into touch with the four most likely people in London and made enquiries. And let me tell you this: in that connection I'm rather proud of this investigation. An appointment had been made with one of these people, a certain Serge Valdar, but it had *never been kept*. The applicant had cried off—the excuse was, through sudden illness. Mark that, gentlemen. Why? Was the claimant Tresham after all? There was certainly the possibility. I determined to keep an open mind for the time being and to watch points.

"The key to the situation, I considered, lay at Tresham, and when MacMorran's men reported that the vultures were gathering there, I knew that I should have to go there too. I enlisted the inspector's help and also the assistance of Miss Wingfield, the late Professor's sister, who lacks neither courage nor intelligence. The estate wanted gardeners, *vide* a local advertisement that I had pointed out to me. Her physique is such that she makes an excellent 'man', and through my offices secured a job there, so that I was provided with an auxiliary, almost within the castle itself, who kept me in touch with several aspects of the case.

"My first call at the castle told me a lot. I telegraphed to myself in Tresham's name, asking for a consultation, and walked in as bold as brass. The name 'Eddington', the man we eventually picked up from Sir Richard Ingle's story, put the cat among the pigeons properly. And then—just as I was going, to return again that same evening, I made a momentous discovery. It was a fortunate thing for me that I made it when I did.

"I discovered the *secret of the spiked lion* . . . the lion of whom generations of Treshams had gone in fear . . . because it had so often spelled death. Not only to their enemies, but also, I am afraid, to some of them. Behind the picture of the lion there is a cavity. The eyes of the lion, in the picture, gentlemen, are movable, so that a watcher may use the vacant sockets to spy upon the people in the room below; the right nostril of the lion had a similar condition; for a revolver to speak through, for example. I suspect, too, that, in years gone by, there were other features of the canvas, since re-modelled, that accommodated certain weapons of the periods. Summerhayes had learnt this secret in the same way, probably, as I did. I saw the right eye move as I looked at it. When he and Tresham quarrelled, because the latter showed no inclination to share the spoils, there was a scene and he cleared out. Or so Tresham and Forbes thought. I fancy Nick had used violence on him. But he didn't clear out. He stayed, hidden in the castle, and used the lion's hiding-place when he chose—as I did later on, during one of his temporary absences. You know how he shot Tresham when he realized beyond any doubt that Nicholas wasn't parting up and meant every word that he said."

Anthony paused. "Any more flats to join for you?"

Sir Austin jumped in. "What brought Raphael to Tresham?"

Anthony scratched his cheek. "I think he suspected the guilty man and was after him on his own account."

"You're right," said Lord Tresham, "he did. He's told me so since. Young Covington, too, got on the track. Recognized the voice of one of the men whose voices he had heard that day on Lashey Down. One of the menservants in all probability. They'd installed him at the 'Plume of Feathers' to keep a lookout for and report suspicious arrivals. You know the idea—'I spy strangers'. Will they hang, Sir Austin?" he asked the Commissioner.

"Summerhayes will without a doubt—for Nick Tresham's murder alone. I think, too, that we can bring the other murders home to him and Forbes. Certain clothes, the poison apparatus and correspondence with Blundell and Wingfield are already in the hands of the police. Yes, I think they'll enjoy the morning walk—more or less."

Chief Inspector MacMorran, for ever practical, also desired information.

"Will you explain this to me, Mr. Bathurst? Why did the murderer 'feature' the spiked lion so? Right from the start of the case, you might say, he has made a rare lot of it. I don't know that I quite see why."

Anthony became all interest. "I think this, MacMorran. I had to consider the same question myself. The lion was sinister and bizarre. It frightened people—even by merely being spoken of—because it was something that they were unable to understand. The unknown and grotesque always do. Children fear the dark because their imagination peoples it. Summerhayes saw the lion on the mother-of-pearl counters, and his imagination seized on it as a means to an evil end. It's an eternal truth that the human mind is prone to despise the simple and the common and will turn almost eagerly to the incredible and the miraculous—let me quote you:

> "'No natural exhalation in the sky
> No scape of nature, no distemper'd day,
> No common wind, no customed event,
> But they will pluck away his natural cause,
> And call them meteors, prodigies, and signs,
> Abortives, presages and tongues of heaven.'

"Those sentiments are just as true here, to-day, gentlemen, as when the magician of Stratford wrote them."

He turned to the inspector. "All clear now, MacMorran?"

"Aye—that's fine, Mr. Bathurst. I can see the point now. That bit of poetry has made it just right for me. I doubt whether I could have put it better myself. And you say the man who wrote that lived at Stratford, eh? That's another coincidence—my mother-in-law lives there."

THE END